DEATH ON THE CHERWELL

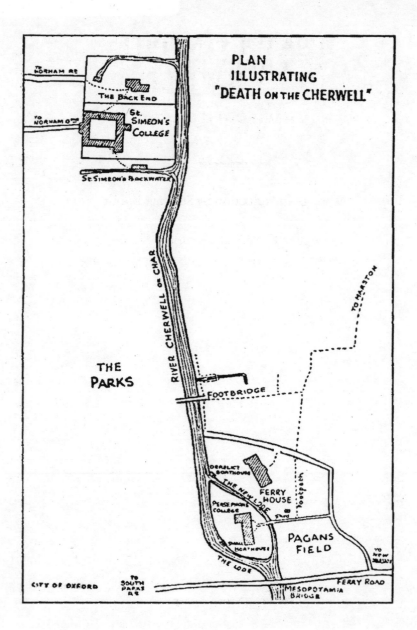

PLAN
ILLUSTRATING
"DEATH ON THE CHERWELL"

TO NORHAM RD

THE BACK END

TO NORHAM G^{DNS}

St. SIMEON'S COLLEGE

St. SIMEON'S BACKWATER

RIVER CHERWELL OR CHAR

THE PARKS

TO MARSTON

FOOTBRIDGE

DERELICT BOATHOUSE

THE NEW LODE

FERRY HOUSE

Footpath

PERSEPHONE COLLEGE

PAGANS FIELD

SMALL BOATHOUSE

THE LODE

TO NEW MARSTON

CITY OF OXFORD

TO SOUTH PARKS RD

MESOPOTAMIA BRIDGE

FERRY ROAD

DEATH ON THE CHERWELL

MAVIS DORIEL HAY

———

With an Introduction by Stephen Booth

THE BRITISH LIBRARY

This edition published in 2014 by

The British Library
96 Euston Road
London NW1 2DB

Originally published in London in 1935 by Skeffington & Son
Reprinted with thanks to the Estate of Mavis Doriel Hay
Introduction © Stephen Booth

Cataloguing in Publication Data
A catalogue record for this book is available from The British Library

ISBN 978 0 7123 5726 5

Typeset by IDSUK (DataConnection) Ltd
Printed and bound by CPI Group (UK) Ltd, Croydon, CR0 4YY

CONTENTS

INTRODUCTION

The tradition of Oxford-based crime fiction stretches back more than eighty years. It began several decades before the arrival of Colin Dexter's Inspector Morse, and is still flourishing today.

Credit for establishing the tradition usually goes to John Cecil Masterman for his 1933 murder mystery *An Oxford Tragedy*, and Adam Broome for *The Oxford Murders* (1929). But one of the pioneers of this popular sub-genre was certainly the long-forgotten Mavis Doriel Hay, whose second novel *Death on the Cherwell* appeared in 1935 and is set in the fictional Persephone College.

It is probably a coincidence that the same year saw publication of Dorothy L. Sayers' Lord Peter Wimsey novel *Gaudy Night*, perhaps the most famous account of life in an Oxford women's college. Sayers' Shrewsbury College (the alma mater of her character Harriet Vane) was based largely on Somerville, which Sayers attended. But Hay's all-female establishment in *Death on the Cherwell* is recognisably similar to another Oxford institution, St Hilda's. There were, after all, only two women's colleges on the River Cherwell – the other being Lady Margaret Hall, which is referred to as 'LMH' in the story.

So it is no surprise to discover that Mavis Doriel Hay herself attended St Hilda's College, which also boasts among its alumnae the crime novelists P. D. James and Val McDermid. Hay was a student there from 1913 to 1916, and she may be looking back with wry recollection in the opening pages of *Death on the Cherwell* when she writes: "Undergraduates, especially those in their first year, are not, of course, quite sane or quite adult."

Unlike her husband Archibald, Mavis would not have come away from Oxford with a degree. It was only in 1910 that Oxford University even acknowledged the existence of female students, despite the fact that four women's colleges had been established in the nineteenth century. And women were not permitted to be members of the university and become eligible for degrees until 1920 – four years after Mavis had left St Hilda's.

In the circumstances, it is understandable that one of the themes of *Death on the Cherwell* is a prejudice against women. Hay's views on women's education are not as explicit as those of Sayers in *Gaudy Night*, but they seem to have been thinking along the same lines.

As with Hay's first novel, *Murder Underground*, violent death is inflicted on a victim who was universally disliked – in this case, the college bursar, Miss Denning. The need to avoid bad publicity for the college leads to the solving of the mystery by a group of students and their friends. In this story, we find a classic tale of the disruption of order in a setting where it's least expected. As the principal Miss Cordell says: "Bursars of Persephone College don't get murdered." But, of course, they do in the world of mystery fiction.

We are reminded of some of the tropes of Golden Age fiction with the description of a local landowner Mr Lund as a man who could not possibly have committed a murder because he comes from "a good, old family." However, Lund is also a misogynist, who won't let a female set foot in his home and has a curse against women inscribed on the chimney piece of his Elizabethan house. For the author, he may represent the University of Oxford itself.

Hay seems to have been pleased with the police inspector who made an unobtrusive entrance in her previous novel, because here we meet Inspector Wythe, a sympathetic and intelligent character, not the typical clodhopping local bobby. He is not quite quick enough to beat the amateur sleuths to the solution, but he gives them a run for their money. The sleuthing becomes a competition between rival groups of male and female students from Persephone and St Simeon's. In the end, it seems none of the people concerned may be capable of crime, though moral guilt turns out to be a powerful thing in Mavis Doriel Hay's world.

It is a shame that there was to be only one more novel from Mavis Doriel Hay after *Death on the Cherwell*. But the approach of the Second World War changed everything for her. Mavis did not marry until she was already 35 years old – her husband, Archibald Fitzrandolph, being a member of a wealthy and influential family of loyalist Canadians. Archibald joined the RAF, but was killed in a flying accident in 1943. Not surprisingly, since she lived through both world wars, her husband's death was not the only tragedy in Mavis's life. One of her brothers had died aged 19 when his ship was sunk during the Battle of Jutland in 1916. Her youngest sibling was killed when his Tiger Moth crashed in the Malayan jungle in 1939. A year later, a third brother lost his life working on the notorious Thailand–Burma railway after being captured by the Japanese.

Although she set aside mystery novels, Mavis returned to her first love, rural crafts. She had taken up a role as a researcher for the Rural Industries Bureau, which was established in the 1920s to encourage craft industries in deprived areas. As Mavis Fitzrandolph, she is still remembered for her work developing the quilting industry in Wales. She was said to be so well connected that she could arrange exhibitions in the homes of the aristocracy. Her aristocratic connections probably came through her husband's family, the Fitzrandolphs. One of Archibald's cousins had married Sir John Dashwood and became a lady-in-waiting at the court of King George V.

From 1950 onwards, Mavis published several more books, including *30 Crafts* for the Women's Institute, and *Quilting* in 1972, only seven years before her death in Gloucestershire, where she had made her home in the village of Box.

Mavis Doriel Hay's short career was a loss to mystery fiction. Even sadder is the fact that she was almost forgotten for so many years after her death. I am delighted these British Library editions are finally remedying that oversight.

Stephen Booth

DEATH ON THE CHERWELL

CHAPTER I

THE BURSAR COMES DOWN
THE RIVER

A SLOPING roof of cold, corrugated iron, above the sliding, brownish waters of the river Cherwell and beneath the stark boughs of a willow, might not appeal to a sane adult human being as an ideal resort at four o'clock on a gloomy January afternoon. But Sally Watson had declared that it was the perfect spot for a certain mysterious confabulation, and her fellow conspirators had accepted her judgment and were all gathered there. Only Daphne Loveridge had, with her usual air of unspoken criticism, ventured on a qualification of Sally's chosen rendezvous by bringing a thick travelling rug, which slightly mitigated the chill perfection of the boathouse roof.

Undergraduates, especially those in their first year, are not, of course, quite sane or quite adult. It is sometimes considered that they are not quite human. Emerging excitedly from the ignominious status of schoolgirl or schoolboy, and as yet unsteadied by the ballast of responsibility which, later on, a livelihood-earning career will provide, they enter the university like beings born again with the advantage of an undimmed memory of their former lives. Inspirited by their knowledge of the ways in which authority may be mocked, they are at the same time quite ridiculously uplifted by the easy possibility of achieving local fame in the limited university world during the next three years. Conscious of the brevity of their college life, they are ready to seize every opportunity to assert their individuality. The easily acquired label of "originality" is so much more distinguished than the "naughtiness" of their out-passed schooldays, and quite a lot of wildness may be mixed with a modicum of work and form a sound basis for a highly respectable later life.

The formation of esoteric societies is one of the favourite pastimes of undergraduates, and these societies are on a definitely higher plane than the secret alliances of the school period. Each has its great idea, of which the passwords or rituals are symbols. Daphne Loveridge, Gwyneth Pane and Nina Harson were gathered on the roof of the small boathouse of Persephone College, Oxford, to meet Sally Watson for the purpose of inaugurating the Lode League. The League owed its name to the Oxford habit of giving special titles to sections of its rivers, for the part of the Cherwell on this side of the island on which Persephone College stands is known as the Lode.

Sally came racing across the lawn to join the others a few minutes after four o'clock had chimed from Sim's tower higher up the river. Five rings of twisted silver wire, slung on a yellow cord, dangled from her wrist as she settled herself on Daphne's rug.

"Five?" cried Gwyneth in shrill dismay. "You haven't asked Draga, surely?"

"How could I?" Sally retorted in withering tone. Gwyneth must be made to understand that communal decisions of the League were sacred and could not be flouted even by its leader.

"But I've got another idea. We're the Lode League so the Lode is our patron saint and must have a ring too!"

"What waste!" Gwyneth commented.

"We can use the worst one," Daphne suggested, examining the rings critically.

"Your souls are of the earth earthy," Nina told them. "I think it's a stupendous idea, Sally. It will make it all much more sort of binding."

"It's awfully unpractical!" Gwyneth grumbled, unconvinced.

"Can't you understand symbolism, my poor girl?" asked Nina sadly. "You're reading the English school and yet you haven't a drop of poetry in your soul!"

"Let's get on," Daphne suggested. "It's chilly."

"We'll inscribe the object of the League in our secret code books in my room, after tea," Sally decreed. "It's getting too dark here."

"So much more suitable," Daphne pointed out, "for mysteries."

"Anyway, who kept us waiting?" demanded Gwyneth.

"Of course, I was pleased to find you so punctual, dears," said Sally approvingly, "but you could hardly expect me to ask the Morter to cut his coaching short because I had a pressing engagement——"

"Not at all the sort of thing our revered Cordial would approve of," Daphne interrupted.

"——but, 's a matter of fact, he seemed in quite a hurry to get away himself——"

"Always thought you were lacking in S.A., my poor girl," Daphne interrupted again.

"—and I was here half a moment after four. The Morter was definitely gloomy, I thought; didn't appreciate my essay as much as it deserved."

"Probably missing his usual afternoon nap," Gwyneth suggested.

"Now that's not a bit like the Morter," Daphne declared. "He's quite a he-man really; more likely to take a brisk swim or run round the Parks in shorts."

"Or perhaps have a canoe race with Burse," said Gwyneth.

"No," Sally announced firmly. "The Morter is a white man—though I don't know how Daphne is so sure about his he-ness. He wouldn't associate with the dregs of the university. Anyway, it was decent of him to fit in this extra coaching for me because I missed the other through flu."

"Which reminds me that the boathouse roof isn't the health resort which our solicitous bursar would recommend for your convalescence," said Nina. "We'd better hurry."

"Remember," Sally reminded them; "that after the League is well and truly formed none of us may mention Burse without a fitting imprecation."

"I believe it's rather a pity," Daphne mused, "that we didn't include Draga. She's so good at curses. They're part of the romantic tradition of her old Slavonic family."

"You all agreed—" Sally pointed out.

"No, we couldn't have her in," declared Gwyneth. "She's serious about all the wrong things and flippant about what's really serious. And you never know how far she'll go—she'd be committing a crime on Burse and bring us all to the gallows. Besides, she can't keep anything secret."

"And by the way," Daphne inquired, "how are we going to keep the League secret if we are to be for ever flaunting these gaudy circlets on our fingers?"

"Surely you can wear a ring without telling everyone all about it?" said Nina.

"Couldn't we wear them on our toes?" suggested Gwyneth.

"Even toes aren't secret in summer," Daphne pointed out.

"You can have your nose pierced if you like," Sally conceded.

"Burse would declare it was unhygienic and make a new rule against it—with fines for breach of same," declared Nina.

"But apart from the rings," Gwyneth inquired, "how do we really keep it secret? If we are being interviewed by the Cordial and have occasion to mention Burse, do we have to say, *Miss Denning, Curse her*!"

"You have to exercise some commonsense. But seriously—" Sally leant forward earnestly—"I do believe that if you are cursing a person quite sincerely all the time, she's bound to get a sensation of something unhealthy in the atmosphere and begin to wilt, or think of trying whether it wouldn't be pleasanter elsewhere."

"I simply can't understand how a fungus like Burse was ever allowed to take root in a comparatively decent establishment for young ladies like Persephone."

"Pull yourself together, Gwyneth," Daphne advised. "If you learnt any botany at school you'd know that fungus grows spontaneously in damp spots—such as Oxford, and especially Perse Island. It's a survival of the Primeval Slime. And even if we eradicate Burse, she'll doubtless grow again, but nevertheless we must do our best to bring about Peace in Our Time. By the way, do you know——

"Persephone once had a Bursar,

"There's really no need to asperse her;

"But her influence rife,

"Has blighted our life,

"So we're forming the Lode League to curse her."

"Good," commented Sally. "We'll inscribe it in our code books. Incidentally, it's getting very dark; let's take the oath quickly and go and toast the crumpets. Gwyneth—I suppose you really do want to join—you've done nothing but criticize?"

"Oh, rather!" declared Gwyneth. "I'm all bubbling with enthusiasm, in spite of the chill of this corrugated iron striking up to my innards."

"And you, Daphne?"

"I'm all for it—though I want to know to what extent my oath will bind me to wage war to the death on Burse. F'rinstance, if I saw her struggling pathetically in the cold waters of the Char, should I fetch her out?"

"I'm sure she can swim like an otter," declared Nina.

"We can settle details later," declared Sally sternly. "But I think actual crime is barred. Now, we ought to stand up; it's more ceremonious."

"But more dangerous," Daphne pointed out.

From Sim's tower the chimes for 4.15 strayed through the twilight.

"An auspicious moment," said Sally. "It's always a good thing to know when any important event takes place."

Gwyneth scrambled dangerously on the rug. "It's slipping," she squeaked. "We shall all be a watery sacrifice!"

"Owing to Daphne's epicurean propensities," declared Sally sternly. She was on her feet, rather unsteadily, on the sloping furrows and the others staggered to the upright and chanted after her:

"We hereby declare ourselves to be striving for the illumination and uplift of life in Persephone College and especially for the eradication of all evil influences and fungoid growths, genus Burse, and the improvement of morals——"

Sally had untied the knot in the yellow cord and solemnly held out the rings in her open hand, but as the others reached to take them Gwyneth proclaimed excitedly:

"Someone coming!"

The prow of a canoe came swaying gently round the bushes which bulged, dark and untidy, over the water at the turn of the Cherwell just above the boathouse.

"Probably *her*," whispered Daphne. "Draga said she had gone up the Char in her canoe."

"Don't let's stand here like Serpentine bathers waiting for the photographer—if it really is Burse—" Nina suggested, and she sat down, trying to look as if she were there to study the view.

There was a scratchy noise, of stiff twigs brushing the side of the canoe. "Rotten steering!" someone muttered. Down that dark channel between the thick brushwood on the banks, faintly lighted by a dull winter evening sky, the canoe floated uncertainly. No one was paddling it.

"It's empty!" exclaimed Gwyneth in a high squeak. "Must have upset!"

"No—she's lying down——"

"Dreaming away the summer afternoon," murmured Daphne.

"Floating down just like the Lady of Shalott! Some new romantic stunt of hers!" Nina was scornful.

"There's something wrong!" Sally stated in a flat, practical voice, which masked the horribly real fear flickering in her mind. "A boat-hook—no, a punt pole—quick!"

She plunged from the boathouse roof on to the steps that led to the water at one side of it and, bending under the roof, stepped into a punt moored there and from that into another punt farther out, setting them all splashing and knocking against one another. She had been so quick that the others were still moving thunderously on the roof above her. What a din! But it did not disturb the occupant of the floating canoe.

"Hurry! Hurry!" Sally yelled. "A pole!" But she found one for herself, slung in the straps at the side of a punt, and got it out with a great deal of splashing and banging. Daphne arrived on the steps with another pole; Nina and Gwyneth, stumbling down behind her with paddles, almost pushed her into the lapping water. The canoe drifted down on the sluggish stream; now it was nearly level with the steps.

Sally poised her pole. "She's drifting farther out; are any of those punts unlocked?"

Nina, in a rocking punt, clinging to the roof, tried the padlocks. "Of course not—when we want them."

No one felt inclined to leave the scene of action and run to the house for a key.

"Hold me—" Sally leaned dangerously across the water reaching out the heavy pole. "I'm slipping—hold hard—I've got her! She's turning broadside on—hook the stern, Daphne!"

"It's the *Faralone* right enough," Gwyneth was murmuring.

"And it's *her*," Nina corroborated.

They dragged the canoe in alongside a punt. In it lay a woman stretched at full length beneath the thwarts and partly covered by a long tweed coat. Her green jersey and tweed skirt were sodden and her wet, fair hair was looped rakishly over one eye and streaked across her pallid face that was smeared with dark mud. Her partly open mouth and the one free eye horribly upturned, gaped vacantly.

"She's drowned!" gasped Gwyneth in a frightened whisper.

"How can anyone drown *in* a canoe?" demanded Sally severely. "P'rhaps she's only ill. We must haul her out. No, tie up the canoe first."

Myra Denning, the bursar of Persephone College, was not a big woman but it was with difficulty that the four girls, crowding each other on the narrow steps, heaved the inert body and its weight of wet clothing from under the thwarts of the canoe and up the steps on to the gravel path.

The suddenness of what had happened and the horror of it had sent all thoughts of the Lode League from their minds for the time being. It was only when the cold body lay on the path that the grim connection between it and their reason for being there struck Gwyneth.

"We can't do any more; hadn't we better clear out?" she suggested in a shaky voice.

"Artificial respiration," said Daphne doubtfully.

"But it can't be any good!" wailed Gwyneth. "And *we*—" she shuddered.

"Don't be an ass!" Sally commanded. "Don't breathe a word, of course, about the League. It has nothing to do with—what has happened." She was already at work with Nina on the unresponsive corpse. "Run like mad to Miss Cordell and tell her to phone to a doctor."

Gwyneth sped away across the wet lawn and round the end of the house towards the garden door.

CHAPTER II

MISS CORDELL FACES PUBLICITY

MISS CORDELL, Principal of Persephone College, Oxford, looked up from her tea-tray at the pale, breathless figure of Gwyneth Pane, who had hurled herself into the principal's study and now stood grasping the door handle, with her mouth open. Miss Cordell's first feeling was annoyance; she cherished some old-fashioned ideas about the desirability of being "lady-like," and hated to see any of her students looking gauche.

"Miss Cordell! There's been an accident—Miss Denning—in her canoe—" Gwyneth gasped out.

"Not serious, I hope—" (Surely not serious, Miss Cordell was telling herself, to contradict Gwyneth's startling appearance. Miss Denning—such a strong swimmer and so used to the river.)

"Yes, we're afraid so—we're afraid—she's—drowned! I think you'd better ring up the doctor—Oh!—your tea!"

Gwyneth had interrupted Miss Cordell just as she was about to enjoy the first delicious sip from a teacup which she still held in her hand; the tea now slopped messily over a plate of bread and butter and even down Miss Cordell's neat brown dress. She set down the cup with a little cluck of annoyance.

"But where is she, Gwyneth? How——"

"She was in her canoe—we got her out—down there, on the garden path by the small boathouse—the others are trying artificial respiration."

For a moment Miss Cordell hesitated. Her vision of under-graduate life was always slightly distorted by the suspicion that "this may be a rag." She could never get away from the fear that she might be "had" and made to look publicly silly. But no; Gwyneth's agitation was surely genuine.

Miss Cordell asked her telephone anxiously: "Is that Doctor Shuter? Miss Cordell, Persephone, speaking. There's been an accident—Miss Denning—in her canoe on the river—*in* the river—*very* serious— Yes, we're doing that. Thank you—good-bye." She hung up the receiver with an uneasy feeling that "good-bye" was not quite the appropri-ate expression at the moment.

When Doctor Shuter arrived some ten minutes later, Sally and Nina were working unavailingly at the saturated corpse in the dark garden.

"You did the right thing but I'm afraid it's too late," he told them, after a short examination of the body. Miss Cordell had brought him out through the french windows of the drawing-room, from which a shaft of light now struck across the gar-den, showing them each other's faces, pale and strained, as they stood in an awkward group on the path.

"How long have you been at this?" he asked the girls.

"Since— Oh! soon after a quarter past four was when we first saw her," Sally told him.

"You saw her body in the river?"

"Yes—no; in her canoe."

"In her canoe? Then you saw the accident happen?"

"No; we saw the canoe floating down the river and then we found that she was in it."

"My dear girl, I'm not blaming you; I only want to know what happened," exclaimed the doctor in annoyance. He looked round at the others. "Will one of you tell me plainly what occurred?"

"We don't *know* what happened," burst out Gwyneth in a voice which, through distress and anxiety, sounded petulant. "But we found her, as if she had been drowned, in her canoe. I know it doesn't sound sensible."

The doctor looked round at them rather grimly. They realized that they were damp and cold and that what had happened now seemed incredible. Sally was so offended by Doctor Shuter's remarks that she maintained a dignified silence.

Nina broke the awkward silence by stating: "We saw the canoe floating down the river, just drifting. We saw something was wrong, so we pulled it in to the steps with a punt pole. Then we saw Miss Denning and we got her out——"

"Out of the river?"

"No. Out of the canoe. She was lying flat in the canoe, simply soaking wet, as if she had been drowned." The doctor frowned and shook his head meditatively. After all, it wasn't his job to investigate this affair.

"I'm afraid there's nothing for it but to ring up the police, Miss Cordell. May I use your telephone? And perhaps—would you mind waiting here? I shan't be more than a few minutes."

He strode off to the house. Miss Cordell turned doubtfully back to the girls. She had a sedate academic affection for Myra Denning, who had been her colleague for fifteen years, but she was still too violently shocked to be sensible of grief or loss. In a crisis she instinctively became official. The doctor's last remarks were like squibs and crackers exploding suddenly in the quiet garden of Persephone College. Police—publicity! Publicity was Miss Cordell's bugbear. Respectable publicity was bad enough because newspaper reporters, however carefully instructed, were liable to break out into some idiocy about "undergraduettes" or "academic caps coquettishly set on golden curls." But shameful publicity! A death mystery! This was terrible! But these four students had apparently been at the scene of the accident. Surely they could explain it. The doctor had frightened them by his brusque manner. She must extract the truth from them tactfully. They would realize that undue publicity must be avoided and that "mystery" was always a keen scent to the hounds of the Press.

The doctor was soon back and turned his attention to the girls, ordering them to go and change their damp clothes quickly and get something hot to drink.

"When you have changed, will you all go to my room and wait for me there," Miss Cordell directed. "I will send for some fresh tea for you. And I must ask you to say nothing whatever of this to anyone."

As the girls walked solemnly away across the lawn, Doctor Shuter tried to reassure Miss Cordell.

"Fortunately the superintendent, Inspector Wythe, was in and is coming at once. You will find him very discreet. Can you understand what exactly happened, Miss Cordell?"

Miss Cordell's tactful questions had failed to make matters much clearer, but she felt that some criticism of her students was implied and rallied in their defence.

"They are all in their first year and they have had a most unnerving experience, but I am sure they will be able to make it clear when they have had time to collect themselves. Sally Watson, in particular, is a most sensible girl. Of course this is all quite unprecedented and very shocking."

"Hm! Hm! Well, I mustn't keep you standing here, Miss Cordell. There's nothing further we can do, but I'll wait here till the superintendent comes."

The principal returned to the house and the members of the half-formed Lode League were assembled in her room, gulping hot tea thankfully, by the time the superintendent arrived. Two constables with a stretcher accompanied him, and after a survey of the scene by the river steps he had the body carried into the drawing-room.

"She was drowned, within the last four or five hours, so far as I can tell," Doctor Shuter told him. "But there's this mark on the back of her head—a pretty hard blow, it looks like, which may have stunned her though it could hardly have killed her."

"Striking her head—no; it was a canoe, you say; not a punt," the superintendent mused. "A canoe isn't heavy enough to give a hard blow. And then all the mud—face, hair, clothes! That looks like something more than straightforward drowning. And you may have observed that although her clothes are saturated, the overcoat is only damp. And found *in* the canoe, you say? Are you sure?"

"No, I'm not," said Doctor Shuter with some asperity, annoyed at having this fantastic story foisted upon him as it were. "You'd better see those girls. They had her lying on the path when I came, just as you found her. Of course one can't name the cause of death for a certainty, or give any idea of when the blow occurred, without a post mortem."

The four girls were not sorry when their tea party was broken up by the arrival of Inspector Wythe, who asked them to accompany him to the boathouse. Already a whisper of mysterious events had spread through college, and an unusual number of maids and students found it necessary to pass through the hall or linger on the staircase which mounted from it, just opposite the door of Miss Cordell's room. The flashing of the superintendent's torch over the path, the river steps and the boathouse was watched by dozens of eyes from the college windows.

The torchlight swept the boathouse roof and showed the abandoned rug.

"Whose coat?" queried the inspector sharply.

"It's my rug," muttered Daphne. "We were sitting there."

Miss Cordell's eyebrows rose.

After a hasty inspection of the place and a few questions, the inspector left his two men to examine the canoe and the surroundings and walked with the rest of the party towards the house.

"I must ask all you young ladies to wait somewhere, so that each of you can answer some questions for me in turn," he said slowly, as if he were still thinking things over. "No one else was with you when you found her?"

"No. We didn't see anyone else in the garden at all," Sally told him.

"Do you know if any other student saw Miss Denning start out in the canoe, or saw her during the afternoon?"

"Didn't Draga say she saw her start?" burst out Gwyneth.

Miss Cordell's frown was invisible in the darkness. Draga Czernak! How—how—*unsuitable*! Just the one student she would not choose as a witness. So unrestrained! So unlikely to do credit to Persephone College!

They were crossing the narrow terrace to the drawing-room door—they must pass through that room, where Miss Denning lay on a sofa. Miss Cordell wondered why she had not led them round to the garden door at the end of the building; but then such a procession tramping all through the college would certainly have aroused the wildest curiosity of any students whom they might have met. Instinctively they trod very quietly through the drawing-room. Miss Cordell took them all to the small common-room, where Sally had coached with Mr. Mort from three to four that afternoon.

"If you will conduct your interviews here, Inspector, the others can wait in my own room, next door," Miss Cordell announced. She felt that the chief witnesses would be "safe" in her sacred apartment. They were still rather pale and quiet, but shudderingly she imagined them, as soon as they were set free, the centre of interest, relating all the horrid circumstances of their discovery to gaping groups round their firesides. Of course it was bound to happen before long, but at least she would have time to talk things over with Miss Steevens, her vice-principal, and decide with her upon some line of action. An announcement to the students at dinner; a warning against gossip. . . .

The inspector elected to interview Sally first and the other three retired to the principal's room. Here, in the warmth and light of the college, they were self-possessed and placid again; what had happened out in the dark garden was definitely shelved in the past. They felt as if they had clambered out of a pit of horror back into the normal world and would have liked to discuss their adventure. But it seemed almost improper to discuss what had happened to Burse while sitting in—perhaps—the very chair in which she had often sat while recounting their crimes to Miss Cordell—that, according to undergraduate opinion at Persephone, being her chief form of conversation. Except for a moan from Gwyneth—"I suppose we can't even smoke"—they said little.

The inspector had purposely curbed his curiosity whilst they inspected the boathouse because he wanted to get the whole story first from the individuals separately, rather than as a hotch-potch of comment and counter-comment and contradictory chorus. Now he surveyed Sally Watson with approval as she settled herself in the small arm-chair opposite to him. Trim and self-controlled she looked now, although her usual buoyant self-confidence had not quite returned. She had sleeked her brown hair and had donned—hastily, yet with a vague sense of fitting herself for a sombre occasion—a tailored, navy-blue frock. A nice, sensible girl, thought the inspector, as he looked directly into her brown eyes.

Rather a stupid-looking man, thought Sally after a brief inspection of his square, stolid face and reddish, toothbrush moustache.

"Now, Miss Watson, will you tell me all that you saw and everything you know about this—er—accident?"

Sally frowned slightly in her effort to remember everything. She realized that the boathouse roof was going to be a little difficult to explain as a natural resort, and characteristically she plunged at once into this difficulty. "The four of us were sitting on the boathouse roof—I was there from four o'clock; I know the time because I'd just come from a coaching——"

"The others came later?"

"No; they were there first; I joined them——"

"Were you going on the river?"

"Oh, no! We arranged to meet there; it's a favourite place of ours to sit; there's something awfully attractive about that river, even when it's cold and half-dark," Sally rushed on, hoping that this was convincing.

"Were you meeting someone there?" The superintendent thought he was on the track of a clue to one phase of the mystery.

"Oh, no; only ourselves. We just met to talk something over and we talked from four to a quarter past; we heard Sim's chimes."

"You were expecting Miss Denning?"

"Oh, *no*!"

"But you knew she was on the river in her canoe?"

"No—oh, I think Daphne knew, but we didn't know when we arranged to go there."

"Did Miss Denning keep her canoe in that boathouse?"

"Yes—but we didn't notice it wasn't there. We didn't go down the steps, only on to the roof."

"So the fact that you were sitting on the boathouse roof had no connection with Miss Denning?"

This took Sally by surprise. She felt it was not quite fair. Obviously this policeman must not be told about the Lode League; he might think it was silly or, worse, he might take it as an implication that they had something to do with whatever had happened to Burse. So she answered firmly, though not quite promptly: "Oh, no!" She wondered if she were blushing under the superintendent's steady stare. An inquisitive man!

"Would it strike you as unusual that Miss Denning should be out in a canoe at four o'clock on a January afternoon?" was his next question.

"No, not really; not for her. She often goes out in the *Faralone*—that's her canoe—and at least once I've seen her come back about tea-time." Sally was relieved to be embarked on the safer subject of Burse's habits.

"So it was not unusual. Now, Miss Watson, will you continue and tell me just what happened after you joined your friends on the boathouse roof at four o'clock."

Sally told her story, from the moment when they saw the canoe; she described calmly, though her lip trembled, how Myra Denning's body was lying, slightly on one side, stretched out under the thwarts, with the grey overcoat covering it.

"Whilst you were on the boathouse roof, before you saw the canoe, did you hear any scream or splash or anything unusual?" Inspector Wythe asked her at the end.

"I don't remember anything; there didn't seem to be a soul about."

"And there's nothing more that you can tell me, Miss Watson? Nothing that might in any way be connected with the accident?" The superintendent put on his most fatherly manner, which he thought ought to draw confidences from any woman.

"I can't think of anything that has anything to do with it," said Sally unsympathetically, rising from her chair.

Wythe rose too and not only opened the door for her but followed her out—quite politely, but with horrible watchfulness—to the door of the principal's room, where he asked

Miss Gwyneth Pane to join him. Sally had no chance for the whisper of "Nothing about the Lode League" with which she had intended to put the next victim on her guard, but she did manage to catch Gwyneth's eye with what she hoped was a "warning look"—commoner in stories of intrigue than in life. Gwyneth merely took it to be an expression of hatred of the unfortunate superintendent.

"Blast him!" said Sally as she sank into a chair. "Gwyneth's so—so ebullient! She'll blurt out something! Why couldn't he take one of you next?"

"Sharp lad, that policeman!" said Daphne composedly. "But we're not guilty of anything. It doesn't really matter what she says."

Meanwhile Inspector Wythe was summing up Gwyneth in his mind as "one of the excitable kind; easily startled into giving something away." She was small, with an impertinent nose and not much chin; she had a pop-eyed look, as if she found life permanently amazing.

"How did you come to witness this accident?" he began magisterially.

"We *didn't*," Gwyneth assured him, her voice rising into a squeak. "We saw Miss Denning—well, I mean her body, in the canoe."

"And you were not expecting anything of the kind?"

"Well, really, would *you* expect it?— But of course, being a policeman, I suppose you might."

Wythe made a good recovery. "Did you expect to see her alone in the canoe?"

"We didn't expect to see her at all." Really this man was incredibly stupid.

"But your presence there on the boathouse was not entirely unconnected with Miss Denning?" If the question had been less ponderously worded, Gwyneth might have been caught, but it gave her time to think.

"It had nothing to do with her being on the river. We didn't know she *was* on the river."

He detected an evasion, but was still baffled. He asked Gwyneth a few more questions about what had happened, and then released her. Accompanying her back to the principal's room he found that Draga Czernak had arrived and decided to deal with her next.

Draga, installed in the small common-room, spelt her name for him and explained that she was a native of Yugo-Slavia— "of the Czernaks of Stara Gora" she added proudly. The superintendent looked blank. He was pardonably vague about Yugo-Slavia, but connected it dimly with Russia and thought its inhabitants ought to be immensely tall, with black hair, burning eyes, a wild manner and a bomb under the arm. So with some surprise he surveyed Draga's short, rather thickset form, her wide face with big greenish-grey eyes and her flat, fair hair.

"Probably you have heard, Miss Czernak, of the accident in which Miss Denning has been involved? You are the only person, so far as I know, who saw her go out this afternoon. Can you tell me the time when, as I understand, you noticed her setting off in her canoe?" Wythe's distrust of foreigners made him anxious to be fair to Draga, so he spoke very slowly and distinctly, since it did not occur to him that as Draga was an undergraduate at Oxford she probably understood English quite well.

Draga's reply poured forth torrentially. "I have seen her—yes, because she passed before my eyes and I must see her, but I was not looking for her and I did not wish to see her. I have seen her because I was sitting to read in the library and she went across the terrace from the drawing-room door, with her paddles, and across the lawn and through the little gate to the steps on the water."

"To the boathouse in fact?" suggested the superintendent.

"Yes, to where she keeps her little boat, her canoe. That is all I know." Draga stopped abruptly.

"Can you remember the time?"

"How can I know the time?" Draga was indignant. "Is it so important to me when I see Miss Denning that immediately I must look at my little clock?"

"It would seem to you quite ordinary, then, that Miss Denning should go out in a canoe on a cold January afternoon?"

"To me," Draga declared earnestly, "it seems finally extraordinary to go forth in a canoe on the water on a day so cold and without sun. But here—you do it. I learn to consider it a thing quite ordinary."

Wythe was a little disconcerted to find himself classed amongst people who went canoeing on the Cherwell in January. He returned to the time question.

"You may remember when you went to the library?"

"I know quite clearly that I went to the library just after lunch."

"Which would be at what time?"

"Perhaps two; perhaps sooner; perhaps later."

"Was anyone else in the library with you when you saw Miss Denning?"

"I saw no one; I do not know. The library is full of—what do you call them—such—such little—alcoves! It is possible."

"And you cannot think of anything else which would help to fix the time? Had you been in the library long when you saw Miss Denning?"

"Not long; not hours; minutes. I had found my book and I had found the chapter I wished to read."

"Can you tell me anything else that may help? How was Miss Denning dressed and was she carrying anything?"

"Her dress—" Draga was scornful; "—she was dressed in a long grey coat that I think you call a raincoat—a thing so English and here so necessary. It has no shape—just long and straight."

"And a hat?"

"Yes, a hat—grey—such a mannish hat."

"A felt hat, perhaps? And was she carrying anything— paddles, I think you said? More than one?"

"Perhaps two paddles. Perhaps also a book—how do I know?"

"Can you remember for certain that she had a book?"

"No. Perhaps no book. How do I know? I tell you I did not take notice so particularly. I was not told that she was going then to die."

This remark was made in the most matter-of-fact voice, and Draga's expression indicated nothing more than boredom.

"What do you mean?" demanded the superintendent sharply. "Who could have told you?"

"The one who killed her, I suppose. I mean only that I did not know this was a special occasion, and I must look diligently at our bursar."

"So you are sure someone killed her?"

"Surely she would not kill herself in the river and then get into her canoe?" inquired Draga, unperturbed.

"Accidents happen," said Wythe.

"Ah! An English accident! I learn another strange thing."

"Are you sure she was wearing a hat?" the superintendent asked coldly.

"I saw a hat on her head," Draga replied deliberately. "She always went in her canoe in that hat."

"And she was alone?"

"Oh, yes."

"Then that seems to be all you can tell me?" Wythe congratulated himself that he had been so tactful with a difficult witness. "If you think of anything else that may help you to fix the time, will you let me know?"

As he opened the door for her one of the constables came forward from the hall.

"Nothing much, sir, but we found these on the rug which one of the young ladies said belonged to her." He held out a yellow cord and four rings of silver wire.

The superintendent took them. "Hm! Hm!" He opened the door of the principal's study and held them out in the palm of his hand. "These have been found on the boathouse roof—perhaps they belong to one of you?"

"Yes—they're mine," said Sally after a moment's pause. She looked at the rings carefully. "Is that all?"

The superintendent's hand closed over them. "Have you lost anything else?" he asked sharply, and beckoned to the man in the hall. "This all you found on the young ladies' rug, Barnett?"

"That's all, sir."

Sally had recovered her composure. "There were four."

The superintendent opened his hand again. "Oh, yes; that's all," she told him. "One each, you see."

"Something to do with your little talk on the boathouse roof?"

"Well, yes, in a way. I made them for my friends you see. We thought it would be nice to have one each, all the same."

"I think you can have them back. By the way, do any of you remember finding anything else in the canoe—besides Miss Denning's body?"

They looked at one another. "Paddles?" queried Gwyneth uncertainly.

"Were there paddles?" the superintendent asked.

"We didn't take any out," said Sally firmly. "I don't remember anything else—but if there were, it would still be there. I'm sure we didn't take anything out."

The constable came forward again in response to a sign and a question.

"There was a plain felt hat, sir, but no paddles; not in the canoe. There were two in a punt."

"You're sure none of you took a paddle out? Snatched it, perhaps, to pull the canoe in?"

"If we could have reached a paddle out of the canoe, we could have reached the canoe," Daphne pointed out.

"We fetched paddles from the shed," added Gwyneth. "Those would be the ones in the punt."

"You're sure about that? How many did you fetch from the shed?"

"I took two," said Nina, "and I gave one of them to Gwyneth."

"And I had a punt pole from the shed," added Daphne.

"Miss Denning's own paddles had her initials on them—M.D.," Sally pointed out; "and she was very particular about them. She kept them in the house."

The superintendent made a note. "Check all the poles and paddles carefully," he told the constable; "and have a search made on the river for two paddles with initials M.D. Now, Miss Loveridge, will you come along?"

Wythe noticed how Daphne settled herself comfortably into the arm-chair, looking down at her very pretty hands folded in her lap, and waited for him to open the conversation. It did not occur to him that her plump figure, her oval face with longish nose, and her black curls, might have belonged to a seventeenth century beauty.

Her story tallied with the others. When she mentioned the boathouse roof, the superintendent asked: "By the way, is that against the rules?"

Daphne looked up at him quickly. "I believe not," she told him solemnly, with a gleam of amusement in her eyes at this naive idea of the rules to which such responsible people as undergraduates must submit.

"But it was a curious place to choose to sit, especially when you were missing tea, which is at four, I understand?"

"Not missing it. We were going to have crumpets in my room—they're sitting there now," said Daphne sadly.

"Then why not have your talk over tea and crumpets in your room—unless you were waiting there for some particular person—or event?"

"The one thing that might have prevented us from meeting on the boathouse roof," declared Daphne, exasperated by his implications, "would have been if we'd have known that the bursar would appear."

"I still fail to understand why you *should* meet there," said the superintendent coldly.

"We met for a private conversation," Daphne replied with dignity.

"Which was going to be lengthy—you took a rug."

"Corrugated iron is cold to sit on."

"Exactly. And a hearthrug in front of the fire in your own room is warm—and private."

"Well, I didn't suppose you would understand," said Daphne in an aggrieved voice. "But we're on an island here and islands are romantic, and so we like to remind ourselves that it really is an island, by sitting beside the river."

Wythe remembered that islands had a romantic fascination for him in his boyhood, and began to wonder whether he was being unnecessarily suspicious about what was perhaps just the usual unreasonable behaviour of undergraduates. But—dash it all, why not have their look at the surrounding water in daylight, instead of at tea-time. "I may tell you," he remarked in his heaviest police manner, "that I am not at all satisfied with this 'explanation' of your conduct. I do not mean to imply that there is anything wrong about what you were doing, but there is something which none of you have seen fit to explain, and I can only say that you are not helping our inquiries by holding back the true explanation. Even details that may seem to you quite irrelevant may be of importance to us. Is there nothing more you can tell me?"

"Really, I can't think of anything," declared Daphne. "I'm just as stymied as you are about this affair, and I'd be awfully glad to throw any light on it."

With his air of severe disapproval unsoftened he indicated that the interview was at an end. He had an uneasy feeling that this girl saw jokes in all sorts of things that he did not find at all amusing, and that he might be making her a present of a joke at any moment. So her exit, with a slight upward curl at the corners of her mouth, did not improve his temper. Nina, who took Daphne's place in the arm-chair, found him rather snappy, but no new facts transpired during her short interview.

CHAPTER III

THE LIE OF THE LAND

MISS CORDELL, the principal of Persephone College, delighted the eyes of American visitors to Oxford, especially if they happened to see her in cap and gown, because she seemed to them the typical "Ahxford Dahn" of the female sex. Actually one will find more variety in the appearances of any collection of dons than in a collection of bankers or stock-brokers, and Miss Cordell was not in the least typical. She was tall and thin and stooped, had rather straggly, sandy hair, wore pince-nez, and clothes that appeared to have been made some ten years ago by a country dressmaker of conscientiously "good" material. Her vice-principal, Miss Steevens, was young, rather plump, rather untidy, and very good-natured. The two of them sat, not quite at ease, facing the superintendent, when he had finished questioning the five students.

"Forgive me," began Miss Cordell, "if I ask for information which you do not feel at liberty to impart, but you will realize our natural anxiety to know if you have any idea as to the cause of this terrible accident. So unprecedented!" In Miss Cordell's opinion nothing should be unprecedented. Even an accident, even a murder (though she did not usually consider murders) should follow some documented precedent, so that one would know how to behave.

"By all means, Miss Cordell," Wythe reassured her. "I'll tell you all that I've been able to gather, though I must confess that at the moment I can only make a guess at what happened. Doubtless with the information which my men are now collecting I shall be able to piece things together this evening.

What seems to me the most probable explanation at present is a particular kind of accident—a practical joke which went wrong. Obviously this cannot be an ordinary accident; you cannot fall out of a canoe and drown and then get back into the canoe. But undergraduates have before now indulged in pranks which have led to tragedy——"

Miss Cordell gripped the arms of her chair and gazed at him in horrified amazement. "But surely, not—not——"

"No, Miss Cordell. I don't think your own students had anything to do with the affair; anyway, nothing that you could call an active part, but I can't get away from the suspicion that they know a little more than they have seen fit to tell me."

"But, Inspector, this is a grave suspicion; you really have grounds——?"

"They were a little what you might call evasive in their answers to my questions, and what in—er—on earth were they doing on that boathouse?"

"Undergraduates behave so very oddly, Inspector. Even I, who am forced to contemplate their odd behaviour every day, never cease to feel surprise at much of it."

"I feel sure I've seen them—those very four—sitting on that boathouse before," Miss Steevens announced. "It's just like them, you know, to choose to sit in the sort of place you would never dream of sitting in."

"Well, ladies, I can't get away from the impression, at the moment, that their sitting there had something to do with Miss Denning, but I certainly don't think they expected to see her dead body come floating down in the canoe—which is what we must assume did happen."

He took no notice of a little gasp of indignation from Miss Cordell, but continued: "As regards the drowning, I was thinking of the young men. They may have staged an 'accident' in which, contrary to their plans, Miss Denning was drowned. Having rescued her too late and realized the terrible result of their so-called rag, they put her body back in the canoe. Very foolish, I admit; but these young men *are* foolish. It has happened before now that persons who have committed manslaughter get into a panic, and in their clumsy attempts to cover up their tracks, land themselves in danger of being put on trial for murder. But rest assured that we shall get to the truth before long. Now can you tell me, Miss Cordell, if Miss Denning could swim?"

"She was a strong swimmer," Miss Steevens told him. "I know that for a fact, because I bathed with her at Deaconesses Delight last summer; she was quite unusually good. That makes it all the more difficult to understand."

"Hm! There was a blow on the head, which may account for a good deal. There are many ways, of course, in which a blow may be caused accidentally; but we can't ignore the possibility that it may have been caused deliberately. That brings us to quite a different explanation of the affair—which, I may say, I do not really consider very likely, at present—murder."

Miss Steevens seemed to consider this idea calmly, but Miss Cordell felt that her mind was disintegrating. Undergraduates, a rag, manslaughter, murder! An insane, an incredible sequence. "Murder!" she gasped. "But no—no one could contemplate—What reason could there be? Murder?" Her real thought, which she was unable to express, was: "Bursars of Persephone College don't get murdered."

"We are bound to investigate every possibility," Inspector Wythe continued earnestly. "It would help me, Miss Cordell, if you would explain briefly Miss Denning's position here as bursar, her everyday occupations and routine, the people with whom she came into contact, and so on. She lived here, I take it?"

Miss Cordell drew in her breath, bit her lip, and seemed to make an effort to direct her mind towards the superintendent's question, but her eyes looked dazed. Miss Steevens glanced inquiringly at her principal and, receiving a vague nod of assent, launched into explanation.

"Yes, Inspector, Miss Denning lived in college. I suppose you will want to see her room. As bursar she was responsible for all financial and business affairs of the college, and the papers relating to college business are kept in the office. The secretary, who is not on duty now, will be able to show you those, if you need to investigate them, though I should hardly think it would be necessary. Miss Denning was also responsible for the domestic management of the college, the catering and supervision of the household staff, and so on. Her status in college was the same as that of the fellows and tutors, that is to say she was a member of the senior common room, though she did no coaching."

"Quite so. Thank you. You have explained the position admirably. I can only wish that all members of the public from whom we have occasion to seek information could give it so lucidly." The superintendent sighed. "Now I am afraid I have to ask rather—er—delicate questions. You have no reason, I suppose, to suspect any irregularity in the college accounts or any difficulty of that kind?"

"I am quite confident," declared Miss Cordell with dignity, "that Miss Denning's business affairs are beyond reproach."

"Miss Denning was a very good business woman," Miss Steevens added soothingly. "She has been our bursar for fifteen years and has managed college affairs most competently."

"Quite so. You will realize that we are bound to make these inquiries," Wythe explained. "Can you tell me whether, in her relations with the dons or the domestic staff, or with people outside the college, Miss Denning may have made enemies? I gather that she did not have very much to do with the students?"

"Oh, I didn't mean to imply that," said Miss Steevens. "Miss Denning had nothing to do with their work, but being in charge of all domestic affairs, rooms and meals and laundry and so forth, she had a good deal to do with them from time to time. She managed the household very efficiently, but people always complain about housekeeping, you know. I suppose it's because, at heart, we all care more about our personal convenience and comfort than anything else. It is useless to deny that Miss Denning was unpopular with the students; if you begin to make inquiries about her you are sure to hear that before long. But I really don't think you need pay much attention to that aspect of the matter. Undergraduates must always have an object for their grumbles and sarcasm. I feel quite sure none of them would ever contemplate anything serious in the nature of revenge."

"I have always had the greatest respect for Miss Denning's work *and* character," declared Miss Cordell.

"I think I understand the situation," said Inspector Wythe. "I know a bit about these undergraduates, one way and another. But apart from the young ladies——?"

"Yes, among outsiders—" Miss Steevens began, obviously with something to disclose. She hesitated and looked at Miss Cordell. Miss Cordell looked at Miss Steevens and again gave a slight nod of assent, in what seemed to be a mood of resignation.

Miss Steevens continued: "I think we ought to tell you, Inspector, of two people who might be called enemies, though not, I should have thought, to any murderous extent. But you may hear of these people in the course of your inquiries, and you had better have the full story."

"Quite right! Quite right!" Wythe agreed.

"You probably know Mr. Lond—Ezekiel Lond?"

"The owner of Ferry House, on the other side of the New Lode? Quite so."

The history of Ferry House and Persephone College was a favourite subject with Miss Cordell, and at the mention of Ezekiel Lond she roused herself from the state of horrified disapproval in which she had, up to the present, kept herself detached from the conversation. Miss Steevens had paused, as if she expected that her principal would now take a hand, and Miss Cordell resumed the narrative.

"You may also know that Ezekiel Lond's father, Adam Lond, owned this land on which Persephone College stands. In fact, this land, now vulgarly known as Perse Island, once formed part of the Ferry House grounds, before the backwater, known as the New Lode, which now divides us from Ferry House, was cut. The filling in of the Old Lode, which ran on the far side of Ferry House, and the cutting of the New Lode, were part of a drainage scheme of considerable extent. If you have ever studied the old maps of Oxford, you will have observed the alteration of the innumerable watercourses and the creation or elimination of islands, through the centuries, a most fascinating subject for study."

"Pardon me," begged Inspector Wythe in his most propitiatory voice, "but—er—you will realize how important it is to gather information quickly——"

This sharp reminder that the superintendent was not merely an earnest seeker after knowledge, but a police officer investigating something that might be murder, recalled Miss Cordell momentarily from the peaceful field of geographical history. But even in this unprecedented situation she could not be false to her favourite dictum that to understand the present one must study the past.

"You must excuse me!" she murmured, a little flustered. "But the connection between Miss Denning and Mr. Lond has its roots, one may say, in that remote past of which I was speaking. The island in its ancient form was known as Londle or Lundle—it is variously spelt in the old maps, but the name seems to have been a corruption of 'Lond's Isle,' since Mr. Lond's family had held it since the sixteenth century. Mr. Lond's late father sold this piece of land, under severe financial stress, to the founders of Persephone College—the well-known—but no; that is of no interest to you. It is commonly said that Mr. Ezekiel Lond never forgave his father for selling part of the family estate, nor Persephone College for occupying it. That is the first cause of ill-feeling. The second difficulty arose out of the use by us of a footpath across the garden of Ferry House, which forms a short cut from our private lane to the road leading to the Parks. There was said to be an understanding with the late Mr. Lond, when the land was bought, that we might use this footpath, but there is no conclusive documentary evidence, and Mr. Ezekiel Lond strongly resents our use of it. Miss Denning firmly maintained our right to use this path, which she believed to be part of an old right of way across the island to a wooden footbridge on its far side, and so through the fields beside the upper river. As you may be aware, there is still a public footpath through those fields, continuing, beyond a stile on the opposite side of the lane, the line of the disputed path. Miss Denning was, in fact, engaged in research on this subject and had told Mr. Lond that she intended to prove our right of way. I was entirely sympathetic with her research—a most interesting subject—but I would have been willing to waive our possible right to use the footpath, to avoid any unpleasantness. It would be difficult, however, to prevent the students from using it, especially while the house remains unoccupied."

"Exactly," put in the superintendent. "Lond doesn't live in Ferry House now, so how can this affect him?"

"Certainly he does not usually inhabit the house, but he visits it from time to time. There is an old man who seems to be employed to keep the garden from running utterly wild, and perhaps as a sort of caretaker, but he does not live there."

"You don't happen to know whether Lond is at Ferry House now?"

"I have no idea. Please do not think, Inspector, that I wish to cast suspicion on Mr. Lond. He is eccentric and—well, not very courteous. We have found him distinctly difficult, but I do not imagine that he can be in any way connected with this terrible accident."

"He is the sort of man," explained Miss Steevens, "who will use abusive language and utter violent threats, but he has never made any show of violence, even when he has met us on the footpath. Besides, he is an old man, quite tottery."

"Quite so," agreed Wythe. "Violence from his own hand does not seem very likely to my way of thinking. I know the man a bit. By the way, was there ever any quarrel about landing from boats on his island? Has that ever been done, do you know?"

"I don't think so," said Miss Steevens. "There is a derelict boathouse, with landing steps, at the corner of Ferry House garden, but I never heard of anyone using it. It looks as if the overgrown bushes almost block the way to the steps from the garden."

"Well, this path business seems a small thing to fuss about when he doesn't live in the house—unless he contemplates selling it and thinks that would hinder the sale?"

"Mr. Lond is eccentric and definitely a misogynist," declared Miss Cordell severely. "He regards his family estate as a sacred inheritance and the loss of part of it and the trespass—as he regards it—of women on another part of it, he looks upon as a form of insult."

"Hm! A bit crazy!" was Inspector Wythe's judgment. "Well, that sort is sometimes dangerous."

"The question of the sale of Ferry House *has* arisen," announced Miss Steevens. "In fact, I'm not sure that it hasn't caused more ill-feeling than the footpath."

"I was about to explain that," continued Miss Cordell. "We are considering the purchase of land for extensions to the college. I believe it is common knowledge that there are two possible sites for our building. One is the piece of land on the side of our private lane opposite to Ferry House, the land known as Pagan's Field—another interesting instance of nomenclature—*most* interesting; its origin—but no, I must not pursue that subject now. The other possible site, which for many reasons is preferable for our purpose, is the land on which Ferry House itself stands. It is known that Mr. Lond is not in affluent circumstances, and we have therefore approached him with a tentative offer to purchase, only to be met with what I can only describe as abuse. Miss Denning, as bursar, conducted these negotiations; she is—was—an excellent business woman."

"Quite so. So Lond might well feel particularly unfriendly towards Miss Denning, if he resented this suggestion so strongly?"

"Undoubtedly he did," declared Miss Steevens. "He regarded her with a fanatical hatred and seems to have had the idea that she was determined to obtain the land from him by some underhand means. He's quite obsessed about it—but all the same, I'm sure he's not the man to do any violence—and I haven't seen him about since last term."

"Murder!" murmured Miss Cordell to herself. "Oh, no! And after all, he comes of a good old family."

"Quite," agreed Inspector Wythe. "And what about the other piece of land—no trouble there, I suppose?"

"The owner of Pagan's Field," put in Miss Steevens rather quickly, "is a Mr. James Lidgett, a farmer of Marston, who has sold a good deal of land for building and was anxious to sell this plot to the college. In fact, he offered it to us when he heard that we had approached Mr. Lond. He's a difficult man too, though of quite a different type from Mr. Lond. Miss Denning was against accepting his offer because she had not given up hope of getting Ferry House—after all, Mr. Lond is an old man. But Lidgett realized that we didn't want to see Pagan's Field covered with cheap, ugly houses and he tried to use this possibility as a threat."

"To force you to buy and at the same time put up the price? And Miss Denning in this case also conducted negotiations?"

"Yes; and not only that; she roused the Preservation Trust to the danger of ill-considered building development on that property——"

"*Of course!*" murmured Inspector Wythe. "That's why I know the name of the field so well. Quite a lot of talk about it, wasn't there?"

"There was a great deal of publicity," the principal agreed, with some asperity. "But at least public opinion proved that it *can* have some power for good. I believe that Mr. Lidgett has been finally prevented from defacing that site. Financial profit seems to be of prime importance to him, and he feels considerable animus towards Miss Denning."

"But you can see," added Miss Steevens, "that neither Mr. Lond nor Lidgett could have any real motive for attacking Miss Denning because, in the first case, she only represented the college council, which is unanimously in favour of the Ferry House site, and in the second case the damage—from Lidgett's point of view—has been done and even the death of Miss Denning can't give him back the freedom to build his nasty little houses."

"Quite. But undoubtedly, from what you tell me, they both had a spite against her—a spite which might possibly drive either of them to sudden violence."

"I trust, Inspector, that the details of this unfortunate relationship between Miss Denning and these two owners of property need not be publicly advertised. I can assure you that no blame whatever attaches to Miss Denning. They are two most difficult men," Miss Cordell declared.

"You can rely upon me, ladies, to conduct the necessary inquiries with the utmost discretion. Let us hope that we may find some solution of the problem which involves no criminal responsibility. There is one thing more I must ask. Can you tell me what relatives Miss Denning had?"

"Yes, of course. I intended to ask you what should be done. Miss Denning was singularly alone in the world, so far as my knowledge goes. She has—had—a niece, Pamela Exe——"

"X?" queried Inspector Wythe.

"E-X-E. A Devonshire name, I believe; or is it merely that I connect it with the river? In any case, probably a surname of place origin. But I must not digress. This girl is an undergraduate at Girton College, Cambridge. Miss Denning was very devoted to Pamela, who is an orphan, the only child of Miss Denning's sister. I have only seen the girl once or twice, for Miss Denning did not wish her to form any attachment to Oxford as she thought it better that she should go to the other university. Miss Denning's parents were dead and I believe she had no near relatives alive. I will telephone to the mistress of Girton and ask her to break the news to Pamela."

"Yes; say a drowning accident."

"Will it be necessary for Pamela to come here? She is certainly the next of kin."

"Not essential, so far as I can tell at present. I can run over to Cambridge by car and see her. Of course she may wish to come."

"We could put her up here of course. We are all strangers to her, I fear, but naturally we would do all that is possible for her comfort. But that dreadful railway journey! One would not, of course, expect constant traffic between the two universities, but communication might at least be less forbidding!"

"I could run the young lady back in my car, if that would help."

"That would be very kind. And—Inspector, I suppose it is inevitable that this accident will be reported in the papers, but doubtless you have influence in the matter. If you could restrain the reports as far as possible; I do not feel that blatant publicity can serve any good purpose."

"Quite. I can assure you that I shall keep a pretty strict hold on the press. At the moment I'm particularly anxious that the papers shan't say too much; it might hinder me from getting at the truth, if the truth is some undergraduate foolery. I think you had better forbid your young ladies the use of the college boats for the present; girls are as inquisitive as cattle and we don't want anyone messing up possible clues on the banks. And warn them not to give interviews to reporters. *If* the press scents a mystery—mind you, I don't say they will—but if they do they'll spare no pains to get a story from someone."

"Indeed, I know. I can assure you, Inspector, that we will take every precaution. I trust it will not even occur to our students that clues might be found on the river banks."

After some instructions about Miss Denning's room, Inspector Wythe departed to sift the facts he had elicited, to gather other pieces of evidence which his subordinates might collect from the Cherwell's sluggish waters and bushy shores, and to try to fashion them all into some coherent chain.

CHAPTER IV

THE BLOOD FEUD

GWYNETH, Daphne and Nina automatically followed Sally towards her room after dinner that evening. Passing through the hall, Sally seized a letter from her pigeon hole.

"Betty!" she exclaimed. "I'd forgotten all about her."

"Your sister—why, she's coming to-morrow!" exclaimed Gwyneth. "You could still catch the post and put her off."

"I don't want to put her off. She may be useful," Sally announced slowly as they went up the stairs.

"Useful?" Gwyneth caught up the word. "What for?"

"Give me a chance to read this. Oh, I suppose it's just about what time they'll arrive." Sally skimmed it hurriedly. They reached her room and she knelt before the fire and attended to it assiduously while the others grouped themselves round the hearthrug on humpties and cushions.

"There are the crumpets," Daphne suggested. "They want eating."

"Any butter?" inquired Sally. "We can't get it now."

"Yes, I got it," said Daphne. "I feel ready for crumpets. I was saving up for the Friday suet pudding at dinner, and then it was all evanescent flimsies and I've an awful hole inside."

"It was a putrid dinner," Gwyneth proclaimed. "Curse—Oh! How awful! We can't curse the bursar now. Well, that dinner was her last act, I suppose. Pity it couldn't have been a better one."

"Gwyneth, you're a ghoul!" Sally was disapproving. "And Daphne ought never to eat suet pudding, with her figure."

"My figure stands comparison with any in Oxford," declared Daphne. "All those straight up-and-down, can't tell whether you're going or coming affairs, have definitely gone out. The crumpets are in my bureau, Nina, if you *are* being so kind as to fetch them."

When they were at last settled round the fire, with a crumpet on Sally's toasting fork, Gwyneth asked:

"What about the Lode League? Does it just lapse?"

"I think not," said Sally very earnestly. "There'll be an awful tamasha about this, and we've got to try to help clear up the mystery. You'll find the four rings in my bag, Nina. The Lode got his all right, apparently, and we'd better have ours." Nina produced them and Sally solemnly handed them round and put one on her own finger. "Now what the Lode League has to do is to try to find out the truth of this mystery, and to find it out so that Persephone doesn't look silly. We had a rotten bursar and now she'll have brought us into the limelight by getting herself drowned in her canoe. I'm awfully sorry for her relatives, and all that. I'm even sorry for Burse—something horrible must have happened and one wouldn't want it to happen to anyone. But I can't help feeling that it had something to do with—well, with all her rotten bursing. There may be things that we don't want to come out."

"We'd better be careful," declared Daphne warningly. "Already that inspector thinks we're hiding something and if we do anything to make him more suspicious, he'll think the worst."

"You must have messed up your interview," said Sally. "You or Gwyneth."

"Of course I'd rather have Burse alive and bursing her worst," declared Nina hastily. "I'd rather lose all my washing and live on gruel for the rest of my three years, than have Burse drowned. But I don't see what we can do. Amateur detectives only do any good in thrillers."

"You don't know anything about it," Sally told her. "My sister Betty had a lot to do with clearing up the Pongleton case."[1]

The others looked awed. "How did she do it?" inquired Gwyneth. "Do you mean she *really*——"

"I'll tell you some other time. But you'd better not ask her when she comes to-morrow, because Basil, that's her husband, doesn't like to talk about it. You see, his Aunt Phemia was murdered on the underground stairs and—well, it isn't a thing you talk about."

"Sally, do tell us," pleaded Gwyneth.

"Not now. We've got to consider the great canoe mystery."

There was a loud knock on the door, which was opened before the knocking finished, and Draga Czernak whisked in.

"And is this another English meal?" she inquired calmly, looking with interest at the group round the fire, the crumpets, plates and butter.

"This is called a snack," Daphne informed her. "Taken in the best society to fill up the yawning gap between dinner and supper."

"And that is called a 'have,'" suggested Draga serenely. "I am not so green! Yes, I get your slang very well. Sally, may I have

---

1 See "Murder Underground," M. Doriel Hay (Skeffington).

your notes from Professor Windle's lecture this morning? You said you would lend me——"

"All right." Sally handed the toasting fork to Daphne and went to rummage in her bureau. "But they're awfully scrappy and you'd really understand the thing much better if you went to a lecture now and then yourself."

"Per-haps. But I had other occupation."

"Have a crumpet?" suggested Gwyneth.

"A snack? No, thank you. I think my Slav stomach would not appreciate the English snack. Thank you, Sally."

"What did the inspector ask you, Draga?" inquired Gwyneth bluntly.

"The inspector?" Draga, half out of the door with Sally's notes, hesitated. "Ah, the police! My God! That *I* should be the one to see that woman last of all!" She returned to the room and shut the door abruptly. She clenched her hands, frowning. Her placidity was broken as though by an electric current.

"You shouldn't say 'My God,'" Sally reproved her. "It's quite a swear in English."

"A woman so bad and so cunning deserved to die," Draga declared.

"That's a beastly thing to say," Nina reproved her. "You have no right to say anyone deserves to die. And besides, being drowned, it's horrible."

"But I say it. She insulted me—per-haps she then drown herself in remorse." The correctness of Draga's English was always impaired by excitement.

"But she didn't drown herself! How could she?" demanded Gwyneth.

"How do you know?" asked Draga excitedly.

"How do we know?" Sally echoed. "She was *in* her canoe. It's a mystery. She may have been murdered."

"I thought she drown herself in the river by mistake," Draga told them. "But in either case she insulted me. She say I am a pig—I, a Czernak of Stara Gora."

"It's nothing to call anyone a pig in English," Nina explained soothingly.

"What happened?" asked Gwyneth, with her usual thirst for information.

"She comes to my room—I have branches on the floor——"

"*Branches?*"

"Yes, of the fir trees. I am—lonely; yesterday was the day of a festival in my country, when we lay branches of the fir trees on the floor of the big hall in our castle. I think I will have my own small festival here in my room, and the servant girl tells Miss Denning this morning that my room is untidy. Miss Denning comes and tells me, 'I do not care for what a state you live in at home in Yugo-Slavia; you may live in the pig—' what is the word—'the pig-house——'"

"Pigsty!"

"Yes, pigsty! 'But,' she say, 'while you are here in Persephone College you must try to attain the English standards of cleanness!'" Draga repeated all this with ominous calmness. Then she burst out in fury: "That she say to *me*! In my country a blood feud has been started for less than that!"

"You simply mustn't take it so seriously, Draga," Sally declared. "Of course, Burse could be pretty rude, but in English it really isn't so bad as you think."

"A pig is a pig, an English pig or a Slav pig. It is all one," said Draga earnestly. "It was an insult. While she lived it could not be washed away."

"Well, it's been washed away now all right, and you really might forget it," advised Nina.

"And don't go about saying she deserved to die," added Sally. "In England we don't say that sort of thing and it might get you into trouble."

"You mean—they might think I have drowned her? Then I would go home and there be secure. I care not a bit." Draga whisked abruptly out of the room.

The four gazed at one another.

"Could she have done it?" whispered Gwyneth in an awe-struck whisper.

"No. I don't think so. I'm not sure that she wouldn't have done it if she had the chance, but how could she?"

"She said, 'How do you know?' when we said Burse didn't drown herself," Daphne pointed out.

"I don't think that meant anything. After all, she hadn't heard how we found her. She doesn't know any more than the rest of the college knows—what the Cordial told us at dinner, that Miss Denning had been drowned in a boating accident."

"Then why should she think it was suicide?" inquired Gwyneth.

"That's just her Slav mind, dwelling on the macabre and trying to find a connection between the accident and the pig-sty incident," Daphne explained.

"And anyway, Draga's a rabbit on the river. She couldn't have anything to do with what happened there," Nina pointed out.

"Not herself—but—good Lord!—she was telephoning to Matthew Coniston this evening!" shrieked Gwyneth.

"What of it?" demanded Sally coldly. "Draga's always telephoning to Matthew. And don't squeak so; they'll think I'm keeping guinea-pigs in my room."

"Guinea-pigs be hanged! I tell you, Draga was telephoning to Matthew in Yugo-Slavian—or whatever she calls her foul language—and she was all het up and it was about Burse!"

"So you were perfecting your knowledge of Yugo-Slavian—only I think it's usually called Serbian—this afternoon?" inquired Daphne sarcastically.

"This is really an important clue," urged Gwyneth. "I wish you wouldn't be such idiots. Draga was telephoning in Serbian, and so it must have been to Matthew, because you know he talks it and she does telephone to him in it, so that no one can understand, sometimes. I was passing and I noticed that Draga was all in a doo-dah and seemed to keep saying something over and over, as if he couldn't understand it, and at last she said in English, 'bursar,' two or three times, and then she went on and told him a lot more, but as if she was in an awful state about it."

"Gwyneth passes—pretty slowly, I gather," remarked Daphne.

"I don't see that there's anything criminal in it," said Nina. "Draga was naturally a bit agitated when she heard what had happened, and it doesn't seem extraordinary that she should ring up Matthew and tell him—not when you consider Draga. He probably didn't know the Serbian for bursar and so she had to explain it in English."

"Well, I think it's queer," Gwyneth insisted. "Draga seemed awfully agitated, but at the end she seemed relieved, as if he had told her that it would be all right in some way."

"You're simply letting your imagination run away with you," said Sally. "When did this happen, as the detectives always ask?"

"After our interviews. After I had gone upstairs I went down again to see if there was a letter for me. I couldn't help noticing, because Draga was yaddelling away into the telephone as if it were a matter of life or death."

"You know how excitable Draga is, and probably she was asking Matthew if she would be arrested because she had said Burse had insulted her, and she was relieved when he said she wouldn't. They might do that sort of thing in Yugo-Slavia," Nina explained.

"We can make a note of it," suggested Sally, "in case it does turn out to be at all vital when we find out more about the mystery. But we've got to be frightfully careful. Remember what the Cordial said about 'harmful gossip or sensational press publicity?' She's quite right. We don't want the papers to get hold of anything they can make headlines of. If we find out anything that seems to bring Draga into it, we may have to cover her tracks."

"But ought we?" Gwyneth inquired. "After all, if it *was* murder——"

"No English jury would understand a Yugo-Slav blood feud," Sally declared. "Would you like Draga to be hanged? I don't believe Draga had anything to do with it, but we've got to watch our step, not only with outsiders but with everyone in college. Everyone will soon know that we found her and will be asking us all about it, and we'd better say as little as possible. In fact——"

Sally put a half-eaten crumpet on her plate and went to her bureau, where she wrote a large "ENGAGED" notice, which she pinned to the outside of her door.

"Now, we've got to be systematic," she announced, with her mouth full of crumpet, having returned to her seat on the hearthrug. "Each of us must take one line of investigation. It's a good thing to-day's Friday; we shall have lots of time in the week-end, and my sister will help. In fact, I think you'd all better come and have lunch with her and Basil and me at the Mitre to-morrow; one o'clock."

"Won't your brother-in-law mind all of us barging in directly they arrive?" inquired Daphne.

"He'll be charmed. And anyway, this is serious; we can't waste time. Now, let's allocate the jobs. The first thing is to find out all about Burse yesterday afternoon. When did she start and who saw her on the river. Gwyneth—no; it means talking to everyone and you'd be sure to say too much."

"Bilge!" declared Gwyneth. "I'll be as discreet as the grave."

"Well, all right. You get a line on that. And I think some-one had better find out—fr-r-rightfully tactfully—about Draga—what she was doing all afternoon. Nina, can you get that taped? And someone ought to scour the river for clues——"

"We can't take any punts or canoes out," Nina reminded the director of operations. "I don't see how else you can do any scouring."

"You ought to search the banks, as far as you can. You can go through the Parks, and through the fields on the opposite side. You might find something—Burse's paddles, for instance."

"A pretty thin job," Daphne remarked. "Squishing about in those muddy fields! The police are sure to have found the paddles. Do you want us to measure the footprints and collect all the cigarette-ends and scraps of paper?"

"You search with an open mind, for anything that *might* be a clue. It's a job that needs brains. Daphne, will you cope? And I," Sally concluded firmly, "am going to investigate Ferry House!"

"Ferry House!" the others echoed. "But why?"

"Old Lond might have something to do with it; he had a special feud against Burse—almost like Draga's blood feud— over the footpath and over something to do with buying that land to build on."

"That's a *brilliant* idea!" Gwyneth declared. "He's mad, too. But, Sally, do be careful. He swore at me terribly yesterday."

"Yesterday? So he was there then—and may have been there to-day."

"I was awfully late for a lekker and my tyre was punctured," Gwyneth explained. "I don't really like meeting him and I wouldn't have gone otherwise. He jumped out from behind a tree and said something about an island in an awful voice; it sounded like a rhyme."

"But even if he was there to-day, how could he murder Burse? He's awfully doddering," Nina objected.

"Hired assassins, perhaps," Daphne suggested.

"The trouble about this case," declared Sally, in her best Scotland Yard manner, "is that the people who would certainly have liked to murder Burse, such as Draga and old Lond, don't seem really capable of doing it."

"Don't you think it might have been an accident after all," suggested Gwyneth. "Couldn't she have lain down to read in the canoe—I know it sounds silly, but it's the sort of thing she might do—and the canoe turned over and drowned her and somehow got right side up again?"

"You've got to bring *reason* to bear on this problem," said Daphne. "She'd have kicked herself free and swum."

"Besides, didn't you hear the bobby say that her hat was in the canoe?" Nina pointed out. "Someone must have put it there."

Sally announced that it was time for coffee, and went to fill her kettle. Conversation became desultory, ranging over the possibilities of murder, accident and even suicide, but it never touched the inspector's theory of an undergraduate rag which had turned to tragedy, because undergraduates, in their own eyes, are responsible individuals.

CHAPTER V

TRESPASS BY NIGHT

SALLY'S party broke up early—that is to say at about eleven—since both Gwyneth and Daphne declared that they must do a spot of work before going to bed, if they were to devote the rest of the week-end to detection. Nina lingered and helped to clear away the crockery. Sally's room was at the south end of the college building and looked across the narrowest part of the garden, towards the boathouse. The shed itself was hidden by trees, but the iron gate leading to the steps could be seen.

The discussion of the mystery had become rather wearisome, because both the girls had completely exhausted, for the time being, their stock of bright ideas, and it was impossible to discuss anything else. As if to seek inspiration from a survey of the scene of the gruesome discovery, Sally parted the window curtains and put her head through, holding the curtains closed behind her so that the light in her room would not make the darkness impenetrable.

"Why, it's cleared up; there's quite a bright moon!" she informed Nina. After a pause there was an urgent whisper from behind the curtain. "Nina! Turn out the light and come here!"

Nina obeyed. "Don't start seeing ghosts!" she remarked soberly.

"Sh! Look at the gate; I'll swear I saw someone climb over it."

"Going or coming?" inquired Nina, joining Sally behind the curtain.

"Coming in. I think it was a man. Look! Can't you see someone moving in the shadows there, by the lilacs?"

"One of those bobbies, probably. Daphne said they had brought the canoe up and left it just inside the gate."

"Then why should they come back? Besides, they don't go climbing over gates. Somebody's come in, I'm sure, to get something or do something to the canoe. *Look!*"

"Y-e-e-s; I thought I saw someone then," Nina admitted.

"Nina, you must go and put on rubber shoes and hitch up your frock, or take it off; and you've got a torch, haven't you? Be as quick as lightning, and don't let anyone see you, and meet me near the garden door."

"But—" began Nina, faintly protesting.

"Quick!" urged Sally. "If you're not there, I'll go alone."

A very few minutes later, Nina arrived on tip-toe at the appointed spot, to find Sally cautiously pushing up the lower sash of a window in the corridor, beside the door leading into the garden. "I wonder they've never put bars on this! Rather high, of course, but we'll get in again all right."

"Suppose someone comes along and latches it?"

"They won't. That's it!" Sally was on the window-sill, and quickly disappeared into the night with a heavy thud. Nina followed.

They crept towards the group of lilacs which hid the boat-house and the shed nearby where paddles and poles were kept. Suddenly Nina gripped Sally's arm, startling her so that she let out a squeak. They stopped dead.

"Ass!" hissed Sally under her breath.

"A light!" whispered Nina. "Didn't you see? Someone's there, with a flashlight."

They stood silent, trembling with excitement, afraid of the mysterious trespasser and uncertain what to do. They heard a little indefinite sound and then a slight crunch of gravel. It was dark, but seemed to be growing less dark.

"Moon's coming out," muttered Nina. "We shall be awfully obvious."

This was true, since they stood in the middle of a small lawn. Sally seized Nina's hand and, pulling her along, moved carefully to the left to reach the shelter of the lilacs. But that brought them on to a gravel path, and here, in spite of their care, every movement produced a creak, crunch or rattle. The moonlight now clearly showed them the gate and, beyond it, on the water, a canoe. But the spot from which the other noises had proceeded was still hidden. Then one of them trod on a dry twig, which seemed to explode with a reverberating crack. They stood still, clutching hands.

There were sudden, scuffling noises from round the corner of the bushes and then a figure appeared for a moment, a head was turned towards them, a man rushed at the gate, scrambled over it and seemed to slide, rather noisily, into the canoe. There was the sound of the chain being pulled in, and of a paddle brought into action.

They rushed forward and peered over the gate and could just see a canoe disappearing round the bend of the river to the right, being propelled strongly by the bowed figure in the stern.

"Certainly a man, and not a policeman," said Sally.

"Is he getting away with Burse's canoe?" asked Nina.

"I don't think so. He must have come in that one—and he came to get something. I think we disturbed him. He was scared. I wish we'd rushed out sooner; we might have seen who he was."

"I was too petrified to move," Nina confessed.

"I wasn't sure what to do," was Sally's way of expressing the same thing. "If he's the—murderer—well——"

"You mean, there might as well be two murders—or three—as one? Anyway, *he* was scared."

"Let's see if Burse's canoe is really there," Sally suggested. She glanced at the college anxiously. "No one seems to have noticed anything. I expect those noises that sounded so terrific were awfully small, really. Got your torch?"

The moon was again behind clouds. Nina swept the torch-light towards the place behind the bushes from which the intruder had emerged.

"Yes! There!"

They crept towards the canoe, which lay there forlornly, bottom upwards. They advanced very cautiously, as if they suspected that the unknown might have left a bomb behind him.

"It's the *Faralone*, and it looks all right," said Sally quietly. "There seems to be nothing else here, but the police would have taken away the hat, and anything else they found. I'm sure that man wasn't carrying anything."

"I don't see what he can have been doing," said Nina in disgust. After all this excitement, she felt, there ought to be something to discover. "Perhaps we prevented him from doing it."

"He had quite a lot of time, from the moment I first saw him. Oh! Here! Light this way again! Look!"

Sally bent down and picked up something; she held it in her hand in the torch-light. It was a penknife, with one blade open.

"So he *was* doing something—but what?"

Investigation by torch-light of the canoe and the gravelled space around it failed to reveal anything unusual, and Sally and Nina retraced their steps towards the house. Sally had to crouch down outside the window and let Nina climb on to her back, in order to open the window, but fortunately no one had latched it. Nina climbed through, and after a lot of effort, and with the help of a pull from Nina, Sally also reached safety. The two of them, Sally with a grazed knee, returned to Sally's room and sat down to examine their find.

"It's nice to be back again," said Nina appreciatively, basking before the fire.

"I don't mind telling you I really was scared lest the window might be latched," Sally admitted. "When you suggested it, before we started, I did think of leaving you behind, to let me in."

"Indeed! You didn't think of staying behind yourself, to let *me* in?"

"You weren't so keen on going."

"I wasn't sure, at first, that it was necessary," Nina replied with dignity. "But let's look at that knife."

Sally handed it to her; then suddenly exclaimed: "Oh!" in a tone that seemed to indicate horror.

"What's the matter? Not blood!" inquired Nina, dropping the knife.

"Worse," declared Sally gloomily. "We *have* made a mess of things. Fingerprints! There would have been some, but I've mauled it all over!"

"Fingerprints wouldn't be any good to us. You mean you were going to give it to the police?"

"We might have. It depends. But now, I don't know; they'd probably be awfully mad with us for having smudged the marks."

"He probably wore gloves," suggested Nina. "I believe murderers generally do."

"But he naturally didn't mean to leave the knife behind, and nobody would look for fingerprints on the bottom of the canoe, so he may not have bothered. Anyway, let's not paw it any more."

Sally fetched a clean handkerchief and carefully picked up the knife without letting her fingers touch it. They gazed at it intently. It was rather large and the handle was made of a curious brown streaky material, that seemed to be stone.

"It's not quite ordinary," said Sally hopefully; "but I don't see how we can find out whose it is, unless we can think of who the man might have been and then try to find out if he has lost his knife, or if anyone recognizes this as his."

"He went up the river, along by the Parks. Or, of course, he might have started that way to put us off——"

"I don't think so. He was in too much of a hurry to think of that. He may have been going to land in the Parks."

"Gates would be shut. Of course, he might climb over them, but he'd have to leave the canoe, and I should think it could easily be traced. What's beyond the Parks? Fields on the other bank, and nowhere to hide a canoe; there's L.M.H., of course, but it certainly was a man. Then there's——"

"Sim's!" Sally screeched. "Matthew! Draga's telephone message!"

"Gosh!" They gazed at one another in a sort of triumphant horror.

"Do you really think—?" began Nina at last.

"See how it all fits together," Sally pointed out. "Draga is up to some fishy business. There's something on, or in, or near that canoe which will give her away. She phones Matthew and says he's got to come and take it away—or something. He probably expects to find the *Faralone* just moored to the steps, where we left it, but he has to climb over the gate——"

"Yes, but *what* could Draga want him to do? If she had left anything that could be taken away the police would have taken it. Matthew would realize that, if Draga didn't. And anyway, how could Draga have been near the canoe? The police were still there when we went in to dinner. Besides, she wouldn't want to do anything to the canoe after we found it. And what could she have done, anyway? And then, what Matthew had to do needed a knife. What on earth!"

"It does seem a bit of a problem," Sally agreed. "We'd better sleep on it. But, look here, Daphne is pally with that man Vellaway, who's a friend of Matthew's. She must find out from him if that's Matthew's knife. I'll tell her in the morning, but better not say anything to Gwyneth."

CHAPTER VI

LUNCH AT THE MITRE

SOON after twelve the next morning Sally was loitering on the Parks side of Mesopotamia bridge, which leads over the Cherwell to Ferry Road and so into the private lane to Persephone College. Before she had been there long a low-built, cream-coloured touring car with green wings approached, slowly because the road is narrow. She waved at it wildly.

"How are you, pets?" she inquired, as the car drew up beside her. "Can you manage to reverse, Basil dear? I've a lot to tell you both and we must go rapidly to the Mitre. There's a side-road, where you can turn, about a hundred yards back."

"*Can* I reverse?" inquired Basil sarcastically, doing it rapidly.

Sally came up with them again when they had backed into the turning and stepped neatly into the back of the car without troubling to open the door.

"Now go ahead and turn left at the end of this road, and remember that Oxford, being very advanced in its ideas, *already* has a speed limit."

"Why all this punctuality and hurry?" Basil asked. "What's up, kid? Have you been sent down?"

"Don't call me that ridiculous name. There's nothing up with me, but there's an awful affair at college. And, by the way, you're having three other charming young ladies, as well as me, to lunch. I've ordered a table and so on."

"Very kind of them," said Basil, "and most thoughtful of you."

"Sally, you really haven't got yourself into some mess?" inquired her sister, Betty, anxiously.

"No, really, Betty. I'll tell you all about it in a minute. Right, here, Basil, then first left. This is the Broad, Trinity on your right. I'm afraid I shan't have much time to show you round, after all."

"Keeping your nose to the grindstone; that's a diligent little scholar!" chuckled Basil.

"Don't be odious! Now, the Mitre is hellish to get at from this direction. At the bottom of this, which is the Turl, turn right and keep on the wrong side of the road, and there you are. I might have brought you a better way if you had been a better brother to me."

They arrived safely at the hotel entrance and Betty and Sally followed the porter upstairs whilst Basil garaged the car.

"It looks an expensive sort of place," Betty remarked, when they were alone in the bedroom. "Couldn't you have found us a room in some more modest pub?"

"Well, I could, but it's a question of my reputation. The Mitre is *the* place for one's people to stay. Of course, Gillian Waring's people stayed in some mouldy boarding-house in Banbury Road, but then Gillian's definitely a personality, and her father's quite famous, so she can carry it off. And, by the way," she added, with elaborate casualness, to conceal her anxiety lest this plan should not be approved, "I've said you'll probably want a private sitting-room, because now that this mystery has happened it is absolutely essential to have some secluded spot to talk in."

"*Really*, Sally; Basil isn't a millionaire, and you shouldn't swank."

"You'll understand, when I tell you the news, that it is quite definitely necessary. And if Basil grumbles about the bill, I'll make it worth his while by telling everyone how frightfully good his books are and sending up his sales enormously."

At this moment Basil arrived. Sally hung about impatiently, urging both of them to hurry up, and as soon as they were ready she led them to their sitting-room. It was a cosy spot, well supplied with deep arm-chairs and cheered by a heaped-up fire.

Basil whistled. "I'd better telephone to my bank at once for an overdraft!"

"Basil, lamb! Don't be so cross. I must tell you this story quickly!" Sally implored. "Now listen, our bursar has been drowned!"

"Your bursar? Drowned—an accident? When?"

"Yes, bursar. Miss Denning; generally known as Burse. It happened yesterday afternoon, and how it happened is a mystery."

"Denning—bursar. Basil, wasn't that the woman we met in Wales last summer?"

"Woman we met? Oh, yes! The one with the pretty daughter."

"Daughter?" began Sally incredulously. "She couldn't——"

"It was her niece," Betty explained. "Pamela. A nice girl. Miss Denning seemed quite agreeable at first, and then, whether she thought Basil was an undesirable character, or what, I don't know, but she sort of sheered off and kept Pamela under her wing, and we didn't see much more of them. It was at Bala, when we were touring."

"Yes, I remember vaguely that you said something about it, but I didn't know Burse then, so it didn't impress me much. I don't know about Pamela. Well, we found the bursar yesterday afternoon, drowned in her canoe."

"Who found her?" Basil inquired. "I suppose you mean drowned in the river?"

"I and the three others who are coming to lunch." Sally told the story. "So you see, it's a mystery," she finished. "And we—the four of us—are a league, and we're trying to solve it, and I thought you might help us."

"Gosh!" groaned Basil. "I thought this was a holiday."

"So it is. Don't talk as if you were a detective every day. I don't suppose you can do much, anyway, but your car may be useful. But I thought Betty might have some ideas."

"What you mean, you're a league?" Basil asked. "Nations, or football?"

"Ass! It's a secret league. The four of us were forming a league to—well, to curse the bursar, and before we'd quite finished forming it, she came floating down the river. So now the league is going to try to solve the mystery. But, of course, no one else in college knows anything about it."

"But look here, aren't there some people called police—or don't you have them in Oxford?" inquired Basil.

"Of course we do; we've a marvellous police force that's always getting bright new ideas about the traffic—but private people can often find out things that the police can't—you ought to know that, both of you. And there may be things the police mustn't find out. But it's one o'clock—I'd better go and see if the others have arrived. We'll tell you the rest after lunch."

Sally rattled down the shiny oak stairs of the Mitre and found Nina, Gwyneth and Daphne, trying to look like women of the world, in the lounge.

"I've told them about finding the canoe; we mustn't say any more till after lunch, for it's sure to be all over Oxford by now, and we don't want everyone listening."

"All over Oxford! I should think it is!" said Nina. "Have you seen the local rag—just out?" She produced a copy of the *Oxford Mail*.

"Mystery Death of Ladies' College Bursar—Tragic Drowning Accident—Undergraduettes' Sensational Discovery—" thus the *Oxford Mail* called attention to the news of Miss Denning's death.

"Foul language! But they don't really know anything about it," Daphne pointed out. "They only say that some students—'undergraduettes'—ugh!—found the body *in* the river, and it is not yet known how the accident occurred, and 'what makes the tragic occurrence even more mysterious is that the deceased lady was a strong swimmer.'"

"Throw the nasty thing away!" advised Sally. "Here's Betty and Basil."

Introductions followed, and cocktails. Conversation was rather sticky, because of the one subject which everyone was trying not to mention.

"Did you motor down?" Gwyneth asked Basil politely.

"We did—but I thought it was always called 'up?'"

"Well, of course, you *come up*, if you come to college, but when you motor from London on a visit I think you motor down."

"Very subtle! But of course, Oxford thought *is* subtle."

Gwyneth laughed uncertainly, fearing that Basil was a high-brow being obscurely witty.

"How long did it take you from London?" she inquired.

"An hour and forty minutes," Basil told her with some pride.

"You're pretty fast!" exclaimed Gwyneth admiringly.

"I? Oh, no, not really," Basil disclaimed. "Nothing to my sister, who married a Talbot."

"One of the Worcestershire Talbots?" asked Gwyneth, who knew a good many of the best people.

"No; I'm afraid not. This one came from the suburbs; six cylinders, you know. I believe there was a young man inside, who became a passenger, but the Talbot had my sister's heart."

They were moving to their table for lunch and Gwyneth was swept on ahead.

"Basil," murmured Sally earnestly, "have you really got a sister?"

"Sister?" he inquired, with the utmost surprise. "Heavens, no! Oh, *that*—just the art of conversation! Not taught at Oxford, I suppose?"

Betty Pongleton, who could usually produce a flow of easy chatter, sat in constrained silence during the first course because every subject that came into her mind deliberately struck her as having some bearing on Miss Denning's death. The river—no! What have you read?—The latest murder mystery! What are we going to do after lunch?—Hear more horrid details about Miss Denning's death, of course. All hopeless subjects. Moreover, she was rather awed by Sally's gang of friends and afraid lest she might let her young sister down by some gaucherie which would show her unfamiliarity with the university world.

Sally was also feeling the strain imposed by the unmentionable subject, and decided that the ban might be lifted slightly.

"Do you know," she announced in a pause, "that my sister met Burse and her niece in the summer vac in Wales?"

"Really? What was the niece like?" inquired Gwyneth. "We've never seen her, but I've heard something about her."

"I thought the niece was charming," said Betty. "She was pretty, too; fair. I gathered that she was an orphan and lived with Miss Denning."

"Poor devil!" Gwyneth sympathized. "She's at Cambridge now, isn't she? Girton?"

"Yes, she talked about going. I wonder why she didn't come to Oxford."

"Ah!" exclaimed Gwyneth knowingly. "Her aunt didn't want her to have anything to do with this place. Kept the girl away even when she herself had to be here in the Long Vac for summer schools."

"There's something to be said for not mixing business and home life," suggested Basil.

"If you were a definitely frightful bursar you mightn't want your niece to know," agreed Nina.

"But Burse thought she was a lovely bursar," Daphne pointed out.

"I begin to have an idea why Pamela was snatched away from us so sternly at Bala," said Betty.

"I thought the idea was that her aunt saw through me," put in Basil.

"Do you remember," Betty continued, "it was Pamela who told us her aunt was bursar at Persephone College, and then one evening after dinner, when we were talking to them, I said my sister was going up to Persephone next term? I'm quite sure that the coldness dated from that. I felt a little icy breeze creeping towards us almost at once."

"You didn't say anything," Basil remonstrated.

"It seemed too absurd. But sure enough, next morning Pamela and aunt were up and away for an all-day picnic before we were down to breakfast."

"Do you think," said Gwyneth, "that Pamela is really Burse's illegitimate daughter?"

"Rats!" said Sally.

"And I gather," said Daphne, "that people here know about the existence of Pamela, so that wouldn't be a reason for keeping her away from Oxford."

"Pamela was rather like Miss Denning," said Basil; "but that would be natural in a niece. Your bursar was a handsome woman and Pamela was a softened version, and slighter, a regular sylph."

"Softened?" queried Nina. "Do you mean the girl's *soft*? Of course, that would be a reason for sending her to Cambridge."

"You mistake my meaning," Basil told her solemnly. "The grey matter's all right, but she seemed a kind-hearted wench, whereas Miss Denning struck me as a trifle flinty."

A party at a neighbouring table was evidently discussing the news in the *Oxford Mail*, and in a lull which fell over the League's table, a shrill affected voice rang out:

"Quite dretful! *So* glad Linda went to Somerville and not to that Persephone place. I suppose it will be quite full of those dretful reporter people taking photographs for the *worst* papers!"

"There you are!" murmured Sally gloomily, with a movement of her sleek head towards the offending voice. "We've become a byword! Burse's final achievement."

Betty looked a little shocked. "Sally," she said, to divert her young sister's attention, "I feel awfully sorry for Pamela. Do you think she will have to come here? I believe she said she had no other relatives, and if she never came here she probably doesn't know anyone at Oxford. Do you think we might drive over to Cambridge and fetch her and have her here with us? That's to say, if she really has to come. We both liked her, and we might be better than nothing if she's alone and wretched."

"Good idea," Sally agreed. "You'd better go and see the Cordial about it, I should think. Now—" hastily swallowing a last mouthful of biscuit—"if those others have finished gorging, what about moving on?"

When they were all settled in the well-padded arm-chairs of the private sitting-room, Sally opened the proceedings.

"We decided last night that each of us should explore an avenue, as Prime Ministers say, and now we will all report. Gwyneth first, on Burse's movements yesterday afternoon."

"There hasn't been much time yet," Gwyneth pointed out; "and apparently very few people, apart from Draga, noticed Burse. Theo was in the library with Draga and saw her, Burse, I mean, and says it was before two, she's sure, because she rushed through lunch and dashed down to the library to look up some date or something. And Bronwen Evans saw Burse going through the hall with paddles just as she came out from lunch—about a quarter to two, she thinks."

"We'll put it as between one-thirty and two." Sally made an entry in a businesslike note-book. "Anyone see her on the river?"

"Was it likely anyone would be on the river yesterday afternoon, except Burse? I didn't find anyone. But I heard quite a lot more about Burse from Hermione Blair."

"How did you gate-crash into third-year society?"

"As it happened, Hermione ran into me as I was coming out of the Schools—I *had* to go to a lekker because no one else who goes to that one takes decent notes—and she asked me about how we found Burse. You know, she was rather a friend of hers, and she's terribly upset, and I think the Cordial told her that we found her. She had heard all about Pamela from Burse, who was frightfully fond of the girl, Hermione says, but even Hermione has only seen Pamela once. It's quite true that Burse didn't want her to have anything to do with Oxford, but Heaven knows why. Burse didn't seem to want to conceal the fact of the girl's existence, but only to keep her away from here. Hermione isn't really so bad, but she's utterly shattered by Burse being drowned, and walked beside me, all weepy, right along the High, with everyone looking."

"I s'pose Hermione didn't know any more about when Burse went on the river or anything?"

"No—but she knew she was going, because Burse was going to tea with Hermione and said she'd be back in the canoe about four."

"And so she was—how awful!" said Daphne.

"But that's a bit queer, isn't it?" inquired Basil. "I mean mentioning that she meant to go on the river in a canoe by herself at this time of year? What I mean is, you might go off on a sudden impulse, if you had nothing better to do and wanted to eat worms, but it's a queer thing to plan it definitely and say beforehand you were going."

"Burse was definitely queer," said Nina.

"There's something in what Basil says," Sally pointed out, as if this were an unusual phenomenon. "We know she did go off in the canoe by herself quite often, but it does look rather as if she had some special reason for going that afternoon."

"The only thing I can think of is to meet someone," Betty suggested.

"I wonder. I suppose the police might find out who else had a canoe or anything out on the upper Char that afternoon, but I don't see how *we* can."

"Could she meet someone who was not on the river?" asked Betty. "I mean, is there a path or road, or anything?"

"Marvellous place for a secret meeting," Basil pointed out. "One goes by water and one goes by land. Only one set of footprints, y'see, for the police to follow; trail consequently confused."

"There's the Parks, and then higher up there's Lady Margaret Hall and St. Simeon's College; and on the opposite side there are fields, with a footpath," Sally explained.

"Probably pretty well deserted at this time of year?" Betty suggested.

"Mm, yes. And how could we find out who might have been there?" Sally pondered for a moment. "Well, Nina, what about Draga?"

"She went out yesterday afternoon," declared Nina dramatically, "and she won't say where."

There was a long-drawn gasp.

"Of course, I was very tactful," Nina explained. "She told me how she was sitting in the library, reading *The Golden Bough*——"

"Witchcraft!" commented Basil. "Who's Draga, by the way?"

"She's a Yugo-Slav and she's rather odd," Gwyneth explained. "But she may be quite normal for a Yugo-Slav. Burse insulted her yesterday and she says it was enough to start a blood feud."

Basil whistled. "Nice lot of ruffians you seem to have at Persephone College! Is it your idea that she's carried the blood feud to its logical conclusion?"

"Not really," said Sally; "but Draga will go about saying that Burse deserved to die, so we thought it best to make some inquiries."

"Draga seems to think that she was almost insulted again by the bare fact that Burse passed within her range of vision on the way down to the river," Nina continued. "She will hardly mention it, but she did tell me that she only read for half an hour or so and then went out. 'I had affairs,' she said. There may be nothing in it, but I don't see why she should be so secret."

"Lady goes up the river in canoe, apparently with an appointment; another lady, who has a blood feud against the first, goes out shortly afterwards on 'affairs.' Seems to fit," said Basil.

"Oh, but it doesn't fit," cried Sally. "No one could possibly imagine that Burse would have an appointment with Draga on or by the river."

"I don't want to suggest that one of your students has murdered your bursar, but I want to eliminate possibilities," Basil explained. "Suppose Miss Denning had some other reason for going up the river, and this Draga girl, seeing her go, gets another canoe and goes haring after her——"

"Hopeless!" Sally declared. "Draga's as likely to swarm up the Martyrs' Memorial as to take out a canoe. Let's go on to the next point—Daphne, what about the river?"

"I had a pretty thin job," Daphne told them. "I suppose you didn't expect me to swim up and down? I mooned around the garden and talked to William and I did find out from him that the police have found the two paddles—Burse's paddles—in the New Lode, I gather, nearly at the top of our island, one floating and one in the bushes. Also William saw her start and says it was just beginning to rain. He remembers that, because he had decided that it was too detrimental to his rheumatics and although as he said, 'Miss Denning was a rare one for the river, wet or fine,' all the same it struck him as a bit queer the way she got into her canoe as calmly as if the sun were shining."

"That looks like an appointment again," said Sally. "But did you look along the Parks bank, and the fields?"

"I did not," said Daphne firmly. "If there's anything to find there, the police will have found it, and I wasn't going to be seen mooning along there, like Ophelia looking for a willow tree."

"I dare say there wouldn't be much," said Sally, rather displeased. "And have you got a line on what I told you this morning?"

"Not a chance yet, but I may see Owen this afternoon."

"Between eleven p.m. and midnight yesterday," Sally announced impressively, "Nina and I did our first piece of investigation." She related to a startled audience their adventure with the unknown trespasser. "We can't explain it," she confessed at the conclusion, "and they've taken the canoe away this morning. To-day I made some investigations at Ferry House. First of all I took the footpath through old Lond's garden, making a bit of a detour to go to a lekker. I found that old beetle—Lond's gardener—hoeing the right-of-way path, if you please! I shouldn't think that path's been hoed since Persephone was built; they'd hardly defile a Lond hoe on gravel where the accursed women students' feet have trod. Anyway, there he was, scratching away first at the gravel and then at his head; just keeping a lookout to see who passed, I'm sure. He gave a sort of snort as I came along. I stopped and said 'Good morning! Nice weather for hoeing!' Snort again. 'Making the path nice and tidy for Mr. Lond?' I suggested. The Beetle jumped and snorted louder than ever. 'Expecting Mr. Lond here soon?' I asked. 'That's none o' your business,' he snorted. 'I thought I saw him about here yesterday,' said I. 'Master don't tell me when he comes or when he goes.' I thought he sounded a bit threatening, so I went on."

"You didn't see old Lond?" inquired Gwyneth.

"Wait a bit——"

"I don't quite see why you should walk through old Lond's garden, whoever he may be," said Basil.

"It's all a bit difficult for you to understand," said Sally kindly. "It's supposed to be a right-of-way, and Burse fought for it like a tiger and old Lond disputes it. I'll make you a map this evening, to help you. The right-of-way is a sort of tradition and the women's colleges have so few traditions, we hang on to any we *have* got."

"And old Lond is another suspect?" asked Betty.

"Possibly. Anyway, when I returned I came by the footpath again and passed the Beetle near the first stile. When I got to our lane I took a good look round; the Beetle was hidden by the orchard trees and no one else was in sight, so I crept along the fence towards the river, very cautiously—still inside Lond's garden; round the back of that shed in the corner and then along the bottom of the garden, on the bank of the New Lode—only there was a shrubbery and a wall between me and the river. When I got to the boathouse I had a good look round but I couldn't see any clues. It's all very tumbledown and the bushes grow close round."

"What did you expect to find? Footprints?" inquired Daphne.

"Well, there were a lot of those—police presumably. You see, it seems to me that just that point where Lond's boathouse is, at the top of our island, is where you might expect whatever did happen, to happen. I don't believe the canoe would drift very far, it would probably get caught in bushes and stick, especially at the top of our island where the stream divides. And now Daphne says the paddles were found just there."

"And of course," said Nina, "you'd think that even in the winter there'd be someone in the Parks to notice a canoe drifting down the Char with a corpse in it."

"Exactly," Sally agreed. "I thought the boathouse and garden of Ferry House might hold some clues, so I sleuthed around, beyond the boathouse, among a lot of bushes on the bank, and there I found a long slidy mark right down the muddy bank into the water!"

"One of the police got his feet wet!" was Basil's suggestion.

"I'm sure it wasn't!"

"Any sign of a cloven hoof on the slide-mark?"

"Basil, I wish you'd be serious about this. And that's only the beginning of my discovery."

"Well, hurry up with it—but of course don't leave out any important details. If you found any shreds of clothing on the bushes they ought to be analysed."

"*Well;* I couldn't see any other clues, so began to make my way back to our lane, when I caught sight of someone up by the house dodging about behind bushes; I thought it might be old Lond, so I crept in behind the shrubbery, close to the wall on the bank."

"Hold hard!" interrupted Basil. "You say there's a wall along the bank, but farther on you found a slidy mark down the bank. Does the wall stop?"

Sally meditated. "It's all very overgrown, but I think the wall stops at the boathouse and beyond there's only a broken fence and willows leaning over the water. Anyway, I crept along between the bushes and the wall and suddenly I butted into something stretched across in front of me—I was going along with my head down. I almost let out a shriek, it gave me such a shock. It was a rug!"

"What sort of rug?"

"How did it get there?"

"What did you do?"

"I didn't move it, but it seemed to be a small rug with a brownish sort of plaid pattern; the kind anyone might have for a car or the river. It was caught up on the bushes; I should think it had been thrown in there by someone who wanted to get rid of it."

"Don't you think," said Daphne slowly, "that it may have been there for ages; thrown up over the wall from the river, by someone larking?"

"No, I don't." Sally disagreed indignantly. "It would need a pretty hefty throw to hurl it over that high wall from the level of the river, and it didn't look as if it had been there for ages. It was dampish; but if it had been there long it would be soaked, and full of dead leaves and things."

"Did your bursar take a rug with her on the river?" asked Betty.

The girls looked uncertain. "I don't *think* so," said Nina at last. "She was rather Spartan, and then she always went in that long Burberry; she wouldn't need a rug."

"It seems to me, my girl," declared Basil paternally, "that at this point you hand over your two clues—the penknife and the rug—to the police, apologize for messing about and perhaps spoiling the footprints and fingerprints for them, and then go quietly about your work and your play and leave them to carry on."

"I'm not 'your girl,'" Sally told him indignantly. "As for the police, they can find the rug if they're doing their job properly. I'm not sure that it's safe to give them the knife—I mean, it may implicate people we don't want implicated."

"I quite see," said Betty soothingly, "that you don't want to find your fellow students mixed up with this affair, but if they *are*, you can hardly hope to put the police off the scent, and you had much better not be mixed up in what may be a nasty business."

"But look here, Betty," Sally urged. "Draga's a perfect ass; *we* understand her, but the police won't. We must try to protect her from her own idiocy."

"There's no harm in your keeping an eye on her and try-ing to persuade her not to make incriminating remarks. Also it's true that you may in the course of conversation gather information that the police wouldn't get by questioning. But I'm quite sure that you ought to hand over to them any clues whatever—material things or information. For heaven's sake don't hold back what may be important information—it might get you into quite serious trouble."

"Well, I'll think about it," Sally agreed, rather downcast.

"And I don't see what this rug can possibly have to do with the crime," said Daphne. "Lond can hardly have strangled Burse with a rug."

"And then poured water over her to look as if she'd been drowned," added Gwyneth.

"And of course there's the time difficulty," Sally pointed out. "If Burse set out at about 1.45 and her body came drifting down in the canoe after four, she would have had time to go quite a long way up the river, unless she talked to someone for ages."

"No one could talk to old Lond for ages. His usual con-versation is a stream of abuse and then he bolts away," Nina pointed out.

"Could old Lond have decoyed Burse into the house and murdered her there, with the help of the Beetle, and then put her back into the canoe, to get her off the premises?" hazarded Gwyneth.

"Apart from the fact that Lond is ancient and tottering and the Beetle incredibly old and bent, I don't believe he would ever have let her into the house, much less enticed her there," said Nina authoritatively. "Mary Wentworth once told me a lot about him—you know she has a North Oxford aunt and so knows all the local gossip. The reason why Lond's so furious about the footpath is simply because we're *women*; he's a misogynist and won't ever let a woman set foot in the house. It's Elizabethan you know, supposed to be rather special, and once some old archæological johnny got permission from Lond to go and see over it, but he turned up with his wife and Lond met them at the door, and went off the deep end when he set eyes on the lady, and almost pushed them out of the place, yelling curses after them. Since then it's said that he's never allowed anyone inside. He'd never let Burse in—not even to murder her."

"I don't want to throw mud or cold water or other chilling substance," said Basil. "I think you've all been pretty smart, but see how you're up against it! You may be no end bright at theories but the police are bound to have you beat when it comes to facts. You don't even know, for instance, what killed your bursar. The police, having analysed everything within reach, probably know by now whether she was really drowned or poisoned or smothered, or what. Hadn't you better hand over to them what you've got, which they may be able to make more use of, and go on using your wits as hard as you can, but leave the sleuthing to them?"

"I don't really see what more sleuthing we can do," Daphne agreed, rather pleased to think there was now no reason for her to go squelching about on muddy river banks. "Of course, I can see if Owen knows anything about the knife and we might be able to find out something more about the rug. But I agree with Mr. Pongleton that the outdoor work had better be left to the police."

"I think so too," Gwyneth concurred. "We might construct a perfectly magnificent theory to explain how Burse was drowned and then Sir Bernard Spilsbury would decide that she was killed with a blunt instrument."

"I think we'd better go back," remarked Sally rather coldly. "Betty and Basil, you can come with us and be introduced to the Cordial and see if you can do anything about Pamela. I do feel awfully sorry for that girl. First she had Burse as an aunt and now she's had her removed by a horrible mystery."

CHAPTER VII

AUTHOR OF "DUST"

"Daphne, have you bought my new poem?"

A young man, who seemed to have been washed up to the pavement by the noisy tide of traffic in Cornmarket Street, intercepted Daphne as she walked back with the others to Persephone College. He had a charming smile, an air of being well-pleased with himself, and regularly waving hair.

"How can you expect me to attend to literature—even yours—when our bursar has just been murdered?"

"Lord! Really? How, when, where?"

"That's just what we're all trying to work out."

"But—I say, does anyone know about it? You're not serious?"

"Quite definitely serious. Everyone knows about it and even you would know about it if you weren't too grand to look at the posters." Daphne waved a hand towards an old woman who shambled down the street with a bundle of papers under her arm and an untidily flapping poster on which the words "LADIES' COLLEGE DROWNING MYSTERY" were intermittently visible.

"Good Lord! Is it a University sensation? Will it spoil the sale of my book?"

"Really, Owen, of all the egoists——"

"Dash it all, if your bursar's dead the fuss can't matter to her, and a little fuss about my book would matter a lot to me. Definitely you must buy it. Come along now—you buy a copy and I'll treat you to coffee—Oh, what's the time of day? Tea then. Come along."

Daphne hesitated, standing there, looking down demurely at her feet. The others had gone on.

"There *was* something I wanted to talk to you about," she admitted. "But I think you might give me a presentation copy."

"There are no presentation copies," said Owen Vellaway firmly. "Mr. Blackwell isn't taking any chances, and we've got to sell five hundred copies before I see my money back."

"So it's merely a commercial venture? I thought you were an inspired bard whose genius simply poured forth to refresh the arid universe—and damn the expense!"

They had strolled to the end of the Corn and Owen, taking her by the elbow, propelled her round the corner into the Broad.

"If genius is going to pour forth in print, someone has to pay for it, and I don't see why I should be out of pocket so that the world can read the lines I have penned by the sweat of my brow."

"What's the price?" Daphne inquired.

"Half a crown—it's a gift, the poem alone, not to mention a woodcut by Jopling."

"But no one will buy it. You know that nobody buys new books in Oxford. They'll go to Blackwell's and read it there."

"Don't I know their charming habits! But that's provided for—sealed copies! And I have several trusty friends on duty in Blackwell's in the rush hours; if they see anyone breaking a seal they stroll up, disguised as one of Blackwell's assistants, and say 'sir—or madam,' as the case may be—'would you like it wrapped up? Two shillings and six *pence*.' Neat idea?"

"Doesn't Blackwell mind?"

"His original idea, you know, was to run a bookshop and actually to sell books. The undergraduate population of Oxford turned the shop into a reading-room, but it is believed that occasionally an elderly professor gets into a panic at the idea that he may die—or at least become utterly cobwebbed and so immobile—before he can finish Blankenstein's ten volume treatise on The Intangibility of the Actual, and deliberately buys the book. Oh, yes, they've got all the gadgets—a concealed till, complete with change, and what not——"

"But I mean, what happens to my half-crown if one of your pals takes it?"

"They're all honest lads. Straight into Mr. Blackwell's till it goes, not a hair of its head harmed. Here we are—but I don't think any of the gang is there now, so you'll have to shock one of the genuine salesmen into activity. Be a brave girl. Go in and say nicely, 'Please, I want a copy of Mr. Vellaway's *Dust*.'"

"*Dust?*"

"Snappy title, what?"

Daphne paused, irresolute. "I think I'll get it out of the Times Book Club."

"Done again! No copies sold to lending libraries! Such is the reluctance of the modern man or woman to buy a modern book, that they'd even take out a three months' subscription, at a cost of two half-crowns, rather than take the desperate step."

"I never realized that you were so practical!" Daphne regarded him with admiration. "But is it really worth half a crown? Perhaps I could borrow it?"

"Daphne, you shall have a really *good* tea, wherever you like; éclairs unnumbered——"

"Right oh!" Daphne walked deliberately up the steps into Blackwell's bookshop. When she returned a few minutes later, Owen was mopping his brow.

"I begin to sympathize with Mr. Blackwell," he told her. "Now where shall it be—Stewart's, Elliston's, Fuller's?"

Daphne considered her choice. "I think I feel like Fuller's to-day. Blackwell's man bore the shock very well, I thought."

"The booksellers of Oxford will rise up and bless me in years to come. I am creating a revolution! Lord! It's a sweat!"

Daphne's finger was sliding under the paper sash which prevented the opening of the thin volume which she held.

"Good Lord, girl! Don't you know how to treat literature with respect? D'you mean to say you'd glance negligently at an epoch-making poem whilst strolling in the vulgar street?"

"I thought I'd just take a look at Jopling's woodcut," said Daphne innocently.

"Even Jopling is worthy of better treatment."

It was early for tea and they easily found a quiet table near a window. After some earnest concentration on the menu, Daphne turned her attention to the book. *Dust*, by Owen Vellaway, was the title, and below it, on the paper wrapper, was printed: *"You can get the best seat at the movies for half a crown and even see the picture round four times, if you can bear it, but you can't pass the seat on to your friends. For half a crown you can buy the most vital poem and the most significant woodcut which Oxford has produced this century, and you can read the one and look at the other as often as you wish, but if you are a gentleman you will realize that for the pecuniary benefit of the author and the artist it is essential that your friends shall also pay for their seats."*

"I don't see how I can prevent them reading it," said Daphne; "but if they think it's worth half a crown they'll then go and buy it for themselves."

"If you are a gentleman—" said Owen warningly.

"Well, if it's really a slap-up tea——"

"With knobs on," Owen promised.

Daphne slit the wrapper and opened the book. Title page; a blank page; another blank page.

"Nice paper!" said Daphne. "For reader's comments, I suppose."

Another page revealed the woodcut, representing a small conical hill above which drooped a lugubrious figure, oozing large tears.

"Molehills aren't really pointed."

"How true!"

Daphne turned another page, which disclosed the title repeated at its head and in its centre a neat little block of print:

"When I am dead
A rubbish heap
My bones will keep.

"Above my head
If weep you must,
You'll lay my dust."

"Very nice and peaceful." She turned another page. Blank. Another. Blank again. "Not much for the money!"

"Not much—! Look at that charlotte russe—ninepence! Four of those for half a crown, and to-morrow will you feel that you have any value for your money—or rather, my money? Whereas there, in that book, you have genius crystallized!"

"Four nines are more than thirty," Daphne told him. "This was a bit of a shock at first, you know. I expect by to-morrow, when it has sunk in, and the charlotte russe has sunk in too, I shall be able to estimate both at their true worth."

"You do not need time to appreciate it properly."

"It certainly has a beautiful, peaceful finality. I'll tell people to buy it, Owen, so that I can watch their faces when they turn the pages. Will you have some more tea?"

"What was it you were saying about your bursar?"

"Oh, yes! Now listen." Daphne told him the story, outlined their tentative theories and described the "clues."

"What do you think of it?" she concluded.

"I gather that your bursar was the kind of person everyone wants to murder?" Owen inquired.

"Don't keep calling her *my* bursar! I didn't choose her. For our sins, we were fed on her meals and had to submit, more or less, to her domestic tyranny. But to be fair to the woman, since she's dead, I believe she really was efficient, from the college point of view. That's what you'd expect of her—she was one of these hard-faced business women; definitely unsympathetic. Not that we wanted to weep on her shoulder, but she seemed hardly human."

"So any one of you might have murdered her, so far as motive goes?" Owen suggested.

"I wouldn't go as far as that," said Daphne cautiously. "After all, you'd have to feel pretty desperate about a person to go to all the trouble and risk of murder, not to mention mess. We could put up with her; after all, there are things about Oxford to compensate you for a rotten bursar. But it's pretty maddening, you know, to have a woman going about college who obviously doesn't care a hang for any of you. Utterly wrapped up in her own affairs, whatever they were!"

"Now we're getting at it!" Owen declared. "She was one of these superior beings, I take it, who look down the nose at all of us? That sort can drive a man to frenzy much more easily than one who is readily subject to the human emotions. Someone has come up against her and has been infuriated by that aloof manner and has upped and clouted her over the head!"

"Of course, she was infuriating," Daphne agreed. "But that just means that anyone with a hasty temper and a strong arm, who might have had an argument with her, may be guilty. There's old Lond, who was mad with her over the right-of-way and always flies into a rage when he sees one of us—anyone from Persephone, I mean—but he certainly hasn't got the strong arm. He couldn't pull the skin off a rice pudding!"

"You never can be sure," said Owen. "Rage lends strength to a man's arm, you know; probably to a woman's, too. What about this girl Draga you mentioned? Is she the one with the flat face?"

"Flat face! I think she's rather attractive, though it's true she hasn't much nose. You know her—it was at tea with her in Matthew Coniston's rooms that I met you."

"That's the girl! No, not attractive; too bleached. I saw her yesterday in the quad."

"In your quad? When?"

"Afternoon, I think. Let's think; I'd been round to Blackwell's to know when he would have my book on sale and it was as I came back—about three, I should think."

"You've thought three times, so it ought to be right! So that's where Draga went—but why wouldn't she tell Nina?"

"Why should she tell Nina?"

"Nina wanted to find out, and she's a miracle of tact, but Draga was awfully mysterious about it."

Probably she came to see Coniston; he's known her for ages; his father was in the diplomatic service in Yugo-Slavia and he was out there as a boy. Why should you probe into the wretched girl's affairs?"

"Because Draga seems to be mixed up in some queer way with what happened to Burse. We don't think she's done anything really criminal, but she's behaving like a perfect ass and we don't want her dragged into it. If we could find out what her connection with the affair is, we might be able to help her."

"I can't quite see what grounds you have for thinking she's connected with the affair, except that she claims she had grounds for a blood feud."

"There's more than that—and this is where I specially want you to help me. Do you happen to know if Matthew Coniston has a penknife with a brown handle that looks as if it's made of some sort of stone?"

"A sort of streaky brown stone?" asked Owen, before he had time to think.

"Yes, that's it," cried Daphne excitedly.

"But look here," Owen demonstrated, realizing that he had perhaps given Matthew away. "There must be hundreds of men who have penknives with brown handles."

"Not like that. It's rather odd. Handles are usually made of bone, or horn, if not metal. Now can you find out if Matthew *still* has that penknife."

"No, I can't!" declared Owen obstinately. "I'm not going to join your band of sleuths—at any rate, not unless you tell me more about it."

Daphne told him of Sally's and Nina's night adventure in the college garden.

"What are you after, Daphne? Are you trying to scrape up a lot of facts incriminating Coniston and then pass them over to the cops?"

"That is about the last thing we are trying to do," Daphne stated with dignity. "I always think that the front of Grimbly Hughes's shop should be starred in Baedeker as one of the most remarkable examples of commercial Gothic, don't you?" She gazed with great concentration out of the window and across the Corn at the building in question.

Owen stifled an exclamation of protest against the violent blow he had just received on his shin and leant towards the window with a critical air.

"Pure Ruskin! Certainly remarkable." Then, after a few minutes, with a cautious glance over his shoulder: "Do you think they heard anything?"

Daphne regarded with distaste the two ladies who were just leaving the tea-room. "They seemed to be hanging round, under the pretence of putting on their gloves, but I don't think they got anything of value. But look here, you do admit, don't you, that it's a queer episode. Draga telephoning to Matthew in Serbian; someone coming by river late at night, doing something queer at or near Burse's canoe, dropping a penknife and bolting."

"Yes, it's queer. But why Coniston?"

"Well, the telephone message—and the penknife. You know him well, don't you? Can you find out more about it from him? What did he and Draga do yesterday afternoon? Burse would have had time to go up the river as far as Sim's; your garden runs along the river bank, doesn't it?"

Owen looked worried. "Look here, Daphne. I don't like the look of this. Coniston is a peaceable sort of chap, not in the least likely to mix himself in a blood feud. Of course, he feels a bit responsible for Draga, I dare say, and might do a good deal for her, but not murder, or anything like murder. As for our garden, there's a high iron fence all along the bank; they couldn't meet your bursar on the bank except like monkeys looking through a cage. But I will see if I can find out anything helpful, though I'm not hopeful. And don't mix yourself up in this affair too much, Daphne. It's a nasty business and you don't know where it might lead you. Don't let your mind dwell on it; you'll get morbid. Think of something else."

"*Dust*, for example?"

"Yes; uplift is what you need."

"And look here, Owen, when you have found out anything, ring me up and ask me to tea again, or something. That will mean you have something to tell me, but don't dare to ring up unless you really have. I shan't ask you on the telephone, because I don't want anyone to overhear."

CHAPTER VIII

"NIPPY"

WHILST Owen Vellaway was exercising considerably more mental energy in his effort to sell one copy of *Dust* than he usually felt inclined to spend on an essay, the superintendent was meeting the afternoon express from London which brought Detective-Inspector Braydon from Scotland Yard to the scene of the Cherwell mystery.

"Very awkward situation, sir," Wythe explained. "The chief was involved in a motor accident a couple of days ago and sustained severe shock. He's not to be worried, so he doesn't even know that this has happened."

"Most unfortunate," Braydon agreed. "I hope that between us we can get it all straightened out for him before he has to hear about it. What happened to him?"

"Well, to tell the truth, his car got out of control and tried to climb the mound that stands in the centre of one of our new roundabouts. Quite a nasty smash!"

"No wonder he's suffering from shock! Well, how's the canoe case shaping?"

"It's got no shape at all so far, sir, that I can see; or if it does begin to take some shape, it changes again before you can see round it, if you know what I mean," grumbled Wythe. "This is the car."

"A regular Proteus of a case!" remarked Braydon, getting in. "Well, what does it look like at the moment?"

"Quite so, sir," Wythe agreed, guessing that the Yard man referred to some difficult problem of the past, some City financial affair probably, that he—Wythe—could not recall.

"I've been making a pretty thorough inquiry at all the boat-houses on the river to try to ascertain what craft were on the Cherwell that afternoon. I hoped to get the survey completed before you arrived, but there is just one more place to visit, which may be the most important of all, St. Simeon's College boathouse."

"Have you sent someone up there?" Braydon asked.

"Well, no, sir; I wanted to see the boatman myself; I just had word that he's to be found there now—"

"And you want to get along and see him?" Braydon finished. "Quite right. Go ahead, super! You can take me with you and tell me the story on the way. Any suspects yet?"

"I had a theory, sir—well, it's hardly a theory, so to speak, that this might have been the result of some rag by those undergrads. That putting the body back into the canoe—it isn't reasonable! And when we come across anything in Oxford that's a bit funny, like putting crockery on the pin-nacles of the Martyrs' Memorial, we know we've got to look around among the undergrads."

"Without knowing all the details," Braydon suggested mildly; "it strikes me that it might be highly reasonable to put the body back into the canoe. What better way of removing it from your premises?"

"Well, there's that about it, certainly. If it *was* on premises. But I'd better tell you what we've ascertained up to the present."

Wythe outlined the case and had hardly concluded his survey when they entered the drive that leads from Norham Gardens to St. Simeon's College. Leaving the car, they walked across the quad to the right and through a vaulted, dark passage, they skirted a lawn and passed through a green gate in a high wall, beyond which a path led them to a backwater, where they found a stout, red-faced man pottering about with a can of varnish on the landing-stage which sloped from the boathouse to the water's edge.

"You carry on!" Braydon directed, and Wythe began to explain his errand to the boatman. Braydon strolled about, examined a newly varnished canoe which lay out on the landing-stage, bottom upwards, and contemplated another afloat and moored to a post. He strayed into the dark boathouse and inspected the names on the lockers above the two vacant places. Emerging, he observed that the canoe in the water was named *Nippy*.

Braydon approached the two men, who were still in earnest conversation.

"I'm telling Inspector Wythe, sir," declared the fat boatman, who had evidently been informed of Braydon's identity, "that I was here all Friday afternoon from the time it stopped raining until it was dark, having a job or two that I wanted to get on with, and none of the gentlemen could have taken any boat out without me knowing. They was all here in their places."

"Did you notice Miss Denning pass in her canoe on the river?" Braydon asked.

The boatman pushed his broad, red face towards Braydon apologetically.

"My hearing's none so good," he muttered.

Braydon repeated the question loudly.

The boatman shook his head mournfully. "It's not as if we was on the open river here. Nice and quiet, of course, but

I wouldn't notice particular anyone passing on the river, not if I was set close to my work."

"If you were working inside the boathouse someone might come down the path quietly and slip into *Nippy* there and be away before you noticed anything?" Braydon suggested.

The boatman shook his head knowingly. "Ah! You're mistaken there, sir, if you'll excuse me saying so. *Nippy* wasn't in the water on Friday afternoon; she was up in the boathouse. There was no boat in the water on Friday. If she'd been there before I left on Friday, she wouldn't be there now. They're all high and dry and locked up at nights."

"So someone's been out this morning?" asked Wythe.

"I wouldn't answer for that," replied the boatman cautiously; "unless they was out earlier than the gentlemen usually takes boats out in winter. Seeing as it was a fineish day, which we don't have too much of just now, I came down here to get on with that little job of varnishing, and there was *Nippy* in the water."

"So it seems that Mr. Coniston took her out yesterday evening after—what time was it that you went home?" Braydon asked.

"You know all about it, seems," said the boatman, rather surly. "That's Mr. Coniston's canoe all right, but he might lend her to anyone. She came out of that boathouse after four o'clock yesterday, I should judge, and the lady was done away with, so I hear, *before* four o'clock, so there's no sort of connection between the one thing and the other. If you ask Mr. Coniston, he'd tell you all about his canoe, I'll be bound. Proper gentleman, he is, though quiet-like."

"I wonder if he *would* tell us all about it," Braydon mused as they strolled back to the car.

"Anyone owning a boat there has a key to the boathouse," Wythe commented, "and there is free access to the boat-house until nine o'clock, when the college gates are locked. After that this door"—they had reached the little gate set in the high wall—"is shut and anyone coming from the boat-house would have to go round to the main gate and knock up the porter."

"Why did he leave the canoe in the water, I wonder? A bit careless—or hurried. I don't think we'll call on Mr. Coniston just now. I want to have a word with the doctor. Is this the only boat you have traced as likely to have been out on this part of the river on Friday?"

"That's the only one. Several skiffs and fours out on the Isis, of course, but none of them is likely to have gone up the Cherwell, certainly not above the rollers. You've been looking at a map of the city, I think you said, sir?"

"Yes; I've got a general idea of the lie of the land."

"These rollers are not far below Persephone Island; they are for the purpose of getting boats past the weir just there. No one goes on the lower part of the Cherwell for serious rowing; it's too narrow and winding. There's very little boat-ing on the Cherwell at all at this time of year. The women, more than the men, take out a punt here and there on a fine day, but Friday doesn't seem to have tempted them, from all we can hear. My men have inspected all craft in boathouses on the upper river and they report them every one dry as a bone. If there's any question of a so-called rag by undergrads, then of course St. Simeon's seems the most likely college, having this boathouse on the Cherwell not so far above Persephone, so I particularly wanted to take a look at that for myself."

"A rag usually produces a good deal of noise, I believe?" inquired Braydon.

"Well, anything of this kind would, most probably. And to my thinking there would be several men in it. To get worked up to such high spirits that they'd drown someone, there'd have to be a party, egging each other on."

"It's hardly the sort of thing that could be completely concealed. I feel that you would have lighted on some sort of evidence by now, if that were the solution. You've made a pretty thorough survey of the river and boathouses, I gather."

"That we have," Wythe agreed. "This accident theory isn't panning out too well, I'll admit." He was evidently reluctant to abandon it. "The other possibility is old Lond—that is, so far as I have been able to make it out, sir. He lives in lodgings at New Marston, a sort of little suburb on the road to Marston village—not half a mile from Ferry House. The old place is half ruinous and he can't afford to pay the rates, or even to put it into good enough repair for his own needs. He is seen about the place from time to time, and there's an old fellow who used to be gardener there who's allowed to use the land for his own vegetables, and is supposed to keep the garden in some sort of order in return. Lond seems to have been hanging about there ever since Thursday, and that's unusual. I'm not sure about Friday, to tell the truth. No one seems to have seen him there, but he left his lodgings in the morning and won't say where he was. He's there to-day all right, and the gardener too, and we're keeping a watch on them."

"What are they doing?" Braydon asked.

"Gardener's pottering about with a hoe. Lond's doing a bit of pottering too, but he's mostly in the house."

"You haven't been in?"

"To tell the truth, sir, I went up to the door to speak to Lond and thought I might get him to let me in without a fuss, but he was downright abusive; refused to answer anything and slammed the door in my face. I didn't really think there'd be anything to find in the house. What I mean to say is, if there was any funny business there, how could that old man, or even the two of them, carry a body down to the river again? It's a good step, and anyone might pass down the lane to the college and see them at it."

"What about the other man Miss Cordell named to you, the farmer?"

"Lidgett? To tell the truth, sir, I can't see anything to link him up with the affair, and I can't see that he'd have anything to gain by it. Not that old Lond would either, but he's crazy enough for anything. No; of course I've kept Lidgett in mind, but I haven't followed up that line, so to speak. What bothers me much more than Lidgett is those young ladies at the college."

"You think they know more than they've told you?"

"I do, sir. There's something very fishy about them all meeting there by that boathouse at four o'clock and then this morning one of them, Miss Watson, comes across Lond's garden by the footpath and slips between the yew trees and wanders off down to the bottom of the garden, by the ruined boathouse. She moons about there a bit, poking in the bushes—one of my men kept an eye on her—and then out she comes. Now, what does that mean? But here we are."

Inspector Wythe was a careful driver at any time, and perhaps his chief's recent mishap had made him even more cautious. Certainly his mind was occupied with the mystery of Miss Denning's death and watchful for any indication that the Yard man might think he had not been smart enough in following up what clues there were. So their progress through the centre of Oxford to the police station had been dignified rather than snappy.

"Now, sir," he announced proudly, as he led the way in; "we've got the canoe here for you to see, and all the information is tabulated, and I think Doctor Shuter and our own doctor, Odell, will be waiting for you. Yes, here they are."

Braydon listened carefully to the doctors' report, throwing out a question now and again.

"Then the gist of it is that she had a pretty hard thump on the back of the head from the well-known blunt instrument, which might knock her senseless but wouldn't be fatal."

"But you'll not be forgetting," interposed Dr. Odell, "that your blunt instrument may not be an instrument at all in the usual sense. The woman might have hit her head on a post or any hard, blunt object."

"Yes, I see. And then she was drowned whilst she was unconscious—that wouldn't take long, I suppose?"

"A few minutes might be enough, in that condition."

"And you don't think she was in the water very long; not more than long enough to drown her?"

"Probably not. There were actually parts of her clothing, round the waist, which were hardly wet," Dr. Shuter explained. "And moreover—" he launched into technical details.

"Quite so. And the time when her wrist watch stopped, 2.37, is the probable time of her death?"

Both the doctors hesitated. "My impression, when I first saw her, not more than a quarter of an hour after she had been taken out of the canoe," Dr. Shuter explained cautiously, "was that she had been dead some hours. There were various points—When we noticed the time at which her watch had stopped, that seemed good enough. It fits. But I shouldn't like to be cross-examined on it. It's a very tricky thing to decide within an hour or two." Dr. Odell seemed to agree.

"I suppose it is established that the watch was stopped through being full of water, and hadn't just run down?" asked Braydon.

"Yes, sir," Wythe confirmed, full of satisfaction. "I've known watches play funny tricks, and I've had a reliable man to look at it, who reports that it certainly wasn't run down and seems to have been in good order. But whether the lady kept her watch fast or slow or even punctual, who's to say?"

"Moreover, you can't be sure that it stopped dead at the moment when she fell into the water," Braydon pointed out. "It might go for some time before the water stopped it. You might ask your man, Wythe, what he thinks likely, but I don't suppose anyone can say with any accuracy how long it would continue to go after it was immersed. All that it indicates is that she fell into the water before 2.37," Braydon decided. "What about bruises or other injuries, doctor?"

"There's nothing that you'd describe as signs of a struggle," Odell reported. "Her clothing was dragged about a bit and her hair was down, but you'd expect that to happen if the body was hauled into a canoe. There was a good deal of rather blackish mud about on the body; that might just have been collected by dragging the body up a muddy bank, but it looked as if she had been drowned in a shallow, muddy spot, rather than in clear water."

"And whoever hauled her out would be bound to get pretty wet, at any rate about the legs and arms, and pretty muddy, I suppose? That's hardly a medical matter; I was thinking aloud," said Braydon.

"It's a matter of common sense," said Odell rather severely. "I don't see how anyone could haul her out of the water without getting into it, at any rate over the ankles, unless they had a punt."

"What about the weight?" Braydon asked. "Was she a heavy woman?"

"Not particularly," said Dr. Shuter. "I've heard her described as tall, but that impression was given by the fact that she was slim. She had rather a masculine figure, square-shouldered. I should say an average man could haul the body without much difficulty out of shallow water and into a canoe, if the canoe were securely moored by the bank."

"That is assuming that the bank was not a high one?" Braydon asked.

"That would considerably increase the difficulty, of course. It might still be possible, if the water were sufficiently shallow for one to stand in it, but then, in hoisting the wet body up a steep bank, one would get wet up to the shoulders, I should judge."

"Yes; thank you. That was my idea," said Braydon. "Well, the problem at the moment seems to be, if she was drowned before 2.37, where was her body between that time and 4.15 and why wasn't it set adrift at once; or *was* it set adrift at once and did the canoe get jammed in bushes and free itself some time later? Now, Wythe, let's take a look at the canoe."

On the way Braydon asked the inspector some questions about Miss Denning's will.

"That and other papers are ready for your inspection, sir. I've found nothing that seems to shed any light on the affair, to my way of thinking. She left everything to the niece; seemingly there was no one else to leave it to."

CHAPTER IX

THE MAN WHO SAW BURSE

OWEN VELLAWAY walked slowly back to St. Simeon's College, thinking almost as much about Daphne's bursar as about *Dust*. Perhaps for this reason he decided in the Parks to make a detour in order to walk along the river bank, although in the dusk and through the white strands of mist which hung about the Cherwell he was unlikely to notice any material clue, even if there should be one to find. When he came to the concrete footbridge which rises in a steep bow over the narrow river, he climbed the slippery path to its summit and stood there for some minutes, looking downstream towards Persephone College. A little below the bridge, on the far side of the river, lay Ferry House, completely concealed by the row of tall elms which edged the northern side of its garden and by the pollard willows which, with the appearance of heads of hair standing wildly on end, seemed to crouch over the water along the riverside boundary. It was impossible to distinguish the New Lode, the narrow channel which branches off to the left and separates Ferry House from Persephone College.

Owen wished he had listened more attentively to Daphne's story, but he remembered that the girls had found the canoe at about a quarter past four—just about this time. The canoe must have floated down the main stream—not along the New Lode—to arrive at Persephone College boathouse, but that would be natural, for the New Lode was only a sluggish backwater. He looked up the river towards Sim's. The Parks bank is fairly clear, but the other is encumbered with jutting bushes and clumps of reeds here and there. Surely a drifting canoe, even if it had escaped the observation of anyone in the Parks, would not travel far before it stuck in a bush or ran aground? Owen felt sure that whatever had happened to Daphne's bursar must have happened in the secluded grounds of Ferry House. Old Lond's derelict boathouse, which Daphne had mentioned and which, Owen remembered, was just above the point where the New Lode branches off, was now invisible, and would still be so from the bridge in broad daylight, he thought. Even if Draga Czernak's visit to Sim's on Friday afternoon had been connected with the bursar's expedition; even if Draga and Matthew Coniston had, from Sim's garden on the river bank, seen the bursar pass in her canoe; even if, incredibly, they had planned some rag to revenge the insult which Draga felt she had suffered, still, he felt sure, these things could have no connection with the corpse-laden canoe which had arrived at the river steps of Persephone College.

But there was that penknife with the rather odd handle, which sounded like one Owen knew quite well as belonging to Coniston. Owen did not know when Draga left Sim's. She might have had time to hurry back through the Parks, over this bridge and through the grounds of Ferry House to some point on the river bank in time to intercept the bursar's canoe as it passed. But, dash it all, this was absurd. He wasn't thinking about a Chicago gangster, but about a woman student of Persephone College, Oxford, who was foreign, and odd, but still—this wasn't the place in which to think things over reasonably. The silence, the faint glimmer of the brown water through the mist, the melancholy trees, did not encourage a clear outlook upon hard facts. They were more conducive to poetry. Deliberately he switched his thoughts from mysterious deeds to the fascination of words, but "crawling water"—which struck him as a good phrase—inevitably suggested "slaughter," and so his mind jerked back again to the bursar. It also occurred to him that he might find himself shut in the Parks for the night if he did not hurry.

When he passed through Sim's dark archway into the quad which, after the gloom of the Parks, looked festive with its double row of glowing windows, he made his way, without any definite intention in his mind, towards Matthew Coniston's rooms. As he mounted the narrow stone stairs he became aware of a tumult of voices and laughter above him. This was unusual, for Matthew was a solitary kind of chap. Clever, erudite in queer bypaths of knowledge, a worker, a man with two or three firm friends, but not the sort of fellow into whose rooms men were continually drifting at any odd hour for idle chatter. It was not unusual, however, to find some total stranger closeted with Coniston for consultation on some awkward problem of life or work. He had a reputation for *savoir-faire*, due, perhaps, to his cosmopolitan life and experience in diplomatic circles. He was a small, dark, ugly man, with long legs, long, clever hands and dark eyes which glinted through thick-lensed, horn-rimmed glasses.

No good trying to do any tactful detective work on Coniston, if he's got a party on, Owen reflected, but I might as well see what the row's about.

The door stood ajar. Owen, on pushing it open, saw Coniston almost lost in the depths of a long arm-chair and behind a fog of smoke from his pipe. In the centre of the room, and apparently the centre of interest, stood a certain

Dick Bayes who, it was generally supposed, would hardly have attained the status of member of the University if it had not been for his prowess with the oar. On a table and the arm of a chair perched two others, vaguely known to Owen as friends of Bayes, a long-necked, red-haired youth called Nickal and a square, stolid man known as Dumps.

"I tell you I saw that woman paddling her own canoe up the Char like a mad thing," Bayes was proclaiming; "and then, later on, paddling it down again, alive and kicking."

"What's all this about?" cried Owen, startled. "When was this?"

"Come and listen, Vellaway," Coniston hailed him. "Bayes saw the murdered bursar on her last voyage. But I don't suppose you even know we've had a murder in academic circles?"

"The corpse in the canoe! I've just been having tea with the girl who found it," said Owen.

There was a hail of questions: "When was the corpse found?" "Who did her in?" "Where?" "Why?"

"Bayes's story obviously comes first," said Owen. "We must do things in order. Let's have it from the beginning."

"I was takin' Nuts—that's my dog—for a run," Bayes explained. "On the top of the Parks' bridge I noticed a canoe——"

"High and dry on the bridge?" interrupted Owen sarcastically.

"Funny man! With a woman in a bright green jumper-thing, paddlin' away like blazes up the Char," Bayes continued unperturbed.

"What time?" inquired Owen.

"A bit before two, near as I can tell. She'd just passed under the bridge, so I only saw her back; she sat like a ramrod, and from the way she pushed that canoe through the water I'd say she might pull a good oar."

"Too late to think of that now!" Nickal reminded him.

"That's all right as to time," Owen corroborated. "Was she wearing a hat?"

Bayes considered. "Felt hat, I think. Don't remember her hair. I thought she was probably cracked and I went on with Nuts into those fields on the other side. As we came back I thought to myself, that dame must be about at Islip by now, if she hasn't run aground, and lookin' up the river, what should I see but another canoe comin' down."

"*Another* canoe?"

"Well, the same canoe, for all I know; but a grey Burberry-affair at the paddle this time. 'S a matter of fact, I took it for a man for a moment. Then I thought to myself, women's colleges must have a regatta or something on; they've got some pretty hefty paddles. Nuts barked—no wonder! Suspicious of anything out of the ord'nary. I took another look at the female and dashed if it wasn't the same one."

"Well, she'd gone up the river, so it wasn't very odd that she should come down again," Owen pointed out. "What time was this?"

"Round about three, I should think."

"Can't you remember exactly? It's vital," Owen urged. "They found her body at four-fifteen, at Persephone boat-house. You're the witness who can fix the time of the crime."

"Didn't you have a date with anyone?" Nickal suggested hopefully.

Bayes considered. "I heard Sim's strike three, but that might have been afterwards. Now I come to think of it, I believe I heard it from the fields—that'd make it just after three that I saw the canoe again."

"Or it might have been as you put Nuts back in his kennel; that would make it about three-thirty; or it might have been when Nuts had his fourth scrap that day; that'd make it about five minutes after you started out—or——"

"Shut up, Nickal! Vellaway's right; this is important; we've got to get it clear," said Bayes earnestly.

"He's got to report to the police," Coniston reminded them, from the depths of his chair.

"That's what I want to know," Bayes declared. "What do I do next?"

"Police, of course," Coniston repeated. "Quite probably it's important. You may be the only person who saw her."

"Then for heaven's sake, don't muddle me," implored Bayes. "I've got the story quite clear if you don't all keep bargin' in with rotten questions."

"There's a raspberry waiting for you," Nickal assured him. "Cops will barge in with questions all over the shop; that's how they catch you out. You'd better let us help you get the story taped."

"Sure thing," Dumps added.

"To return to the canoe," Owen suggested. "Are you sure it was the same one? The first one had a green jumper and the second one had a Burberry, and you didn't see the first one's face."

"Didn't see the second one's face, either. You know the height of the bridge; I was lookin' down on the top of her head, and she had the same grey felt hat rammed down over her ears——"

"Then the first one *did* have a grey felt hat?"

"Didn't I say so? Same hat all right, and hefty female about the same height and build, paddlin' down just as hard as she went up. Thin, square-shouldered, 's far as I could see."

"As a rowing man yourself, of course, you'd recognize her style when you saw her again?" Owen inquired.

Bayes became very serious. "There's not so much individual style in paddlin' a canoe, of course, as in rowin'. Now I come to think of it, she was paddlin' on stroke side each time and holdin' the paddle good and straight. Anyway, it must have been the same; there can't be two strappin' females mad enough to go paddlin' up the Char on a winter afternoon."

"Look here, you've described her as hefty and strapping and also as thin. Sure there weren't two?" Owen asked.

"Well, she paddled pretty heftily, but now I come to think of it she wasn't outsize," Bayes decided.

"Perhaps one was the bursar and the other was the murderess, hot on her trail," Nickal suggested.

"Though it's not a dead cert that it *was* a murder," put in Coniston.

"What, drowned herself and then got back into the canoe to go home?" asked Nickal.

"I don't know how it could have happened," said Coniston rather slowly. "But no one's found a murderer yet, have they?" He looked towards Owen.

"I don't think so," Owen said hastily, a bit flurried. "This bursar seems to have been pretty unpopular, even for a bursar, but murder isn't usually committed even on the least beloved of our dons. She had a quarrel with an ancient lunatic man who owns Ferry House, but he is reported to be too enfeebled to murder anyone. There doesn't seem to be any definite idea of a motive, except general hatred."

"Why do most women get murdered?" asked Dumps.

"Unfortunately they don't," Coniston informed him.

"But most of those who do——"

"Intrigue!" Owen hazarded. "Some wretched man gets involved with too many of them and has to remove one or two."

"Was this bursar an intriguing sort?"

"I've only seen her slightly," Owen admitted. "Struck me as one of those hard-faced, self-contained spinsters; not much appeal. Of course, you never know. What was your impression, Con? You knew her, didn't you?"

"No more than you did, I suppose. Impression much the same. Not the sort to get entangled, I should have said," Coniston replied.

"I suppose you didn't notice a murderer hanging about, in the course of your walk?" Owen asked Bayes. "Sinister-looking fellow skulking behind a bush?"

"By Jove! Now I come to think of it, I met a rough sort of farmer chap! Gave Nuts a nasty look and said a dawg like that can do a tidy lot of damage, he wouldn't wonder."

"Sure that wasn't another day you saw him?"

"I've seen him before; well, I think I have. Seems to own that land. I'm pretty sure it was yesterday that I passed the time of day with him and he muttered something about seein' if he couldn't get some wire put up before the summer to stop those blankety blank picnic parties from landin' and tramplin' down his hay."

"Was he near the river?"

"Right on the bank."

"There's your murderer!" exclaimed Dumps.

"Hold hard!" said Coniston. "You might as well say that Bayes was the murderer, or Nuts."

"But look here!" Bayes protested. "I didn't even know who the woman was."

"All right; we don't suspect you, yet. But don't go telling the police, or anyone else, that you saw the murderer," Coniston advised him. "Are you sure you saw no one else?"

"Not a blooming soul!"

"Not even a woman, who according to some authorities, has no soul?" Coniston urged.

"I'm dead certain I didn't," Bayes maintained.

"Didn't you say something, Vellaway, about a right of way?" asked Nickal.

"Yes, but that was through Ferry House grounds, lower down, and Bayes's rough sort of farmer chap doesn't sound like the owner. But of course, this bursar may have had a complex about rights of way, and she may also have passed the time of day with the farmer, and on hearing that he was going to put up barbed wire entanglements against her summer picnics, she may have attacked him with a paddle, and he knocked her into the river and then, not wanting her floating about near his property, put her back tidily into the canoe."

"But Bayes saw her again, alive and paddling strongly," Nickal objected.

"Bayes doesn't know what he saw, do you, Bayes?" Owen asked.

"I know I saw that woman twice," declared Bayes obstinately. "I can't say you've cleared things up any with your damnfool questions and ideas, but I'll bet my bottom dollar she passed under the Parks bridge alive, going strongly downstream."

"She was found at four-fifteen, still going downstream, but dead," Owen pointed out. "It wouldn't take more than ten minutes, I should think, to paddle downstream from the Parks bridge to Persephone boathouse—or would it be longer, Con?"

"*I* don't know; haven't noticed particularly. But obviously she was murdered between the bridge and Perse Island. There's a bit more field, isn't there, below the bridge; and then comes Ferry House."

"Yes, I was looking at that this afternoon from the bridge," Owen told them. "Just the spot for a murder; deserted and surrounded by trees. If Bayes really saw her before three the murderer seems to have taken his time, but he may be one of these slow and sure fellows."

"What else did you notice, Bayes?" Dumps asked.

"Yes, we must straighten out your story," suggested Nickal; "and then we do a spot of detection. We piece together the facts and they make a theory."

"Go easy on the theory, for the police," Coniston advised.

"But you must have noticed something more," Owen urged. "You saw the late bursar a few moments before her death. Wasn't there a strange light in her eye? Didn't she grip the paddle convulsively? Wasn't there another canoe slipping quietly but swiftly round the bend of the river behind her?"

"Oh, stow it!" cried the harassed Bayes.

"What about that coat she came down in?" asked Nickal. "She can't have had it on when she went up, if you only saw her back and noticed a green jumper—or was it Danube blue or Isis mauve? Anyhow, was the coat in the canoe?"

"Can't say; easily might have been. I couldn't really see into the canoe. But—by Jove! now I come to think of it, there was something in the canoe when she came down!"

"But that's wrong; you ought to have seen a coat in the canoe when she went up," Owen pointed out.

"I tell you I couldn't see what was in it then, but there was a coat in it when she came down," Bayes insisted.

"But she had the coat on, you said; you've bungled it hopelessly!"

"It might have been a rug, now I come to think of it; yes, that's it; a brown rug!" proclaimed Bayes triumphantly.

> "He thought he saw a Rattlesnake
> That questioned him in Greek:
> He looked again and found it was
> The Middle of Next Week,"

Owen quoted. "Or, if you prefer it:

> He thought he saw a Bursar Dead
> Who paddled a canoe:
> He looked again and found it was
> A yellow Cockatoo.
> You'd better paddle on, he said,
> Your gills are very blue!"

"Fine! Send it in for the Newdigate," Nickal advised. "But to return to our bursar——"

"The more I think about the rug, the surer I am about it," Bayes insisted. "And what's more, there was something under it."

"Poetry has stimulated his imagination," said Owen.

"*What* was under it?" Nickal asked.

"If it was under the rug, how could I see?" demanded Bayes, aggrieved. "Picnic traps, I suppose."

"Picnic traps!" yelled Nickal in derision. "At this time of year!"

"Well, what would you have in a canoe?" Bayes demanded.

"You, with a mind little above that of the beasts, wouldn't think of anything but provender, of course," Owen told him. "But bursars are bent on higher things. She may have been carrying her account books about, to work on them at odd moments. But you know, Bayes, the story's getting too elaborate. All this 'coming to think of it' is fatal to its original charming simplicity."

"There's no sense in the affair, anyhow," grumbled Dumps, who was beginning to be bored. "The bursar was batty and that's that."

"Batty or not," growled Bayes. "She went up the Char in a canoe and she came down again, and that's plain fact worth a dozen of your rotten theories."

"That's a good simple story for the police," Coniston told him. "If you can stick to it and not introduce too many side-lines."

"I'll sum it up," said Owen helpfully. "Just to help you get it clear. You went for a swim up the Char to see a farmer about a dog; a bursar paddled upstream to have a party with the farmer and you saw them both coming down again with empty bottles under a rug in the canoe."

"Oh, cheese it!" cried the exasperated Bayes. "But now I come to think of it——"

The rest was drowned by howls of derision. When calm was restored Bayes remarked, sulkily: "I've forgotten what I was going to tell you. It was something rather vital, but you've put it out of my head with your howling."

"You must at least admit that we've helped you a lot," said Nickal. "Whatever you tell the police they're sure to say 'How do you account for that?' and we've explained all the difficult points. Now have you got it all clear?"

"I had it perfectly clear," Bayes muttered, "before you spouted all your putrid theories."

"I advise you," put in Coniston, "to go and think it out quietly by yourself, trimming the story of all excrescences, and then off to the police before you talk to anyone else."

"O.K." said Bayes, and departed.

Nickal and Dumps made a move.

"Have a heart, my lads!" Coniston urged. "Don't follow him or he really will get so mixed that the police will think he did it himself."

They departed, muttering agreement.

"Wonder what he *will* tell the police," murmured Owen.

"Probably very little; he'll be so afraid of mucking up his story, which is perfectly good, I think, so far as it goes," Coniston replied. "I'm afraid I ought not to have let you bait him so. We really don't want to confuse the trail."

"Do you think that it really was the same woman?"

"Most likely; but I think he invented the 'traps' under the rug. He may have invented the rug. By the way, what do you really know?"

"Practically no more than I've told you. Daphne Loveridge and some of her pals found the bursar's body in a canoe by their boathouse." He repeated a few more details. "Daphne said something about a rug having been found later, I think, so Bayes may be right about that."

"You heard no suggestion as to who really did it?" asked Coniston.

"No. Daphne considers it a first-class mystery. That foreign friend of yours, by the way—Draga, I think she's called—seems to have been the last person to see the bursar, apart from our bright friend Bayes." Owen spoke with elaborate carelessness, keeping a watchful eye on Coniston.

"Yes, I saw Draga yesterday afternoon," Coniston replied with equal carelessness, puffing at his pipe. "She rushed up here, as she often does, to tell me her troubles." He paused; then continued: "I suppose she was here at about the time that the wretched woman was being murdered. She came bursting into my room all unchaperoned, which is just the kind of thing she is liable to do, with a fine scorn of any rules and conventions that are not those of her own country and family. She's a queer creature, but her people were very decent to us when we were out in Belgrad, and I feel rather responsible for her."

"I gather from Daphne that Draga wasn't fond of the bursar?"

"She came to tell me that the bursar had insulted her—called her a pig, which is pretty bad among the Yugo-Slavs.

Draga was very bitter about it and thought she couldn't remain any longer under the same roof with the woman. I had to soothe her and tell her we never mean what we say in English. She departed fairly calm."

Owen had taken out a pencil with which he was making violent strokes on the back of an envelope.

"What's that?" Coniston inquired. "A new poem, expressed in geometrical figures?"

"Blast!" exclaimed Owen. "Got a penknife? I'm trying to draw a map of the scene of the crime and I've broken my pencil point."

Coniston put his hand to his pocket, but withdrew it almost at once. "No, I haven't. Why not use a pen?"

"Can't draw with a pen. Haven't you really got a knife? You generally have."

"Probably lent it to some swine at a lekker," replied Coniston irritably. "Here's another pencil, but you'll break that if you stab at the envelope as you did before."

Owen took the pencil and continued to draw, more gently.

"If that bursar started from Persephone at one forty-five, as she seems to have done, and paddled strongly up the river and was seen by Bayes returning under the Parks bridge soon after three, how far up do you suppose she would have got?"

"Is this higher mathematics? That's just over half an hour each way, and of course she'd go down more quickly. There's quite a strong current now. I should say she'd get up beyond Timms's boathouse."

"That doesn't seem to help much. Anyhow, it isn't what happened to her above the Parks bridge, but what happened below, that's important."

"Exactly—and I'm a bit sick of these idle speculations. You haven't heard from Daphne of any sensational discoveries, I suppose?" Coniston shot out this last question suddenly and raised himself a little from the depths of his chair. Owen was startled.

"Er—no, I don't think so," he stammered. "What sort of discoveries?"

"You know what I mean." Coniston's eyes seemed to bore into him. "Owen, you *may* be a good poet—mind you, I'm not giving a positive opinion—but you're a rotten detective, and now that Scotland Yard is on this job, as you probably don't know, but as I've seen in the latest edition of the *Oxford Mail*, you may find it better to leave the inquiries to them. If I have any information to give, I'll give it to the police, if it's likely to be relevant, but I shan't blurt it out to the world in general, or even to you. If I have lost my penknife that's my affair. Even if someone has found it, it's hardly *your* affair. I expect Daphne has put you up to this, but you'd better tell her not to mix herself in criminal investigation. And if they're hounding Draga, because she disliked the bursar—as most of them did—and has been indiscreet, there'll be the devil and all to pay."

"Sorry, Con. I've been an ass. I did tell Daphne to keep clear of it. But as a matter of fact what they are trying to do is to protect Draga from the possible consequences of her own rashness."

"They needn't bother. Draga's in no danger and I can do any protecting that may be necessary. I don't want to discuss this business, but I'll tell you one thing and that is that neither Draga nor I know a thing that is likely to throw the smallest ray of light on the problem of who killed the bursar."

"I don't know whether it's of any interest to you," said Owen slowly, "but Daphne told me that they had carted away the bursar's canoe, to be exhibit 1 at the inquest, I suppose."

"Oh!" commented Coniston, non-committally. "Inquest's on Monday, isn't it? I suppose the police must have something to gloat on, as there are no blood-stained handkerchiefs nor blunt instruments in this case so far."

"I've been a clumsy ass and I apologize," said Owen shame-facedly, and drifted out of the room.

"What the hell did I want to mix myself up in it for?" he muttered to himself. "Damn Daphne!"

On thinking it over in his own room, however, he decided that it was a pity to damn Daphne outright. She was an amusing girl and he would quite enjoy giving her lunch on Sunday. After all, he could tell her Bayes's story and say that penknives and the rest of it must be left to Scotland Yard.

He sat down and wrote:

"THE BURSAR SPEAKS

"From bursal greed
Catastrophe
Has set my spirit free.

"There is no need
For heartless youth
To seek the muddy truth.

"It is decreed
Since I've been Charred[1]
To call in Scotland Yard."
"But I *can* tell you something if you will meet me
at the George to-morrow at one, for lunch."

"O."

He addressed this to Miss D. Loveridge, Persephone College, and hurried down to put it in the box for the college messenger to collect.

---

1   N.B.—Joke.

CHAPTER X

THE MYSTERY OF FERRY HOUSE

GWYNETH's room, at the opposite end of the college building from Sally's and on the top floor, commanded the best
possible view of Ferry House, and here Sally organized what
she called the "Lond Patrol." One member of the League was
always to be on duty at Gwyneth's window, keeping a watchful eye on the two or three windows of Ferry House, and the
stretch of moss-grown terrace at the back, that were visible.
This system was instituted after tea on Saturday, with protests
from Gwyneth that she didn't see why her room should be
turned into a sentry box and some grumbling from Daphne
that there wasn't anything to see, and if there was, what of it?
Sally could not answer that question. She had no clear idea of
what she was looking out for, nor of what she would do if the
patrol saw anything unusual. But she felt that the Lode League
must continue to justify its existence and for the moment she
could not think of any other steps to take. The others fell in
with the plan partly because Sally was the dominating personality of the League and partly because, after all, queer things
had happened in the last two days and more queer things
might be going to happen, and the house and garden belonging to old Lond, who was definitely queer, seemed the most
likely setting for unusual events.

Sally herself put her name down for early dinner—an
arrangement devised for the convenience of earnest students,
who were thus saved from the waste of time involved in dress-
ing for the regular dinner. They wolfed a hasty meal half an
hour earlier and hurried back to their rooms to work in peace.

Sally hurried up to Gwyneth's room to take up her post at the window.

"Anything to report?" she inquired of Gwyneth, the last watcher.

"Well, of course I *had* to get dressed somehow," Gwyneth explained, "but I did think I saw a light in a downstairs window—in fact, perhaps in two windows. It wasn't a steady light, and not very bright; rather as if someone was striking matches here and there."

"But that's definitely vital!" cried Sally excitedly. "Gwyneth, you are a juggins! Why didn't you keep a proper watch—you can dress for dinner any day, but something positively crucial may be going on in that house."

"I can't dress any day for to-night's dinner," Gwyneth pointed out. She was particular about her clothes. "I did put on my easiest frock, and whatever may be going on, I couldn't really have seen more than I did see. Try for yourself!" She whisked out, switching off the light, and left Sally on guard.

Sally disdained the arm-chair which Daphne had placed by the window earlier in the evening, to ease her spell of stern duty. She sat with her eyes so fixedly focused on the darkness that hid old Lond's property that even the distinction between the intenser gloom which was the house and shrubbery, and the paler shadow which was the open terrace at the back of the house, became blurred. She blinked and shook her head to restore the clarity of her vision and, even as she did so, became aware of a faint ray of light striking out from the house over the terrace. Definitely she saw the edge of a low stone wall and the twigs of a bush jump into visibility. Then all was dark again.

Someone was in the house—but what was the use of knowing that, except that it gave her a feeling of importance, of being in possession of secret knowledge. It might be only those blasted police. Though if they wanted to inspect the house, surely they would do it in daylight. Whilst, if old Lond wanted to hide some incriminating evidence, he would certainly do it at night. She might creep out and investigate—but she was definitely afraid. Betty would be mad with her, of course, if she came to know of it, and in spite of Sally's air of independence, she greatly valued her elder sister's good opinion and had considerable respect for her judgment. It was possible, of course, to ring up the police and tell them what she had seen—but then, suppose they went clumping around and found nothing and no one; they would think she was all strung up and had imagined the light and would doubtless be awfully superior. No, she couldn't tell the police about this—unless she could first make sure that there was really something to tell them.

She was still chewing on this problem when the others came up from dinner.

"What luck?" inquired Nina.

"There's someone in that house, moving about with a light; I'm trying to decide what we ought to do," Sally told them.

"I told you there was a light," Gwyneth reminded her.

"And now I've seen it myself, and I'm sure it's old Lond."

"Well, if he's really there—and you said yourself that he was there this morning—he would naturally have a light," Nina pointed out. "I don't believe there are any curtains or blinds, so you'd naturally see the light. He's probably going to bed."

"But he doesn't live there; there's no furniture; I think he has lodgings somewhere. Therefore he's there for some nefarious purpose," Sally insisted.

They discussed the problem for some time and the more the others opposed Sally's suggestion to investigate and counselled leaving the whole thing alone, or else telling the police and letting them get on with it, so Sally's determination hardened and her courage grew.

"Look here, I'm going," she declared at last. "We're simply wasting valuable time in all this palaver. I'd like someone to come with me; it may be useful to have a witness; but if no one will come, I'll go alone."

"I'm definitely out of this," Daphne announced. "I think it's lunacy."

"What about you, Nina?" asked Sally.

"If you must go, I'll go," Nina agreed reluctantly. "I think you're loopy, and anyway I'm *not* going to follow you into that house. If you go in I shall yell loudly—or else go and try to find some police; I believe there are some hanging about our lane. But I'll go with you if you'll be reasonable."

"If you're going to yell, I'm not sure that I want you."

"I'll come, if you like," Gwyneth offered without much enthusiasm. "But I'm sure I should yell; I hate noises in the dark."

"It's nearly nine," Daphne pointed out. "You haven't got late leave, I suppose, and there'll be questions asked. How will you explain it if you come back at the double, with old Lond at your heels?"

"There's not going to be any need of explanation," Sally replied. "We'll come back by the window we used before, and you and Gwyneth must keep an eye on it, to make sure it's open for us. If the gate is locked we can climb it. Come on, Nina; you must change. Rubber shoes again and dark clothes."

A few minutes later they set forth, after Gwyneth had done some preliminary scouting for them, to make sure they would leave the house unobserved.

"We won't go over the stile," said Sally. "The police may be watching there. There's a gap in the fence before you get to the stile, just stopped up with some branches."

It was very dark and the lane seemed deserted. They found the gap and Sally shoved herself through with some violence and a good deal of noise. Nina followed, accompanied by rending sounds.

"Blast! I've torn my skirt on that branch."

"Sh! Stand here; quiet! If anyone has heard and comes to see what's up, we mustn't make a sound," whispered Sally.

They stood for some minutes, half crouching amongst wet bushes against the fence. There seemed to be tiny noises all around them. Dropping water, scufflings, creakings; but no steps on the other side of the fence.

"We're all right. There are no *human* noises," Sally said at last.

"Wish there were! This is a beastly place. Let's get out of these wet bushes."

"Now, I want to creep round the house, as near to it as we can get. If we think Lond suspects anything, we must just melt into the bushes and freeze. If he should come out after us, we must separate and run for the lane; he couldn't catch us possibly."

"What about the old Beetle?"

"He couldn't catch us either. And he isn't there at night. Anyway, if we separate that'll confuse them and we'll get away all right. But it won't come to that if you keep calm and quiet."

"I'm terrified of old Lond, for all his feebleness. I feel he might creep round behind us somehow and bash us on the head or something."

"Keep a look-out behind you then, but don't get the horrors. Come on!"

Sally led the way, pulling her feet out of the sticky earth in which they had been standing and pushing through the bushes as quietly as possible until they emerged on to a path. They made their way cautiously up to the house. The end nearest to them was quite dark, but as they stepped gingerly over the old, firmly set flags of the terrace round the corner of the house, Sally breathed: "Look!"

A glimmer of light showed through a wedge-shaped slit between the side of a window and the curtain or rug which had been hung over it inside.

They crept along the wall until they reached the window and tried to peer in. They could hear slight sounds from the room, little tapping and scraping noises, but the crack through which the light shone was high up and they could see nothing.

Sally motioned to Nina to withdraw and they crept back along the wall and discussed the situation in breathless whispers.

"We *must* see somehow," Sally declared. "We must find something to stand on. Surely there's something about— flower-pots, perhaps."

"That shed," Nina suggested.

The two girls retraced their steps and rounded the corner of the house, following a path towards a shed which stood near the disputed right of way, and in which they had occasionally seen the old gardener pottering about. The door was only fastened with a hook and, safely inside, Nina produced her torch and swept the beam of light over a jumble of gardening tools, dry bulbs and other litter.

"There!"

A stack of flower-pots in one corner was fenced in behind rakes and hoes. The larger pots were full of smaller ones, piled in lop-sided towers. Sally sighed despairingly.

"I'll have to move all those things, frightfully carefully, one by one, while you hold the torch. Just a mo'; let's make sure it's safe. It would be awkward if he caught us here."

She ventured outside. The garden was silent except for the intermittent drip of water from wet branches. She returned to the shed and closed the door.

Trembling with anxiety and excitement she began to remove the rakes and hoes, one by one. Then, with the utmost care, she started on what seemed the least topply pile of flower-pots.

"Don't waver that torch about so! You must be all of a dither."

"I'm all right," Nina declared stoutly. "I'm just trying to point it where you want it."

As Sally lifted one pot a piece fell out of it and tinkled upon the others.

Nina flicked off the torch and they both held their breath for some moments in terror. But there was no sound from outside.

"It was only a *tiny* tinkle," said Nina, reassuringly.

Sally resumed her work, lifting each pot with the greatest care. At last, one very large one was free from obstructions.

"I should think it's nearly midnight," Sally groaned. "There's not much skin left on my knuckles and we might have done several murders in here for all the police care!"

"Not quite so quietly as this."

"You never know. I think it's your turn for manual labour. Give me the torch. I'll go ahead and warn you of any pitfalls and you follow close behind with the pot. And for Heaven's sake don't let the thing crash!"

Nina obeyed instructions. When she had a firm hold of the pot and a clear route to the door, Sally switched off the torch, opened the door and stepped aside to let Nina out first. A half-stifled shriek horrified Nina so that she nearly dropped the flower-pot.

"Are you all right?" she inquired anxiously.

After the light of the torch the blackness of the shed was impenetrable. A little scuffling sound from Sally; then a low voice, full of apology.

"All right! Frightfully sorry! I thought it was a clammy hand, but it's only a cobweb."

"Sure it was nothing else?"

"Quite sure. All serene. Lead on! I'll shut the door."

The door safely hooked, Sally took the lead, feeling her way carefully, and so at last they regained the back wall of the house and with infinite care lowered the flower-pot on to a level flagstone below the screened window. Sally stepped on to it, gripped the window-sill, and gradually brought her eyes up to the level of the gap through which the light showed.

She looked into a long, panelled room, low-ceilinged, empty of furniture. In the opposite wall, but some way along to the right, she could see an open fireplace with a good deal of heavily carved dark oak above the chimney arch. A few feet from the fireplace, with his back to Sally, stood the old gardener in his earth-coloured clothes, with his legs strad-dled apart, his knees bent and his body leaning uncouthly forward. He held aloft a lantern in a trembling hand, so that its light flicked unsteadily about the fine old room and some-times on to his wrinkled, weather-darkened features which might well have been the work of the Elizabethan sculptor. But the lantern light was chiefly directed on to the point where a chisel and hammer, gripped in the knotted hands of old Lond himself, were at work. Lond was standing on a box in the hearth. The lantern light showed his long, grey hair straggling over his coat collar, and Sally had a glimpse now and then of his rather fine face with the beaky nose and eyes deep-sunk under bristling brows. But mostly he bent for-ward, intent on his work, tapping and chiselling with unhur-ried concentration.

Sally stepped down from the flower-pot, putting a hand on Nina's shoulder for support. She dragged Nina across the terrace and down the shallow steps which led to the lower part of the garden near the river. Here, she felt, it was safe to talk.

"I saw him, and the old Beetle too; old Lond is chipping away with a chisel, as far as I can make out, on some wooden panelling above a fireplace. It looks as though he was carv-ing something—too extraordinary! You're taller; you may be able to see more. They haven't the ghost of a notion that they're being watched and it's quite safe, but don't make a sound!"

They returned to the spy hole and Nina mounted the flower-pot. After some minutes she stepped down again and they retreated to the bottom step below the terrace.

"He's not exactly carving; he's cutting away something that's been carved there before," Nina announced. "I'm quite sure, because I can see the long strip where he's been working. It looks as though there was an inscription all round those panels and he's hacking it off and making it more or less smooth. The wood is lighter where he's taken the top layer off. He must be absolutely batty! But isn't it a lovely room!"

"Can't say I noticed it much; I'd think it a lot lovelier if the window was opposite the fireplace. I must have another look. What makes you think it's an inscription? Perhaps it's bloodstains! Or perhaps he fired at Burse and there are bullet-holes that he wants to hide."

"Sounds very far-fetched to me; besides, it did look like words, though I couldn't see clearly; it might just be a pattern."

"Of course I didn't really mean that about bullet-holes. But it's much more reasonable to suppose he's cutting away some trace of the crime than that he's merely removing an inscription. Especially as he's supposed to be devoted to his old house."

"While we're arguing here, he's finishing the job," Nina pointed out. "It looked to me as if he had nearly got to the end. If you really want to look again you'd better hurry up. But do be careful; that flower-pot didn't feel any too safe."

Sally mounted to the point of vantage once more and peered through the chink. Yes, Nina was right; he was certainly chipping away some of the carving. The chink at the edge of the curtain was wider towards the top and Sally thought she could see more if only she could raise herself higher. She found that she could just reach the moulding above the window and, holding on to this, she raised herself to tiptoe, leaning sideways at the same time. Yes, she could now see the chisel blade, driven by the hammer, peeling off all the raised part of that strip of carving, leaving a rough track paler than the surface of the old mellowed oak.

Then the flower-pot moved.

"Look out!" breathed Nina, too late.

The pot grated on the flagstone, toppled and crashed. Sally landed with a thump, clawing at the window as she fell. Even in falling she saw that the noise, which indeed seemed thunderous, had broken the peace of the lantern-lit scene inside the room.

"Run! Bushes!" gasped Sally, and they ran, across the terrace, pell mell down the shallow steps, stumbling and tripping through the wild garden. Sally went down towards the river and the thick line of bushes inside the wall. There she found a damp, uncomfortable shelter and crouched motionless.

She could see the lantern swinging about on the terrace; the two old men were apparently going to and fro up there, probably looking at the ruins of the flower-pot. Then old Lond began to shout. At his first yell Sally's heart stood still; she thought he had seen Nina somewhere. But no, he did not give chase, but stood there, shouting into the night.

"You damned sneaking trespassers; you—vermin! Clear out and drown yourselves! Drown your*selves*, I say! I'll not touch you, but the curse of the House blast you!"

There was a good deal more; Sally listened, trembling. There was a pause; the lantern remained still; she was terrified lest perhaps old Lond was creeping through the darkness towards her, leaving the Beetle alone with the lantern, as a trick. But no, after a last curse flung down into the unresponsive garden, the lantern began to move steadily along the terrace, showing glimpses of long, striding legs ahead of it. It disappeared round the far end of the house.

Sally still crouched in the bushes for what seemed like half an hour. All was quiet; the light did not even reappear at the window where they had watched. Sally was trembling all over; she imagined footsteps, sounds of someone pushing through bushes, the sound of someone breathing heavily. Where was Nina? And now there were the police to evade. If they were really posted in the lane, they would surely have heard this uproar and would be on the watch. Meeting them might be even worse than meeting old Lond and the Beetle.

She crept out; there was a path here at the bottom of the garden which followed the bank of the New Lode towards the lane. Sally crept along, pausing every few minutes to listen to the indefinite, frightening night sounds. Then a more definite noise; the cracking and creaking of branches.

"Sally!" the faintest whisper.

"Nina! Here! There's a path." Sally stretched out a hand tentatively, as if she feared to meet some horror. In a moment her arm was gripped by Nina's groping hand. They clung together with infinite relief.

"I'm afraid those police may be on the watch!" whispered Sally. "But if we go through the hole again we're bound to make a noise. There's a flower-bed here and I think we might get across it and up to the fence and move along by that very carefully. Then, when we come to the stile, we must nip over it and bolt for our gate."

"Then if they see us they can trace us easily," Nina objected.

"There's no other way. After all, we can't get on to Perse Island except by the gate, unless you want to swim. And all that row was ages ago; they may not be watching now. If we're going to be caught, better to be caught crossing a public stile than crawling through a hole in a fence."

"Golly, what a night! We must have been in there hours! I'm in a frightful mess. Why not go straight up to the stile by the path?" asked Nina.

"Because if they're watching it, they'll see us coming and stop us for certain and ask us awkward questions. But if we go up by the fence we may just get across before they realize we are there. You can go over the fence first and if I'm caught you can run on. After all, I made you come," Sally added generously.

"If we're in the soup, we'll be in it together," declared Nina valiantly.

So they plodded heavily through the sodden flower-bed, close under the fence. When they could make out the stile just ahead they paused.

"Now for it!" murmured Sally and plunged forward. Nina heard her mutter "Oh, hell!" But she vaulted the stile neatly, paused a moment on the far side for Nina to follow, and then they both ran swiftly for the bridge over the New Lode and the iron gate of Persephone College.

A strong beam of light sprang out of the darkness behind them, showing them their own fantastically moving shadows.

"Over the gate!" cried Sally. They climbed it neatly and without hesitation. Sally led on down a path to the left, away from the front door. In a few minutes they stood panting beneath the window which had served them before.

"Let's leave our shoes here!" Nina suggested.

"I've only got one," said Sally. "Left the other in the mud by the stile. I don't think they followed. They saw us, but they surely couldn't recognize us."

"No; but it will be quite simple, if they want to know who we are, to go to the front door and make the Cordial have a roll call; we should never get clean in time. I suppose we had better take our shoes in with us. Hope to goodness Daphne has managed the window!"

Sally drew herself up on to the window-sill. Yes, the sash moved upwards. "All right!" she reassured Nina and, pushing aside the curtains, she dropped into college. Nina followed.

Daphne, neat and elegant in red silk crêpe, emerged from some corner.

"Gosh! You do look sweet! You'd better both come up to Sally's room. I'll see that the coast's clear."

They followed her upstairs, skulking round corners. At last, in the warm security of Sally's room, they looked at each other. Hair tousled, faces smudged, mud everywhere; Nina's skirt with a rough, triangular rent; a muddy and somewhat bloodstained graze on one of Sally's hands. They shivered with cold and their legs trembled.

Daphne surveyed them with disapproval. "You'd better get a bit cleaner as quickly as possible. Scotland Yard has been here and he wants to see you both!"

Their eyes widened, but they found no words for several moments.

"What's the time?" asked Sally irrelevantly, after a glance at her wrist. "Did I leave my watch or did I lose it over there?"

"After ten," Daphne told her.

"I thought it was to-morrow. Look here, are you serious about this man? When did he come?"

"Not so very long after you'd gone out. Cordial sent for me, after having failed to find you, I suppose, and asked if I knew where you were."

"What did you say?" they both gasped out together.

"Well, I tried to be vague and said I thought you might have gone out and forgotten about late leave—I knew they'd soon find you *were* out. I think Scotland Yard knew."

"Is the Cordial mad?" Sally asked with some apprehension.

"Not so much mad as pained. I'll have to let her know that you're in. I think Scotland Yard went away but said he'd come back later."

"Golly! What a pity we didn't come in by the front door, since they know we're out," Nina remarked. "I expect that was Scotland Yard's light; the hound! He'll know we're in all right."

"Daphne! Could you get hold of old Jane and square her?" Sally implored. "She's a good sort. Get her to go to the Cordial and just say we're in. She needn't positively say she opened the door for us; the Cordial will assume that. Oh, Daphne, do! Then we'll have our baths quickly and be all clean and tidy for Scotland Yard. He's sure to follow hard on our heels."

"I'll try!" Daphne agreed. "Nina, I'll get you a dressing-gown; take off those muddy clouts here and go straight to the bathroom. And hurry up, both of you!"

They tore off their mangled garments and dashed for the baths.

CHAPTER XI

SCOTLAND YARD CONFERS
WITH THE LEAGUE

A BRIGHTLY LIT bathroom, a great deal of hot water and steam, and the removal of dirt, restored the self-assurance of Sally and Nina. They were back in Sally's room. Nina, with her brown hair in its customary twist at the nape of her neck, in a long, slim frock of brown velvet, looked very demure. Sally, in the perky yellow jersey which she had not changed for her early dinner, was collected and alert. They now felt that they had achieved something rather remarkable and had startling information to impart to Scotland Yard. Daphne arrived to assure them that old Jane had turned up trumps and that they were to await a summons from the Cordial.

"Now tell me if you've really been dredging the Lode, which is what you looked like, or what," Daphne began, and was interrupted by the violent entrance of a blue silk dressing-gown topped by a red face and a wildly rumpled mop of fluffy, fair hair.

"Gwyneth! You've been boiling yourself in your bath again!" Sally protested.

"You look like a blushing blonde gollywog," Nina declared.

"Have you ever learnt to cook?" inquired Daphne.

"I?" asked Gwyneth in innocent surprise. "Not much more than scrambled eggs."

"I thought not. If you had been properly brought up you would have learnt that when vegetables are boiled all their goodness goes into the water. That's what's happening to you; all your goodness, including the intellect, goes down the drain. You'll never get a first."

"I never would, boiled or unboiled," Gwyneth agreed. "I've been washing my hair. But I want to hear the news."

"The news," Daphne told her, "is that Scotland Yard has applied to the Lode League for help in solving this difficult case, and we are all waiting to meet the nice detective gentleman."

"What—not me?" cried Gwyneth aghast.

"I'm not positive, but I have a hunch that he'll want to see us all."

"*What* am I to do?" squeaked Gwyneth. "I'm sure the Cordial won't let me see him like this, and it'll take weeks to get my hair right."

"Just run a comb through it," Nina advised, "and sleek yourself down a bit——"

A maid arrived to announce that Mr. Braydon wished to see them all. Although Miss Cordell had suppressed the visitor's official title, the girl was bubbling with surmise about this unusual visit at ten-thirty p.m., and after reciting her message and observing Gwyneth's appearance, she retired in a state of hysterical giggles.

"Hurry up and make yourself tidy," Nina exhorted Gwyneth. "We'll tell him you're coming."

Detective-Inspector Braydon was a tall, grave man of scholarly air, with a thin, tight-lipped face. He was waiting for them in the small common-room with Miss Cordell. She went through the three introductions in a flustered manner and asked where Gwyneth was.

"She's just had a bath," Sally explained; "but she'll be here in a minute."

"I owe everyone an apology," said Braydon cheerfully, "for calling at such an unearthly hour; please don't worry, Miss Cordell."

The principal, with an air of disowning the whole affair, fluttered away.

"It's good of you to spare time from your private detective work to interview an old fogey from Scotland Yard," Braydon suggested.

The girls looked at him with suspicion. His eyes, rather screwed up, sparkled amusedly. There was silence for a few minutes.

"What do you want to know?" Sally inquired.

"Who killed Miss Denning, when, where and why. But I don't suppose you can tell me that? However, I think you can tell me something that may be useful; the slightest detail may be of importance. First of all, has anything at all come back to your minds connected with the events of Friday afternoon, which you didn't happen to mention to Inspector Wythe?"

They looked at each other. "We've gathered from various people," said Sally, "that Miss Denning started out between half-past one and two, probably at a quarter to two—I expect you know that?"

"Don't be afraid of telling me what I already know. Until this business is cleared up, every scrap of information may help to throw light."

Sally produced a loose-leaf note-book, extracted a couple of pages and handed them to him. "I've written down the names of the people who saw her and what they said."

Braydon glanced at the neatly tabulated pages. "Very businesslike, Miss Watson, and very helpful. Now, where was each of you that afternoon before four?"

Nina was playing hockey and Daphne was reading in her room, they told him.

"I was coaching," said Sally.

"Here in college?"

"Yes, because it was with Mr. Mort; it was extra, to make up for one I missed through flu. He belongs to Sim's but doesn't live in college and so that's why he comes here to coach me—the proprieties, you know."

"Which way would he come?" Braydon asked.

"His house is on the river, just above Sim's, so he probably walked through the Parks."

"And at what time was your coaching?"

"From three to four; but he's not awfully punctual. I was there at three and he arrived a few minutes later. He's very absent-minded, you know, and often forgets to start in time. Oh!" Sally suddenly laughed. They all looked at her in astonishment.

"I'm sorry," she apologized. "But I just remembered something very funny. But about the time——"

"You'd better tell us the joke," Braydon advised. "Your friends are longing to share it."

"It was Mr. Mort's absent-mindedness reminded me," Sally explained. "He came in the most awful old trousers and shoes and explained that he had been gardening and suddenly remembered the coaching and started straight away and never thought of changing. He was really frightfully upset."

"I suppose he was plastered with his garden mud?" Braydon chuckled.

"Oh, I don't suppose he does much more than moon about the garden and snip at things," Sally explained. "I don't think he was muddy, except his shoes; but that's natural; there's an utter morass just by the stile leading to the Ferry House path."

"And your coaching finished at four?" Braydon inquired.

"Yes; Mr. Mort left a moment after we heard it strike. I suppose he may have seen Miss Denning from the Parks on the way here. *Do* tell us, *when* do you think she was murdered?"

Braydon shook his head. "The obvious inference is that the canoe wouldn't drift very far and that, therefore, Miss Denning's body can't have been in it for more than half an hour at most. You've probably reasoned that out for yourselves already. But the apparently obvious isn't always what happened."

Gwyneth, now cooled to a paler shade, with her dressing-gown neatly arranged and her hair somewhat subdued, arrived.

"I'm sorry about this," she announced, "but I didn't realize that you wanted to see *me*."

"Quite in the best tradition," Braydon assured her. "Sherlock Holmes favoured a dressing-gown. I was just trying to reconstruct Friday afternoon, before we go on to later events. What were you doing before four o'clock, Miss Pane?"

"As a matter of fact I was trying to crochet a tam-o'-shanter and it didn't turn out very well; in my room."

"I'm sorry about that; very tricky things, I believe. Can any of you think of anything further? Do you happen to have heard whether Miss Denning took a rug with her in the canoe?"

They were startled.

"No—she didn't take a rug; we are almost sure," Sally declared. "But do you want to know about a rug?" Perhaps this was her moment of triumph.

"I confess I *am* rather interested in a rug, probably a brown rug," said Braydon.

"Have you found it?" asked Sally cautiously.

"I should like to," he admitted, watching her closely.

"You probably can if you look between the bushes and the wall at the bottom of Ferry House garden." Sally described her discovery.

"I'm glad to know it's there, but I'm sorry you've been crashing about in those bushes."

"I didn't crash!" declared Sally indignantly. "I was awfully careful; I didn't want to make a noise."

"What shoes were you wearing?" he inquired.

Sally held out a foot. "Walking shoes, but not these; I changed them because they were so muddy. Size 5."

Braydon surveyed them and nodded. "Are there any further discoveries you can entrust me with?"

"Yes," said Sally. "Two. Here's the first." She held out the penknife, still wrapped in a handkerchief. "I suppose I'd better tell you," she continued, as he took it carefully, "that we didn't think of fingerprints till rather late and you'll probably find both Nina's and mine on it."

"Where did this come from?"

Sally and Nina told their story. He looked grave.

"I'm glad you've handed this over, and because you've handed it over and have told me about the rug, I won't say much, except that you may have wasted valuable time and you may have obliterated valuable evidence. Any idea whom it belongs to?"

"We couldn't possibly have recognized the man, even if he were someone we know," said Sally. She shot a glance of inquiry at Daphne, who looked deliberately blank.

"The only thing is," announced Gwyneth, suddenly sitting bolt upright, "that I heard Draga Czernak telephoning to someone in Serbian about Burse on Friday evening and the person she generally telephones to in Serbian is a man called Matthew Coniston at Sim's."

"But you mustn't take too much notice of anything that Draga says nor of how excited she gets," added Sally hastily, with a sidelong scowl at Gwyneth. "The Yugo-Slavs seem to have very excitable natures."

"I can well believe it," Braydon agreed. "But how did you know, Miss Pane, what was said in this language? Do you understand it?"

"Oh, no! But Draga said *bursar* once or twice very plainly in English and she seemed to be frightfully worked up about something."

"Did Miss Czernak know that you had found the knife?" asked Braydon.

"Oh no! It was much earlier that she was telephoning; before dinner," Gwyneth explained.

"And this man Matthew Coniston is a great friend of Draga's," Sally explained further. "And because she can speak her own language to him—he was out in Belgrad—she probably feels she can talk to him more easily than anyone else, and she easily gets wrought up, so it isn't very peculiar that she should telephone to him to tell him that Miss Denning had been drowned. After all, it was rather shattering."

"We really don't know a thing about that knife, or what it means," Nina confirmed.

"I quite understand," Braydon told them.

"But as we seem to be coming clean," Daphne remarked; "as they do at the miscalled Oxford Group meetings, I'd better tell you that Draga Czernak did go to Sim's on Friday afternoon. That's only hearsay, but I'm pretty sure it's true. I'd rather not tell you how I heard about it. Sally thinks I'm giving Draga away, but you can easily find this out for yourself—people saw her—and you may as well know sooner as later. Perhaps *you* can sort things out and explain it."

"I think you're right to tell me," Braydon said. "If it should be important it's the sort of thing that I'm bound to hear of. Now what was the second discovery you mentioned, Miss Watson? That, presumably, was made this evening?"

"I suppose it was you who shone a light on us?" Nina asked.

"You didn't mention to Miss Cordell that you saw us running down the lane?" Sally tried to sound unconcerned.

"I really came here to collect information, rather than to impart it," Braydon pointed out.

"It was really because I felt sure you'd been rather decent about that, that I decided to tell you all that we've found out, such as it is," Sally confessed.

"That's really handsome," Braydon acknowledged. "And now will you tell me what you did find out in the garden of Ferry House to-night?"

Sally began the tale but generously gave Nina the honour of describing exactly what they saw through the window.

"That seems a strange procedure," Braydon commented. "Have you any theory to account for it?"

"Not a vestige. You see, when we went we didn't know what we were going to find."

"I suppose none of you has ever been inside the house?"

They all shook their heads. "Nor even looked through the windows?"

"We don't really use the path very much," Daphne explained. "We generally have bicycles. It was the bursar who used it most, because she thought we had a right to use it and wanted to rub it in. And no one's very keen to meet old Lond, or even the Beetle."

"You don't happen to know of anyone who *has* been inside that house?" Braydon asked.

"You mean someone who would know what was carved above the fireplace, where old Lond was chipping?" Sally asked bluntly.

Braydon nodded. "I don't really think Ezekiel Lond is in the picture at all, but I'd like to know why he was defacing his fireplace. Probably some of these elderly donnish people can enlighten me. It's an historic old house, I understand."

"I looked through the guide books when I came up and first heard stories about Ferry House," Nina volunteered; "but they didn't say much and certainly didn't give the words of any inscription—if it *was* an inscription."

"To return to Friday afternoon," said Braydon. "You all met on the roof of your boathouse, I understand, at four o'clock, by appointment?"

"We did," Sally agreed. "We've done it before. It's rather a—well, an impressive place for a private conversation. But we were not expecting the bursar to come down the river. We didn't even know she was out in her canoe."

"I did actually know," Daphne put in. "Someone had mentioned it, but I hadn't remembered it specially, until we heard the canoe coming, scratching past the bushes, and then I thought it might be hers."

"The canoe came down on this side of the river?" questioned Braydon. "Not as if it had been pushed off from the Parks bank, or anything of that sort?"

"It seemed to come round the bend close under the bushes," said Sally. "I haven't really thought of it before, but we heard it before we saw it."

"And you are quite sure there were no other boats to be seen on the river?"

All agreed that no other craft had passed the boathouse, or come within sight of it, after about four that afternoon, until the body was found.

"Now listen," said Braydon earnestly. "You have given me some interesting information, which may be very useful. If you hear of anything else that you think I should know, you can always get in touch with me through the police station here. But I must put a strict ban on further expeditions into Ferry House grounds. Up to the present, our men have only had orders to report on who went in and came out. I don't suppose you realized that you were bringing suspicion to bear on yourselves and on your college by these skirmishing parties? In future, Ferry House will be strictly guarded, the right-of-way must be waived for the present, and unauthorized persons found wandering in those grounds are liable to arrest. As a matter of fact, I particularly did not want Ezekiel Lond disturbed. As I have told you, I think he can be ruled out as a possible criminal. But the man's half crazy and he may know something even if he has done nothing. I want to leave him alone, merely watching him. At the same time you've got to bear it in mind that if he should be guilty of something criminal he may be a desperate man and he might well have done worse than curse you. If our regulations are not respected I shall have to ask Miss Cordell to put very severe restrictions on the comings and goings of all the students in this college—and that would be a confounded nuisance for everyone!"

"We'll keep clear of the place," Sally promised, and the others echoed her promise. "As a matter of fact, I'm not very keen on going there again."

"And you know," Braydon continued, "you might bring your reasoning power to bear on Ezekiel Lond's behaviour. I notice your expressions of polite incredulity when I remark that he is not the criminal! But if he were, would he continue to hang about on the scene of the crime, especially when he has a lodging elsewhere? And granted that he did, then wouldn't he have been more upset when he heard you smashing flower-pots under his window? Wouldn't he either have pursued you, or else have bolted from the house?"

"But then what is he hanging about for?" Sally insisted. "He's not usually there for two or three days running."

"That's one of the things I'm hoping to find out—as well as the explanation of Miss Denning's death."

"Haven't you *any* idea who did it?" asked Gwyneth, stifling a large yawn.

"Have you considered this," he replied. "Some undergraduate rag, which ends unexpectedly in tragedy? Picture to yourselves the position of two or three young men who have somehow, as a joke, upset the canoe. Miss Denning hits her head against something and doesn't come up; after some minutes they realize that this is serious; then they recover the body; they find she is dead. What are they to do? Enough to make anyone lose their nerve and their judgment!"

"And do you think that's what really happened?" Sally asked.

"How awful for whoever it was!" Gwyneth reflected.

Braydon was watching them closely. "Exactly. I don't know if that is what happened, but it's a possibility. A case of manslaughter rather than of murder. By the way, I'm afraid you'll all have to give evidence at the inquest on Monday, but if we are still not in a position to ask for a definite verdict, it is probable that we shall only outline the main points, so far as they are known. I understand, Miss Watson, that your sister is kidnapping one of the possible witnesses?"

"Oh, you mean the bursar's niece, Pamela Exe? There's something rather mysterious about *her*—I suppose you know? The bursar would never let her have anything to do with anyone connected with Oxford. My sister and her husband, Basil

Pongleton, have gone to Cambridge to-day to fetch her, and are bringing her back to-morrow."

"Inspector Wythe has seen her," Braydon told them. "I don't suppose she knows anything that will throw any light on this business, and I don't want to badger the poor girl. But I am about to commit one of the rashest acts of my career." He paused impressively and looked round at their startled faces. "I am going to confide in four ladies and trust that this will go no further. You may be able to help me in two directions. I don't want you to spy on Miss Exe, or anything of that sort, but she may talk to you about this curious ban which Miss Denning put upon any communication with Oxford. If you learn anything which seems to explain it, you might let me know. The other point is the inscription in Ferry House. Perhaps in the course of your academic researches you may light on some information. If so, again let me know."

"We will," they assured him.

"And now, one lady, at any rate, ought not to be kept any longer from her bed. Good night, and thank you all!"

The four girls trooped upstairs in a subdued manner, making their way by common consent, to Sally's room. Gwyneth gave way to yawn after yawn.

"I've had to stifle so many," she complained. "It always makes them worse. If I can get a few good ones off my chest I shall feel better."

"He's quite decent," Nina observed.

"I wish I knew what he knows and what he thinks," Sally remarked. "We must get to work on this inscription business. I think a little research in the Rad is indicated."

"How would you start?" asked Nina.

"Old histories of Oxford, or books about the architecture or the old houses, or something of that sort," Sally suggested vaguely. "You'd better get a line on it, Nina; you admired the house so much."

"All right; but I don't suppose I can do it before Monday."

"Didn't you say something, Nina, about Mary Wentworth's aunt?" inquired Gwyneth sleepily.

"Yes, but I don't think she ever went inside the house herself. Probably old Lond has kept himself and his house so much to himself that nobody knows what was carved there."

"Look here!" said Sally suddenly. "Have you ever thought of this? Perhaps Burse was drowned in the New Lode; it's an awfully narrow, dark tunnel there between old Lond's wall and our hedge and trees; even from our bridge you can hardly see any way at all, because it bends. No one goes round that way in boats, because it's so shallow and muddy. The rug had something to do with it, and was thrown over the wall. Then the canoe with the body in it was towed up to the fork, just below Lond's boathouse, and sent drifting down the other side of our island."

"And why did they leave the paddles afloat at the fork?" Daphne asked. "If they weren't left on the scene of the accident, why not put them in the canoe?"

"Just to confuse the trail, perhaps. *I* don't know," Sally admitted wearily. "I think I'll go to bed."

Meanwhile Detective-Inspector Braydon was conferring with Inspector Wythe, who had met him in the lane.

"Those girls are all right," Braydon assured the local man. "If there was a rag and an accident, they know nothing of it.

All this routing about in which they have been indulging is simply the natural curiosity of the young and their sublime confidence that they are the only people with good ideas. But they have found something. Also, they're certain that no other craft passed their boathouse on Friday between four and about half-past."

"All the same, sir," Wythe insisted, "you've got to bear in mind the fact that a boat could have got away from the scene, without going upstream, by taking the New Lode, the narrow channel on this side of Perse Island. It's usually deserted, but it's navigable."

"Yes, of course," said Braydon with some impatience. "Has Mr. Mort, a don of St. Simeon's College, I understand, given you any information about having been near the river on Friday afternoon?"

"No, no information of any kind from dons, beyond the ladies," Wythe replied.

"He seems to have come through the Parks and over the footbridge rather earlier than that man Bayes. He might help to fix Bayes's time, but of course, his not coming forward looks as if he didn't see anything of Miss Denning. I'll look him up. Any news of our pair of loonies?"

"The gardener has hobbled off in the direction of home, and old Lond himself set off at a good pace towards his lodgings, with one of my men trailing him. The old chap's not so decrepit as you might think!"

CHAPTER XII

JIM LIDGETT

On Sunday morning Inspector Wythe paid an early call on Braydon in the old-fashioned commercial hotel where the latter had chosen to lodge. Sabbath calm hung over the empty coffee room, and in a far corner Braydon sat at a table near the fire, a large-scale plan of the city of Oxford spread before him and walled along its further edge with an array of pots and jugs.

"Had visitors to breakfast, sir?" inquired Wythe, counting the coffee pots.

"Morning, Super! Count the cup before you form any theory," Braydon advised. "I like lashings of coffee. The pot at the end is still hot; shall I ring for another cup?"

Wythe waved away the suggestion. "How much do you believe of that man Bayes' story, sir?" he asked abruptly.

"Bayes is all right. He's not consciously making up anything, though it's unfortunate that he told the story to his pals before he told us. He saw a canoe go up the river and down again; other evidence, or lack of evidence, indicates that it was *the* canoe. I'm inclined to accept his time for the return journey—soon after three."

"Then you wash out what the doctors say about the time of death, and the evidence of the watch?"

"The doctors, you remember, are not prepared to swear to anything. If we tell them the evidence indicates that she was alive at three, I don't think they'll dispute it. The watch is more difficult. It hardly seems likely that a business-like woman would keep her watch half an hour slow. But we mustn't pay too much attention to that watch if it goes dead against all other evidence. When you paddle a canoe rapidly, a good deal of water may run down your arm, and that may have done the damage."

"If that was likely, you wouldn't expect her to be wearing it," Wythe pointed out. "She wasn't a novice in a canoe."

"True. But there's the possibility that she was in the habit of taking it off and forgot to do so on this one occasion, perhaps because it was a very important occasion, about which she was sufficiently anxious to make her omit a piece of routine. There's another point. The watch may have been altered, deliberately, by the murderer. Suppose someone had an alibi for two-thirty-seven, but not for—let us say—three-thirty-seven."

"And banked on no one seeing her after two-thirty-seven?" Wythe considered the problem. "Yes, I see. And what do you think, sir, about Bayes's statement that there was a rug, and something under the rug, in the bottom of the canoe when she came down?"

"The rug, yes, since a rug has turned up. As for what was under it, don't you think that was simply the second paddle, which we know she had, lying in the bottom of the canoe, with its end on one of the thwarts? With a rug over it, it might easily give the impression of 'traps,' as described by Bayes."

"But why the rug?"

"That may be the key to the conundrum. You've found it?"

"Yes; not more than half a dozen paces from the steps of Lond's ruined boathouse, just as it might have caught up on the bushes if someone standing near those steps—or perhaps pushing in a little way between the bushes and the wall—had hurled it away. Wishing to get rid of it, as it might be. You couldn't see it from the steps or the path, which explains why my men didn't spot it. It might have been there for years if that girl hadn't gone blundering in," he added gloomily.

"No means of identifying it?"

"It's a common enough type of rug and no name on it, of course. We've been through Ferry House, and it's as the young lady said: two long strips of carving have been sliced off above the fireplace in the long room at the back. We'd have seen it quick enough without hearing of it from her; regular eyesore it is now. It seems clear that the old man was cutting away something carved there, rather than any accidental marks, because his chisel followed along what seems to have been a sort of border to the rest of the carving, quite neat and deliberate."

"Nothing else of interest in the house?"

"Not a thing. That's to say, there's the hammer he was using with the chisel; useful little tool to knock a woman on the head with, but it seems too small to have made that bruise."

Braydon contemplated his map for a few minutes.

"It seems to me that we have two problems," he announced. "First of all, why did Miss Denning go up the river alone in her canoe? She had done it before; on this occasion—and possibly on others—she had planned beforehand to do it." He paused.

"That's so, sir," Wythe agreed. "From all that's said she wasn't an impulsive sort of woman. She was in the habit of mapping out her plans for the day."

"It looks as if she went for some purpose, presumably to meet someone secretly—unless you can think of any other object of a trip up the Char? She went up above the Parks footbridge and returned. That looks as if she kept her appointment with Unknown No. 1. Now someone else comes into the picture—Unknown No. 2. Possibly he intended to make away with her; possibly he merely wanted to talk to her without having to go to the college. In that case we must assume that the conversation was such as would lead to a quarrel and violence. Unknown No. 2 may have known of her appointment, or may have heard of it after she started out and deliberately intercepted her on her way down. Or he may have seen her, by chance, from the river bank. He may have some connection with Unknown No. 1, or may know nothing of him at all. In either case No. 1 might be expected to lie low because, in the first place, there's something fishy about those secret meetings, and in the second, he might expect to be under suspicion, at any rate until No. 2 is found."

Wythe considered this for some moments. "If it's made known at the inquest that she returned safely under the Parks bridge, you think No. 1 may come out into the open?"

"It's possible; if No. 1 was ignorant of No. 2's intentions and if we throw out some feelers. In fact, I think the press should be given Bayes's story, if they haven't ferreted it out already, with an indication that we hope No. 1 will come forward, making it sound not too sinister."

"I understand, sir. You agree, I take it, that she was knocked on the head and drowned between the Parks bridge and the top of Persephone Island, in fact, near Lond's boathouse?"

"It seems the obvious place; perhaps too obvious. I want you to have a further search made of the banks between that and the bridge, both sides and every inch of the ground. The canoe was presumably brought up to the bank and moored there. The woman, even if she fell out of the canoe into the water, must have been dragged on to the bank; you can't haul a body out of the river into a canoe, I should say, unless the canoe is aground or very securely moored. There ought to be something to show for all that."

"You're not forgetting that mark, sir, on the bank in Ferry House garden, above the old boathouse?" Wythe inquired. "Just the place from which to push off a canoe into the current, so that it would float down the main stream."

"I have not. Nor have I forgotten that the steep muddy bank there is *not* just the place from which a man of between seventy and eighty years old—or indeed anyone else—would drop the body of a fair-sized woman into a topply canoe. Something may have happened there; it's like the mark of one foot slipping down the bank; but it's *not* the place where a body was shipped. I don't even see how it could be done from the steps, lower down. You know what they're like— green and slimy with mud and river deposit; rickety into the bargain. They wouldn't stand the weight, let alone the marks that would be left by anyone struggling there with a corpse. Someone may have landed there, of course; if he was careful to pull himself up to the bank without putting a foot on the steps—which would be possible, with the river at its present height."

"You're not thinking that one of those girls made the mark, sir?" asked Wythe. "You remember we found it before that

Miss Watson made her little survey, and I'm pretty sure none of them strayed down there earlier—unless it was before the body was found."

"No, I rule out the girls," Braydon told him. "If you can find anything to explain that mark, well and good. I only say that I don't believe it indicates the spot where the corpse was embarked, and that's the spot I want you to find, if you can."

"We've been pretty thorough in our search, I can promise you," Wythe grumbled. "But of course, I'll put them on to it again, if you say so. All the town will be mooning up and down the Parks bank and the fields to-day, since it's Sunday, hoping to pick up clues, not to mention those college young ladies."

"I think I've given them something to occupy their attention elsewhere," Braydon told him.

"Old Lond and his gardener are both snug in their beds this morning, to all appearances," Wythe continued. "I'd sooner see them safe in the cells. You don't think——?"

"No, I don't. They're not the sort that can make a quick get-away. You can keep an eye on them, but I don't think it will do you any good."

"Then what *do* you think, sir?" exclaimed Wythe in some exasperation.

"I'm not really thinking yet. I'm going to seek information above the Parks bridge. I want you to concentrate on the banks below the bridge. I also want you to find out where Ezekiel Lond really was on Friday afternoon. Give up trying to prove that he was at Ferry House and see if you can't prove that he was somewhere else. I want you also to see the farmer.

Lidgett. Try to find out what he was doing in the fields by the river, how long he was there, and if he really spoke to Bayes. It would be useful to see if Bayes can identify him."

"Right, sir, I'll get on with that. Bearing in mind, I take it, that someone may have an alibi for two-thirty-seven but not for three-thirty-seven?"

"Yes; remembering, of course, that that *may* have nothing to do with the case. And follow up anything you come across, but try not to put the wind up anyone. I may be back here by lunch-time."

"I've got the car here, sir, in case you wanted it," said Wythe, as they left the hotel.

"No, thanks, I'd rather walk. It clears the brain. And I want to go through the Parks. You'd better take it for your Marston visit, after you've set your men to work on the banks."

The superintendent inserted his bulky form carefully into the black M.G. Midget which stood by the pavement in Cornmarket Street and drove off to the police station. There he issued his instructions rapidly, and before long the little car nosed its way out of Blue Boar Street into St. Aldate's, turned into the High and went snorting away across Magdalen Bridge towards Marston.

On the near side of the village Wythe turned the car into a lane on the left leading to Hall Farm. He had been here on the previous day, only to find that James Lidgett was away at Aylesbury market. He parked the car in the lane, pushed open the garden gate and walked up to the plain square house of red brick.

A small, chubby girl opened the door.

"Is Mr. Lidgett in?" Wythe inquired, smiling at the child.

She pouted at him and twined one leg round the other. "My dad's in bed," she informed him.

"Tell him that Inspector Wythe wants to see him most particularly, and ask him how long he'll be. Say I can come back in half an hour."

The child hesitated. "My dad won't get up till dinner-time to-day," she said at last.

"Now be a good girl and run up and tell him what I said," urged Wythe encouragingly, "or else ask your mother to come."

The child turned away and clumped slowly up the steep stairs which led out of the hall. The kitchen door at the end of the passage stood open and Wythe could hear someone moving about there and clattering plates. Probably Mrs. Lidgett, he thought, and probably she has overheard, but she's not going to give any help. A surly lot, these Lidgetts!

The child came down the stairs again, considerably more quickly than she had gone up, and faced Wythe in the doorway, looking up at him defiantly.

"My dad's cross," she announced.

"I shall be crosser if I don't see him soon," Wythe informed her. "Did he say when he would be down?"

The child shook her head.

"Tell him that I shall be back here in half an hour and if he's not up then I'll see him in bed. Now, mind you tell him, at once!"

The child made no reply, but shut the door emphatically as soon as Wythe turned away. He got into the car, sputtered down the muddy lane and back towards Oxford and drove on till he came to New Marston, the settlement of small new houses at the point where Ferry Road turns off towards Persephone College. Here he turned into a side street and stopped outside one of a row of unattractive yellow brick houses.

"Is Mr. Lond in?" Inspector Wythe asked the stout, untidy woman who came to the door in answer to his knock. She looked rather worried when she saw him.

"He's in his room, read'n' the papers, Inspector. Three or four of 'em he sent my Bobby out for this marnin'. I'd a-hoped you wouldn' be botherin' of 'im any more. He was in a fair way yes'day an' out till all hours an' came home lar' knows what time o' night, knock'n us up an' all, but he's more settled-like this marnin'. It's a shame to upset the pore ol' gennleman, that it is. 'E don' know a thing about it, an' that's a fack!" She made no attempt to let him in, but stood squarely in the narrow doorway, looking at him with an anxious smile.

"I wish I could be sure of that, Mrs. Marley," Wythe replied. "The trouble is, Mr. Lond himself won't help us. I want to ask him where he was on Friday when, as you yourself told me, he went out in the morning and didn't come back till tea-time— about five, I think you said? If he will tell me that, I may not have to worry you or him any further."

"Is that true?" the woman asked suspiciously.

"I'm making no promises," said Wythe cautiously. "But if Mr. Lond has nothing to hide I don't see why he shouldn't tell me what I'm asking. One thing *is* certain, that I shall keep on worrying everyone until I do find out."

She considered this. "'E's not so partic'lar about 'is meals, y'know. It's not the first time 'e's missed 'is dinner. See here;

I'll find out if I can, an' you come rahnd 'ere again later on and mebbe I can tell you."

Wythe hesitated. This was irregular. "I seem to be enlisting her in the force," he thought to himself. But from experience he knew the difficulty of extracting any information from old Lond and perhaps his landlady knew how to humour him.

"All right!" he agreed. "I'll be back some time this morning."

He scattered the little group of boys who had been attracted to his car like wasps to a jam-pot, and aroused their open-eyed admiration by the way he backed and turned, and shot off again towards Hall Farm.

As Wythe had expected, Jim Lidgett was shaved and dressed and downstairs and evidently on the watch for the car, for it was he who opened the door, almost before the inspector's hand had released the knocker. Wythe had not seen him before but had often heard him described as obstinate and bad-tempered, and having met his surly wife and sulky child, had pictured the farmer himself as a heavy-featured, clumsy man. He was surprised to see him tall and well-built, trim in his dress and in his movements, clean-shaven and with very closely-clipped greyish hair.

"Good morning, Inspector," said Lidgett, with a quick smile. "Come in. Surprised to find a farmer in bed at ten in the morning, I'll be bound?"

"A bit unusual, certainly," Wythe agreed, following the man into a chilly parlour in which a fire had just been lit. The room, with modern arm-chairs upholstered in green vel-vet, a gaudy carpet with deep pile, and an expensive-looking gramophone, indicated prosperity. Wythe made a bee-line for the chair with its back to the window, so that Lidgett could hardly avoid taking the one which faced the light.

"I'm making inquiries in connection with the death of Miss Denning who, we believe, was drowned in the Cherwell on Friday afternoon," Wythe explained, watching Lidgett's face closely. In spite of the ready smile, it was not a pleasant face, he decided. The sharp nose and keen eyes gave it a look of cunning. Lidgett's expression at the moment revealed only that he was on his guard.

"You'd better tell me a bit more, Inspector," he said. "All I know is what I've read in the paper—and not much of that. I was at Aylesbury market all day yesterday, as you know, and came home late. Some people seem to think a farmer has nothing to do but mooch about his fields all day; they forget the business he has to attend to."

"That sounds as though you're doing well," Wythe suggested.

"None too bad. Farming's all right if you've got brains, and use 'em," Lidgett replied.

"Well, this is the point; we know that Miss Denning went up the river in her canoe on Friday afternoon. It is important for us to be able to fix the exact times of her movements. I understand that you were in your fields by the river bank and probably saw her, so your information may be of value. You know Miss Denning, I believe?"

"Her at the college on the island?" inquired Lidgett, unnecessarily. "I know her well enough, when I see her. I've tried to do business with her, as you know, but she was so set on getting hold of Mr. Lond's old ruin that she would hardly look at my site."

"That was a disappointment to you, I take it?" Wythe suggested.

Lidgett grinned. "As for that, someone else may be wiser. I don't let it worry me. There's buyers in plenty for the land round here."

"To return to Friday afternoon, I suppose you saw Miss Denning go past in her canoe?" Wythe asked.

"You're supposing too much," said Lidgett, with another quick smile. "I saw nothing of her, though I don't deny I was in those fields."

"At what time were you there?"

Lidgett considered. "I was up here about the rickyard and the byres after dinner, till two or thereabouts, as my men can tell you. Then I walked across to the river and followed the bank all the way down, as far as Mr. Lond's place."

"Where did you strike the river?" asked Wythe.

"About opposite the Rhea."

"That's a bit above St. Simeon's, isn't it?"

"That's right. I may have been there about a quarter past two, but there's no telling exactly. I don't see what good this is going to do you, Inspector," Lidgett remarked pleasantly; "since I didn't set eyes on the lady."

"I don't quite know how you failed to see her," said Wythe. "Do you remember meeting a young man with a dog, as you came down by the river?"

"White terrier? I remember him all right and I shouldn't be surprised if he remembers me." Lidgett seemed amused.

"He was going down towards the Parks bridge, I think, and overtook you?" Wythe suggested.

"You haven't got it quite right. He came across the fields, rather from this direction, with his blasted terrier rampaging about among my cows. Whatever these young undergrads learn at college, they don't learn much common sense. We had a few words and he went on ahead of me, along the bank."

"And you followed, I take it?"

"I went on, along the same path, with no call to move at the pace he was going," Lidgett amended.

"And do you know," said Wythe impressively, "that this young man, Mr. Bayes, as he crossed the footbridge saw Miss Denning come down the river in her canoe?"

"Not having seen the young gent since, I didn't know that," replied Lidgett cheerfully. "But it seems you've got your evidence about her being there, so why come bothering about whether I saw her or not?"

"I want to fix the time, which this Mr. Bayes isn't sure about," Wythe explained patiently. "I also want to know how it was that when Mr. Bayes saw the canoe from the bridge, you, who must have been on the bank a little above the bridge, say you didn't see her at all?"

Lidgett barked a short laugh. "I can't tell you how it was, Inspector. You say she passed me and of course you know. There may have been a hundred canoes passed down the river that afternoon, for all I care. I wasn't there to watch the races; I was there to look at my banks. As long as these here canoers keep to their blasted canoes they can paddle up and down all day and all night, for all I care. But if they come scrambling up the banks into my fields they'd better look out, I say. And that's that!"

"Do you mean to tell me," Wythe persisted, "that you don't know whether one canoe or several canoes or no canoes at all passed down that river whilst you were walking slowly along the bank?"

"That's what I mean to say," Lidgett retorted. "I'm used to seeing 'em and I don't take much account of 'em."

"But you do take account of one canoer who lands in your fields? You can tell me when and where Miss Denning landed on Friday afternoon?" Wythe shot the questions at him quickly and watched carefully for the result.

Lidgett's swift grin again showed a flash of white teeth, but there was also a quick contraction of the brows and a new expression—dismay? or perhaps only surprise—which flickered in his eyes for a moment, like a face appearing dimly at the window of a dark room. "She landed, you say?" he asked, after a pause.

"It's obvious that she landed somewhere," Wythe pointed out, "since she passed under the footbridge alive, paddling her canoe, and was taken out of that canoe, lying dead in the bottom of it under the thwarts, at Persephone boathouse."

"Well, that's a bit of a conjuring trick, I'll admit," said Lidgett cheerfully.

"Are you sure you can't tell me any more?" Wythe persisted. "How far did you go along the bank that afternoon?"

"As far as my south boundary."

"That's the lane along the north wall of Ferry House, I believe?"

"That's so. I turned into the lane and came home by the footpath across the fields." Lidgett looked down at his knees and scratched his head. Then he looked up at Wythe, a little uneasily, the latter thought. "Look here, Inspector, I'm always on the side of the law. It doesn't pay a man to be anything else. If I knew anything about this, I'd tell you, but take my word, you're on the wrong tack."

"Look here," Wythe suggested. "Will you come with me now across the fields, the way you went on Friday, and then down the bank and show me exactly the place where you saw Mr. Bayes. That may at least help to fix the time."

Lidgett glanced at the rain-washed window. "In this weather?" he inquired.

"We can't afford to notice the weather in a case of this kind," said Wythe heroically. "At least it will keep the sight-seers away!"

"Sightseers, d'you say?" asked Lidgett sharply, rising to his feet. "Clumping about my banks and breaking my hedges? I'll sightsee 'em! Come on!"

Wythe fetched a waterproof from the car and envied the leather leggings which appeared beneath the farmer's ancient but effective mackintosh. They crossed the farmyard and entered the fields by a gateway where cattle had trodden the ground into an unpleasant morass. Wythe suspected that they might have joined the field path by another route and that Lidgett chose this one maliciously, but since Wythe had insisted that they should follow the route taken on Friday afternoon he could not make any protest. At his suggestion Lidgett led the way, at his own pace. Wythe noted the time when they started and they plodded through the rain towards the river. In ten minutes they reached the river bank oppo-site Rhea Island, a few hundred yards above Sim's Here they turned and worked their way slowly down the river, Lidgett pausing to poke the bank with his stick, examine the willows and the bushes, and now and then to pace distances. Few words passed between them. Wythe caught a sardonic grin on Lidgett's face now and again and guessed that the farmer was enjoying himself. This did not mitigate the inspector's discomfort, as he stamped his numbed feet in the mud and contemplated the dreary, rain-washed fields. Occasionally they left the river bank to cross by a gateway from one field to the next.

"You see, Inspector," said Lidgett on one of these occasions, "it's more than likely that that there canoe slipped by when I was off the bank, going through one of these gates. There was a hinge gone off one of them and I spent a bit of time at it."

"What was that?" asked Wythe sharply.

"The next one. It was mended yesterday."

They had passed Sim's and Lady Margaret Hall and were now opposite the Parks. Lidgett paused.

"About here it would be that the young feller with the terrier came along, across this field, you see, from the gate over there."

Wythe consulted his watch. It had been ten minutes to the river and for twenty-five dreary minutes they had squelched about on the banks.

"Do you think it was much after two when you started from the farm on Friday?" he asked.

"Might've been five minutes or so after the hour," Lidgett told him.

"And how long did Mr. Bayes stand talking to you?"

"We didn't have a long chat," said Lidgett pleasantly. "I told him he'd better clear out of my fields if he couldn't keep his dog under proper control."

"Wasn't something said about barbed wire?" Wythe asked.

"If you say so, I expect you're right," Lidgett agreed. "I won't deny I had barbed wire in my mind, to keep those blasted canoers from landing here in the summer. There's no right-of-way here; the path from the footbridge goes straight ahead, inland as you might say, and comes down to the riverside again higher up. If they want to go in a canoe, I say, let 'em stick to it, and not come messing about on private property."

"Quite so," said Wythe grimly. "And I reckon you took some minutes to say all that to Mr. Bayes?"

"Likely I did," Lidgett agreed.

"Just wait here a minute, will you, while I walk to the bridge," said Wythe.

There was one more hedge and a narrow backwater, little more than a muddy ditch, which necessitated a detour away from the river to a stile. Walking briskly, Wythe reached the middle of the footbridge in four minutes from leaving the farmer by the river. He added up the times.

"Say he left the farm at 2.5, ten minutes to the river; twenty-five minutes down the bank, three minutes talk and four minutes more to the bridge. That would bring Bayes here at 2.47. Even allowing for a little extra time spent by Lidgett on his way down, it looks as if Bayes crossed the bridge before three. But then Lidgett may be wrong, deliberately or accidentally. In fact," said Wythe to himself gloomily, "he's more likely to be wrong, than right, so far as I can see."

He looked downstream from the bridge and observed several helmeted figures in dripping mackintosh capes moving slowly about the banks, their heads bent, apparently in deep dejection. The sight of his subordinates carrying out his instructions and perhaps having an even more unpleasant time than himself, slightly cheered Inspector Wythe. He returned to where he had left Lidgett and, as he passed through the gate, reflected that it seemed quite likely that Lidgett himself had been crossing from one field to the next just at the moment when Miss Denning's canoe passed down the river.

Wythe considered the muddy ditch which ran alongside the hedge. You couldn't paddle a canoe up it, but if Miss Denning had drawn the canoe up to the bank of the river and disembarked, it would be easy to drag the canoe a little way along the ditch, where it would rest steadily, ready to receive a body. But the ditch was above the footbridge, and she had certainly passed down under the bridge, according to Bayes. Of course if Lidgett, as soon as Bayes was out of sight, had run down the bank, he might have overtaken the canoe, called to Miss Denning and got her to come ashore on some pretext. Having quarrelled with her and knocked her into the river, he could pull the canoe back along the bank, or possibly paddle it back, to the ditch. But what about the body? No, the ditch was tempting, but didn't seem to fit.

He rejoined Lidgett.

"I suppose you don't remember noticing the time at about this spot on Friday?" he asked. "You should have heard Sim's chimes."

"I must have heard them, sure enough, but I'm hearing them all day and don't pay any particular attention."

"You can't remember whether it was before three or after three that you saw Mr. Bayes? According to our times to-day, it would have been just after a quarter to three."

"You can take it that's near enough," said Lidgett ambiguously.

"And now we'll continue to follow your stroll on that afternoon," Wythe informed him. "I believe you went a little quicker after this?"

"Then you know more about it than I do," Lidgett remarked. "I had just as much to see to below the bridge as above. If you know so much about it, suppose you set the pace?"

"Never mind," said Wythe crossly. "Go on just as you say you did on Friday."

They plodded on to the ditch, turned along it and crossed it by the turfed bridge at the gate. There they came in sight of the constables moving heavily about on the bank.

"What's all this?" asked Lidgett sharply. "Is this some kind of a trap? What are those cops doing there?"

"Collecting information," said Wythe evenly. "As I told you, Miss Denning must have landed *somewhere* on these banks; I want to know where."

"If she landed here," exclaimed Lidgett in rising anger, "she'd no right to and no call to, that I can see. I know nothing about her and I didn't see her, and you won't find any information about her in my fields unless you put it there yourself. I've heard tell of such things, when you cops haven't the sense to get on the track of a criminal, and you've got to find something to show for your trouble, you'll frame up a case of some kind and not care whether a man's innocent or not!" The pleasant amenableness, with the hint of a sneer in, with which

Lidgett had formerly met Wythe's questions had turned to fury, which was heightened by the outlet of the man's smothered annoyance at the trouble he had been put to.

"You're talking rubbish, and you know it," Wythe said severely. "You know best whether there's anything here for us to find, and if there isn't there's no cause for you to object to our search. Come on now, we're following your walk on Friday." But he realized that now he could rely on Lidgett even less than before to reproduce his movements and time schedule accurately.

"It's foolery!" Lidgett declared. "I can tell you that I carried on from here all the way along the bank to the lane, which you can see, just as I did higher up. I didn't see the woman. If you say she passed me back there, she'd've gone right on ahead, paddling as she did, and'd be pretty well out of sight by the time I got here by the bridge."

"So you know just how she paddled?" queried Wythe quickly.

"Oh, I've read the papers," Lidgett replied, after a pause.

"Very interesting! I don't remember that any of them described just how Miss Denning was paddling."

"Folks talk. If I didn't read it, I heard it."

As they approached the nearest of the slowly moving, hunched policemen, Wythe saw that he was the sergeant and hurried ahead to speak to him. Lidgett followed at a deliberate pace, passed them and went on.

"Very well," Wythe instructed the man. "Don't stop at the bridge but carry on as far as the ditch that runs up from the river; examine the ditch carefully, and after that you can knock off. Report to me at once."

Wythe overtook the farmer. "I must ask you to come with me to the police station to make a statement about your movements on Friday afternoon," he said.

"If you think I can tell you anything more, you're making a big mistake. I've wasted half the morning already over this play-acting."

"Your daughter told me that you would be in bed till dinner-time, so I assume that I'm not keeping you from any very urgent business," Wythe reminded him.

Lidgett smiled grimly, but made no reply.

"When you have time to think it over, you may remember something further," Wythe continued. "But even if you cannot tell me any more, the information may be important, and I want to have it in writing and make sure that I have it down accurately. We'll go back to your house, where I left my car. I suppose the shortest way is down the bank to the lane and then back by the footpath, the way you went on Friday?"

They followed this route without further conversation, and buzzed back to Blue Boar Street. Wythe remembered to stop on the way at Lond's lodgings in New Marston.

A boy came running round from the back of the house when he knocked on the door and handed him a folded sheet of ruled paper, torn from an exercise book and inscribed: *the inspector*.

"Mummy had to go out and she left this for you," gasped the child, and sped away to the back of the house again.

Wythe unfolded it.

"Dear sir, mister Lond went to the Free Libery
on the friday aftnoon and he sais the gent there
knows him. Yours truly, Alice Marley."

At the police station he took Lidgett to his own office and left him alone for a moment while he gave instructions to another officer, first to bring Bayes, if he could be found, to the station at once and then to identify and visit the official who was on duty in the Free Library reading-room on Friday afternoon and discover if he could remember seeing old Lond there.

CHAPTER XIII

BRAYDON VISITS SIM'S

IT was not yet the hour of church services when Braydon sauntered forth on that Sunday morning, and the Corn and the Broad were deserted. He entered the Parks by the gate at the end of South Parks Road and veered to the right to follow the path along the river bank. As Owen Vellaway had done, he went to the summit of the steep footbridge and looked up and down the river. A few of the more inquisitive of the citizens of Oxford were already hanging over the railings of the bridge and gaping about on the river banks, as if hoping to witness a repetition of the tragedy which, they knew vaguely, had been enacted on Friday on or near the upper Cherwell. Wythe's squad of searchers had not yet arrived.

The wind blew coldly and the aimless loiterers, Braydon noted with malicious pleasure, looked chilled and miserable. A few large drops of rain fell, and he turned up the collar of his raincoat and set off briskly towards St. Simeon's College. In ten minutes he had gained the shelter of the great gateway and was asking the porter if Mr. Mort was in.

"Do you happen to have been on duty here on Friday night?" Braydon inquired as the man led him round the left side of the quad, skirting the walls to gain some shelter from the rain which now drove down.

"That's right, sir," the man replied.

They entered an arched passage and Braydon paused. "Can you tell me who came in late that night, after nine? You would have to open the gate to anyone entering college after that, I think?"

"That's right, sir. Let's see; there was Mr. Peters and Mr. Anderson came in together, not very late they weren't. Then there was Mr. Coniston; I remember him well because he only just made it; nigh on twelve it was. Unusual for him to run it so fine."

"Any others?" Braydon asked indifferently.

The porter mentioned a few more names. "Nothing wrong I hope, sir? I understood, sir, that the—accident—happened in the afternoon."

"That's quite right. In these cases, you know, one often has to trace the movements of a great many people who have only the slightest connection with the affair. You needn't mention that I have made these inquiries; starts gossip, you know, and probably no one need ever hear of it."

"I quite understand, sir. There's a good many things that we find it better not to mention. Now if you go straight across the garden, sir, and through that gate in the wall, you'll see the house. Mr. Mort hasn't been out this morning, not this way, but there's another way round by the road, though he don't often use it."

Braydon, hunching his shoulders against the rain, crossed the well-kept garden by a wide path, opened the gate in the wall and found himself in another garden through which a pergola led up to the door of a small, irregularly built house.

The room into which he was shown by the middle-aged woman who opened the door was a pleasant one, with windows at the far end looking on to the rain-drenched garden. Most of the wall space was filled with bookcases. The furniture was old-fashioned and shabby. Braydon walked over to a desk which stood in front of the window and glanced down at the photograph of a girl which stood on its right-hand corner. Pre-war, he decided, on the evidence of the shirt-blouse and tie. It had been taken out-of-doors, and her hair, which looked very fair, was blown in wisps across her face. She was slim and pretty, with nothing very distinctive about her face except her widely set eyes. Braydon studied the photograph very attentively, and if anyone had asked him why, he might have remarked that a man does not keep a photograph of a girl, who is neither his wife nor daughter, on his desk for twenty years for nothing.

When Denis Mort entered the room his visitor seemed to be rapt in contemplation of the garden.

"Pleasant little country house you've got here," he said, turning round in response to a greeting which held a questioning note. "I must apologize for this early call. My name's Braydon—Detective-Inspector Braydon of Scotland Yard. I think you may be able to help us."

Denis Mort looked worried. He was a slim, wiry-looking man, not so tall as Braydon, apparently in the early forties. He was fair and rather bald, with grey eyes and deeply scored lines between his brows.

"Please sit down. I don't know—" he began uncertainly.

"It's about this drowning affair—the bursar of Persephone College—you have read of it, I suppose?"

"Yes, indeed; Miss Denning. But why do you come to me?"

"We find some difficulty in tracing her movements on that afternoon and in fixing the time of her death. Her body was found—you may not know—by four students of Persephone College, drifting in her own canoe. One of them—Miss Watson—told me that she had just come from a coaching with you. I therefore suppose that you may have walked from here to Persephone College shortly before three on Friday afternoon. There don't seem to have been many people about by that stretch of the river, and anyone who was in the neighbourhood at the relevant time may be able to tell us something helpful."

Braydon paused expectantly. Denis Mort sat gazing into the fire, apparently regardless of what had been said. But he seemed to realize that it was his turn to take part in the conversation. He ran a hand up over his forehead and through his hair.

"I'm sorry; I've got—something on my mind. Yes, I usually walk to Persephone through the Parks; not alongside the river, except after crossing the footbridge. Miss Watson; yes, I coached her at three; three or four. Miss Watson was one of those, you say, who found the body. Horrible business! I don't remember seeing anyone on the river—is that what you mean?"

"You crossed the bridge at what time, Mr. Mort?"

"I'm never very good at time; I believe I'm renowed for unpunctuality, as Miss Watson may have told you. But I don't think I was late last Friday, so I suppose I must have crossed the bridge at about five or ten to three."

"And you saw no craft on the river? You knew Miss Denning, I suppose? You would recognize her if you saw her on the river?"

"Yes, I knew her; I have known her for many years. I should probably have noticed if I had seen her—or anyone else—on the river on that afternoon."

"Do you remember meeting anyone in the Parks or on the bridge?"

"That I cannot remember; one usually sees a few people in the Parks."

"You don't remember a young man with a terrier?"

Denis Mort looked round rather quickly at Braydon. "A young man with a terrier? Not an uncommon sight; one of our men here keeps a terrier, and I have certainly met him at times exercising the dog in the Parks. But I don't remember seeing him on that particular afternoon. I'm sorry; I'm apt to be preoccupied when I'm walking and I don't notice things much."

"Any apology is due from me, for cross-questioning you in this tiresome way," Braydon replied. "There's one more point. Did you take the footpath through Ferry House garden, the disputed right-of-way?"

"One naturally takes that path, approaching Persephone College from this side. I don't suppose I have ever been along the road that rounds the end of Ferry House grounds."

"And you returned the same way?"

"Oh, yes; I came straight home after the coaching."

"So that you crossed Ferry House garden again soon after four?"

"I don't think I kept Miss Watson for many minutes after we heard the hour strike, but she will be more certain of the time than I."

"Did you meet anyone, or see any sign of Ezekiel Lond or his old gardener, or anyone else, on your way back?"

"I cannot remember anyone. It was dusk, and I remember thinking that the deserted house and garden were rather eerie."

"You heard nothing unusual?"

"Nothing."

Braydon pondered. "Can one see the ruined boathouse and the river from that path across the garden?"

"I think not. There is a line of yew trees set closely together along that side of the path, you may remember. And the garden slopes away to the river. The boathouse is hidden from every point of view, I should imagine, but I know it from having passed it on the river."

"I am very much obliged to you, Mr. Mort, for answering my questions, and interrupting your own work, I suspect. You knew Miss Denning, so you also knew her niece, Miss Exe, I suppose?"

"I know of her, but have seen her very seldom; she was never in Oxford, as you probably know."

"That's another point that puzzles me," Braydon said. "Do you happen to know if there is any truth in the idea that Miss Denning purposely kept her niece away from Oxford, and what her reason may have been?"

"She thought it better, I believe, that Pamela should go to Cambridge. Science is her line, and Cambridge is popularly supposed to be pre-eminent in that branch of knowledge," replied Mr. Mort dryly. "I really do not think you will find that anything concerning Pamela has any bearing on this affair, and I hope you will not think it necessary to worry the girl. The situation is hard enough for her as it is."

"It is my earnest wish to avoid worrying Miss Exe," Braydon replied emphatically. "The trouble is that she seems to be Miss Denning's only near relative and therefore the only person with possible knowledge of Miss Denning's private affairs, which may hold some clue to this case."

"Miss Denning always struck me as the type of woman who would keep her secrets, if she had any, to herself."

"Can you tell me this, Mr. Mort—since you say you have known Miss Denning for many years—was there something about her niece's parentage which she was anxious to conceal?"

Denis Mort shook his head at the fire. "Can it do any good to stir up old trouble? Pamela is the daughter of Miss Denning's sister, who died soon after the child's birth. I knew Pamela's mother."

"And the father? This man Exe?"

"He is dead. Miss Denning disapproved of her younger sister's marriage to him. But he is dead long ago; what can it have to do with what has happened now? Pamela never even saw him. She knows less than nothing about him."

Braydon rose and crossed to the window. "I'm sorry to have to behave like an inquisitive brute, but the pursuit of clues often leads into murky by-ways. Is that the river that one sees over there, beyond your garden?"

"Not the main river; only a backwater which leads nowhere. It's the boundary of my garden on that side."

"And you have a boathouse there?"

"Yes; I keep a punt, but I don't often take it out in winter."

"Miss Denning was an all-weather canoeist, I gather?"

"Yes; I suppose she was a familiar figure on the upper Char. She had great ideas about fresh air and exercise."

"Did she always come up this way? With some definite object in view, perhaps?"

"Probably to avoid the trouble of taking the canoe over the rollers, which she would have to do if she went downstream."

"Quite so. Well, I must pursue my inquiries elsewhere."

He reached the door.

"Inspector Braydon!" said Denis Mort suddenly.

Braydon turned round to face the man who stood in the middle of the room, swinging himself slightly from one foot to the other.

"Inspector Braydon! If you should at some later stage of your inquiries have reason to believe that any more detailed knowledge of the life story of Pamela Exe would throw any light on the case, I ask you to come to me for information. I knew Pamela's mother—well; I have, therefore, a special interest in Pamela, although I have seen her so seldom. I feel sure that she herself cannot help you. If you have any definite question in your mind now, I will do my best to answer it."

"Thank you, Mr. Mort. I will remember."

Braydon returned to the quad, and in spite of the rain, which was falling rather less copiously, he wandered round it with the air of a sightseer, examining attentively the curious carving over the archway of the passage he had come through and over the great entrance to the hall staircase. He also noticed the names on the board at the foot of each staircase and was lucky in lighting on Matthew Coniston's name before he had gone far.

He would have said himself that he was visiting Coniston with an open mind. He had in his pocket the penknife which Sally and Nina had found in Persephone College garden. This had already been tested for fingerprints and, as he had expected, this test had disclosed nothing in the nature of evidence. All the prints on it were smeared beyond the possibility of identification. If Coniston did not appear to realize that he had lost it, Braydon was not sure whether he would produce it. Coniston was not yet labelled as a "suspect" in connection with the murder of Miss Denning. Braydon was merely seeking information and above all he wanted to get some impression of this man who had apparently been engaged in some questionable business with the bursar's canoe after her death, and had taken so little trouble to cover his tracks. In this frame of mind Braydon climbed the narrow stone stairs to Matthew Coniston's rooms.

Although the sitting-room had windows on two sides, the spaces between the stone mullions did not let in much light, and the panes were now dimmed by the rain streaming down them. The room was low and gloomy and seemed full of heavy, dark furniture. Braydon had to look all round it before he distinguished the owner embedded in the long, low armchair, with his back to one window and his feet to the fire.

Coniston showed no surprise when Braydon explained who he was, but indicated an arm-chair opposite to his own and regarded the detective quizzically, with an air of faint amusement.

"Have you brought my penknife?" he inquired.

Braydon did not show that he was taken aback. "I think I have." He pulled it out of his pocket, still wrapped in a handkerchief, and held it out. "That it?"

"Fingerprints carefully preserved, I see!" Coniston remarked in a tone that seemed to approve of this precaution. "Yes, that's mine. I should like to have it back. It's an old friend and I didn't like losing it. In fact, I went back for it; that's why I was nearly late in getting in to college, as you probably know."

"And that's why you left *Nippy* in the water?"

"Exactly. I hadn't a moment to spare. I wanted to leave it as late as possible, so that there would be less likelihood of anyone being about, and I timed it nicely, but didn't allow for the time spent in going back. That's why the cleverest criminals are often caught, I expect. They time things too neatly and don't allow the necessary margin for accidents. Isn't that so?"

"I *have* known men who were a bit too clever in that way," Braydon agreed. "At the moment I am collecting information about the death of Miss Denning. Do you care to tell me exactly why you went to Persephone College garden by canoe on Friday night?"

"Am I not to be warned that anything I say will be taken down and may be used as evidence?" inquired Coniston reproachfully.

"That is not necessary at this stage," Braydon informed him. "I do not at present propose to arrest you; I am, as I said, merely seeking information."

Coniston nodded. "I'm afraid I hadn't got the procedure quite clear. Ever since I knew the knife had been found I have been expecting to be asked to explain. It's a queer story. You may find it rather hard to believe."

"My powers of belief are used to a good deal of strain," Braydon assured him.

"Draga Czernak of Persephone College can confirm the story, but she's a good deal wrought up over this business and regards her own part in it far too seriously, so if you frighten her I don't quite know what she'll tell you, and I rather hope you won't find it necessary to ask her.

"I don't know if you've seen her," Coniston continued slowly, when Braydon made no comment. "I understand that one of the local men has. She's Montenegrin; of an old family; brought up on legends and supernatural tales, and therefore, though highly civilized on the surface and educated and all that, intensely superstitious. She had some row with Miss Denning over a domestic matter and considered that she had been gravely insulted; lesser insults than that, she said, had given rise to blood feuds in her own country."

"When did this insult occur?" Braydon asked.

"On Friday morning. Draga's mind immediately flew to the idea of revenge. She cut a lekker on Friday morning; she was much too wrought up to attend to it, in any case. In the garden she found one of those wooden labels used for marking where you've planted things, and on part of this she scratched one of her family curses. She explained to me later that it wasn't the worst sort of curse; it wasn't supposed to kill the victim, but only to make her hair fall out or her teeth decay or something of that kind. Draga's first idea was to conceal this in Miss Denning's room, under the mattress perhaps. To ensure its efficacy you should fix it to some object which the victim will come into contact with. Draga hung about the room, but there were maids going in and out and then Miss Denning herself came in sight, so Draga cleared off and tried to think of some other plan. Her mind naturally jumped to the canoe; everyone knew of Miss Denning's habit of going out alone in it, and it's a thing that Draga finds particularly hard to understand. I'm not sure that she doesn't consider it evidence of magical practises on Miss Denning's part.

"Draga strayed into the garden, and there was the canoe chained up in the boathouse—the same one where her body was found later. It's not a proper boathouse, you know; that's a little farther down the river. This is merely an iron roof over the water, beneath which boats are moored.

"Draga managed to fix her curse securely to the canoe, just under the gunwale, with some sticking plaster. It was a small thing and it was unlikely that anyone would ever notice it. Having done that, she felt better. I'm not sure if she really expected that the curse would have any effect, but at least she felt that she had retaliated. However, thinking it over later, she remembered that water—particularly running water— has special magical properties, and she wondered whether these might render the curse invalid. After lunch on Friday she rushed to the college library and studied *The Golden Bough*, searching for enlightenment. She doesn't seem to have found anything that helped much, but while she was there she saw Miss Denning cross the lawn with her paddles, obviously going out in her canoe.

"Draga got into a panic. She began to wonder whether the curse was perhaps a stronger one than she had intended; it occurred to her that this is not Yugo-Slavia, and that if there were any mishap the English might misunderstand her intentions."

"So she expected a mishap?" Braydon asked.

"No; I don't think she really did. I don't quite know what she expected, but she imagined all sorts of things. She's not used to water and a canoe has always struck her as a danger-ous thing. Anyway, she worked herself into a frenzy and came rushing up here to tell me what she had done."

"At what time would that be?"

"I expected that question and have been trying to remem-ber, but I can't be sure. I was writing an essay, and I certainly

hadn't done much of it when she turned up. I think she probably arrived about half-past two. I gather that she didn't start
immediately she saw Miss Denning go out; she sat for some
time thinking things over. She did mention that she hadn't
seen any sign of Miss Denning when she crossed the river. If
I'm right, that would be about twenty past two."

"I suppose it's about a quarter of an hour's quick walking
from Persephone College here, through the Parks?" Braydon
suggested.

"About that. Well, I soothed Draga and told her that
a canoe was really quite safe and nothing serious was likely
to happen to Miss Denning. I encouraged the idea that the
waters of the Cherwell might neutralize the curse and even
that a Montenegrin curse might not work in England. I tried
to explain away the insult and generally to get Draga into a
more reasonable frame of mind. I was a bit worried myself,
because women students are not supposed to visit men's
rooms unchaperoned, but Draga would not let a little thing
like that stand in her way."

"You know Miss Czernak pretty well, I gather?"

"I've known her since we were children, and I feel a bit
responsible for her. Her father asked me to keep an eye on
her, and she doesn't settle too easily into the academic life. She
naturally comes to me for advice; for one thing, I can speak
her own language.

"To continue the story, she calmed down a bit and I offered
to take her out to tea, but she insisted on going back to college.
I think she partly wanted to assure herself that Miss Denning
really did return safe and sound. The next thing I heard from
her was that Miss Denning had been found drowned. Draga

rang me up that evening before dinner and, speaking her own language, told me that some students had found the body and that she herself had been questioned. She was in a great state, and although of course they hadn't asked her about curses, she thought they suspected her of something. She had heard that the police had taken the canoe up out of the water; she didn't think they had found the curse yet, not having mentioned it, but they would surely examine the canoe by daylight and were bound to find it and would know it was her work because it was in Serbian. I must go that evening and get it off the canoe.

"Of course I tried to persuade her that if it were found she had only to explain matters; I offered to go and help her over that. But she wouldn't hear of it. She couldn't believe that anyone who confessed to having put a curse on a person who was soon afterwards found drowned, would not be considered guilty of something pretty awful. So at last I agreed to go down by river late that night and remove the curse, if it were still there. I thought it would probably have been washed away by the water. It seemed pretty safe, so long as the police weren't hanging about the boathouse. I made sure of that and I located the curse all right, with a torch. The sticking plaster was amazingly tight and I had to get out my knife to scrape it off. You'll probably find the mark. Then I was disturbed, apparently by some of the students, and had to do a quick getaway and dropped the knife. As I've told you, I went back for it, but apparently they'd picked it up."

"Didn't it occur to you that, rather than embark on this escapade, which would have been difficult to explain if the police had been about, it would have been far safer, for

Miss Czernak as well as for yourself, to leave the curse alone, so that she would be forced to give an explanation when it was found?"

"I had decided," Coniston explained, "that if there was any sign of police on guard, I would do that. But the coast seemed clear, and I didn't think my light could be seen from the college. I think those girls must have been snooping around the garden."

"One of the most curious stories I have ever heard," said Braydon noncommittally.

"I was afraid it would strike you like that," Coniston remarked.

"Do you happen to know at what time Miss Czernak left your rooms to return to college?" Braydon inquired.

"There again I'm not a bit certain. I hadn't any reason to note the time. I've heard the story of that man Bayes, and I gather he didn't see Draga. I expect she crossed the bridge later. It may have been half-past three when she left. I don't know when or where the drowning is supposed to have happened, but I'm perfectly certain, from the way Draga talked on the telephone, that she then knew nothing more of it than she had gathered from the man who questioned her and a few words she had with the girls who found the body. She wouldn't attempt to *do* anything to Miss Denning, apart from the physical impossibility of any such thing. Draga was already rather appalled at what she felt she had done, in the way of the curse, and if Miss Denning had got home safely I'm not sure that Draga mightn't have removed the thing."

"I should like to see that curse, if you've got it," said Braydon slowly.

For the first time Coniston seemed startled out of his composure. "I haven't. I burnt the thing."

"Didn't it occur to you that it might provide useful confirmation of your story?"

"I didn't think of that. My intellect rejects any belief in curses and magic, but I think I have some vestiges of superstition rooted in me somewhere. Who hasn't? After what had happened, I didn't like the thing and was glad to see the last of it."

"A pity. Well, Mr. Coniston, I'm much obliged to you for telling the story so fully. I don't think it need be referred to at the inquest. But I think I must see Miss Czernak. There is a problem of time which she might possibly help to clear up. I promise you that I will be tactful."

"I don't think you'll get much help about times from her," Coniston said. "Her ideas on the subject are not very—English."

"Well, I must try to anglicize them. By the way, I suppose you cannot give me any information about Miss Denning's river trips? They seem to have been a habit and I gather that she usually came up the river. You may have met her when out in your own canoe?"

"Yes, I think I have," replied Coniston rather doubtfully. "But I can't remember any particular occasion or any particular place. Isn't the most probable explanation that she liked that form of exercise? It's not uncommon up here, you know. And after all, you can only go two ways on a river, up or down."

"Quite true," Braydon agreed, and took himself off.

He returned to his hotel and sat there for some time, jotting down notes and drawing apparently meaningless diagrams. Then he rang up the police station and, finding that Wythe was there, strolled down to Blue Boar Street.

Wythe reported on his morning's work. "They can't find a thing, sir. Of course, after all this rain, and people passing, a river bank's not the best place on which to find any sort of track. I wouldn't say that nothing happened because we can't find where it happened, but it's pretty certain, to my way of thinking, that if anything did happen we can only prove it in some other way."

"I didn't really expect much," Braydon confessed. "I gather that your impression of Lidgett is not favourable?"

"I don't know when I had a less favourable impression of anyone," Wythe admitted. "To begin with, that staying in bed; it's not natural, in a farmer. I don't believe he was in bed at all, but he knew from his wife that I called yesterday and maybe he hoped to put me off, or maybe he only wanted to keep me waiting."

"He's the sort of man who might be roused to sudden violence, you think?" asked Braydon.

"I do," said Wythe emphatically. "After being as pleasant as you like all the time we were pottering about those fields—though with a nasty sort of sneer in the background, so to speak—he flew into a rage when he saw my men searching the banks. Then, whilst it's possible that he was out of sight of the river just when the canoe passed, you've got to remember that the river's straight there and you'd see any craft a long way up or down. He'd surely have noticed it when he returned to the bank, and by running he could have caught up with it."

"And you think Miss Denning might have come to the bank to talk to him?" Braydon asked. "But why in heaven's name should she disembark? She could talk to him from the canoe."

"Goodness knows. He may have had some trick. Perhaps pretending he wanted her to look at another piece of land," Wythe suggested. "Or suppose she got out of the canoe of her own accord and he saw her. It's clear that the one thing that riles him is to see people embarking on his land."

"He and Bayes recognized each other?"

"Oh yes; made no bones about it! Not too pleased to see each other, though. I must say, Lidgett's story hangs together except in that one point: saying he didn't see the canoe, when he must have seen it; and then letting slip that he knew just how she was paddling."

"No sign of anything that might have been a weapon?" Braydon asked.

"Not a trace. He carries a stick, of course, but it's not a very heavy one."

"Well, if Lidgett's our man it's going to be confoundedly hard to nail it on to him. How about old Lond?"

"It seems that he's a great reader, sir, at the public expense. The assistant in the newspaper-room at the Free Library knows him well and remembers seeing him there on Friday afternoon, certainly till three fifteen. If he went by the quickest way to Ferry House, that's to say by a bus from Carfax up St. Giles—though they say he never uses them—and through the Lamb and Flag yard and South Parks Road, I should say he couldn't be there till half-past three. That still gives him a chance, and there's the watch which may have been altered."

"But if Miss Denning passed under the footbridge before three, as Lidgett's evidence indicates, or even a few minutes past three, as Bayes said, she'd pass Ferry House boathouse long before half-past," Braydon pointed out.

"That's true, but suppose the fancy took her to disembark there and have another look at the site she was so anxious to get hold of, and old Lond arrived and found her there——"

"Then we go back to the physical impossibility. It won't do, Super! We must think of something else. I'm going to spend most of this afternoon with Miss Denning's papers and the college account books."

"To my way of thinking, sir, there's too many impossibilities in this case, and one or other of them's got to be proved possible if we're to get any solution," said Wythe as, in a very dissatisfied mood, he went off to lunch.

CHAPTER XIV

PAMELA, NIECE OF BURSE

SALLY sat in a carefully selected chair in the lounge of the Mitre on Sunday, shortly before one o'clock, keeping an eye on each party of well-behaved relatives and self-assured undergraduates that entered. She wondered what Burse's niece would be like, whether she could really have been fond of Burse and what it would be like to have Burse as an aunt. Anyhow, all this affair must be perfectly beastly for Pamela, so one ought to be decent to her.

"Here's Sally already!" cried Basil's voice. "Depend on her to be on the spot when a meal is due!"

Sally shot up out of the deep chair. She achieved this neatly by swinging her legs up in the air and bringing them down again with enough leverage to raise her from the low seat. There was Betty in a large mackintosh with the collar turned up and a great woolly scarf round her neck; beside her was a slim, fair girl in a fur coat. The girl was pretty, undoubtedly, though her nose was rather red from the cold air; Sally noted enviously that she was one of those people who can still look attractive with a red nose, instead of quite awful. Betty introduced them and Pamela smiled at Sally shyly.

"Yes; this *is* your sister's coat; she insisted on lending it to me because she thought I should be cold. But I do hope you're not simply perished, Mrs. Pongleton."

"Betty, please. I simply can't bear to be reminded that I married such a name! I'm positively hot! There's nothing like a hideous solid mac. for keeping the wind out and

I, knowing Basil's *penchant* for rapid movement through the cold air, put on *layers* of Jaeger undies."

"Betty always goes motoring with half a dozen spare coats and a few hot water bottles in case the passengers are cold," Basil declared. "There was one occasion when she padded a passenger to such an extent that when they got home the poor woman couldn't be pushed through the front door. Moreover, in the extreme heat, the rubber hot water bottles had melted and fused her garments into a solid mass, so we had to cut away the door frame and knock a few bricks out of the wall before the wrappings could be cut off the victim in the decent obscurity of the house."

"Basil writes novels," Sally explained, "and unfortunately he's not able to distinguish truth from fiction; but his printed stories aren't at all bad."

"Name your drinks," Basil commanded. "I must buzz off; I'm lunching with a man and leaving you three to feed yourselves."

Pamela confessed complete ignorance of cocktails. "But I'd like sh-sherry, please." There was a slight hesitation in her speech when she was a little nervous, which Basil found ravishing.

"Are you going in the Riley?" Sally asked in her most off-hand manner.

"Lord no! I understand it costs you about £4 an hour to leave your car standing by the kerb in this place; wonderful how many millionaires you must have, to judge by the cars that line the streets! But what's your plan?"

"I just thought I might drive it," Sally suggested. "If it was doing nothing. I haven't got any plan."

"Marvellous!" said Basil.

"I should think Pamela has had enough of the car for one day," Betty suggested.

"I loved it!" Pamela declared.

"But, Basil, if we *do* want a drive, may I take the Riley?" Sally insisted. "You know I really am careful and you don't know how well I drive because when you're there I'm all of a dither, but when you're not I'm as steady as the rock of Gibraltar."

"O.K.," said Basil with resignation. "But look out for the one-way streets!"

He departed, and the others gathered in the private sitting-room in which Sally had already ordered lunch to be served. Betty had resigned herself to this extravagance with the thought that, after all, this visit to Oxford would be less of an ordeal for Pamela if she didn't have to be on view in public rooms all the time.

Sitting opposite to Pamela at lunch, Sally studied her in detail and finally approved. She was rather tall and—as Basil had said—a regular sylph. Her hair was of flaxen fairness which is so often seen on children and so seldom on grown-ups, and which, therefore, gives those who have it an air of innocence. It was fastened in thick coils low down on her neck and soft strands of it waved round her forehead and over her ears. Her eyes were blue and set very wide apart; her nose quite undistinguished, freckled and slightly tip-tilted.

"Do you know a don here called Mort? He belongs to Sim's, I believe," Pamela asked Sally.

"I should say so; I'm coaching with him this term; he's rather an old stick, but a good sort. Do *you* know him?" Sally was surprised, remembering how Pamela had apparently been kept from any association with Oxford.

"Ye-es," Pamela told her eagerly. "He came to see me last term at Cambridge. H-he had to be there on some business he said; something to do with research, I think. He said he looked me up because he was a friend of my father. I didn't think he was sticky at all." She was a little indignant.

"Of course I've only seen him in coachings," Sally explained. "He's all right, but—I don't know—sort of shut up. As if he was on his guard all the time against anyone being too personal. Not that medieval history leads much to personalities; it's more a feeling I had about him than anything he says. Have you known him long?"

"That was the first time I'd seen him, but I hoped I'd get to know him quite well. He was that sort of person, I thought; you feel he's nice and he'll be nicer still when you know him. I thought he'd have written when—when this happened. It made me feel awfully alone, you see, and I felt he was a dependable sort of person who could help. I was most awfully glad when I heard you were coming to fetch me," she added to Betty.

"I don't think he would have had time to write," Betty suggested. "You see, the news wasn't in the papers until Saturday afternoon."

"No—I see. Do you think I might call on him? He won't know I'm here, and I feel almost sure he will write or go to see me or something. It may seem rather odd, but he said when he came to see me that I was to let him know if ever I was in trouble. It seemed a queer thing to say, but I thought of it when—I heard."

Sally had been trying hard to readjust her view of Mr. Mort and consider him as someone who might be regarded as a friend, a human being. "I wonder he hadn't looked you up before," she suggested.

"Well—" Pamela seemed a little embarrassed. "P-perhaps he d-definitely waited till I was grown up; and then, you see, Aunt Myra didn't want me to know him." She became rather pink and stopped.

"Why not go to see him this afternoon?" Sally suggested, to create a diversion. "Dons are always at home on Sunday afternoon. I think they inaugurated the Sunday tea festival to demonstrate that they really are human and can eat buns with the best of us."

"Won't there be crowds of people there?" asked Pamela.

"Why not ring him up?" Betty suggested. "Sally could do it, as she knows him, and tell him you're here. Of course you don't want to be landed in the middle of an Oxford tea-party."

"And I could drive you up in the Riley," Sally agreed, delighted at this heaven-sent opportunity to take out Basil's car. "Unmarried dons generally live in college, but the Morter lives in a little house, called the Back End, just outside the college walls. I've heard that he was the sole support and comfort of an aged mother and wanted to live with her, and that was why he got that house. Probably there's no great run on it by the married dons because it's so small. His mother died some years ago and there's a rumour that the Morter's working on some great scholarly tome and has his notes laid out all over the house and can't move for fear some of them would get lost. The Back End's an awfully out-of-the-way spot, reached by a road that goes nowhere else, and he has his own backwater that runs alongside his garden, with a boathouse." She paused in her flow of explanation, suddenly realizing that boathouses were not a good subject of conversation. "I tell you what! I'll go and ring him up now. Sure to find him in. Keep my ice from melting!"

Denis Mort was considerably surprised to be rung up by Sally Watson; in fact, at first he seemed to have difficulty in remembering who she was. Just like a don, thought Sally in disgust, not to know you out of hours. "You coached me on Friday afternoon," she reminded him reproachfully.

"Yes, yes," he answered wearily.

Well, really, thought Sally, he needn't speak as though my essay gave him a pain. It was rather a good essay.

"Miss Denning's niece, Pamela Exe, from Girton, is staying here with my sister and would like to see you—you remember her? I wanted to know if I could bring her round some time to-day. But she doesn't want to meet masses of people at tea, you see."

"Pamela? Here in Oxford? Yes, of course; I should like very much to see her. Will you bring her at four, or earlier if it suits her. I'll see that she isn't bothered with people. Tell her, please, that I shall be very glad to see her."

Sally's indignation was not lessened by the fact that he obviously remembered Pamela, whom he had only seen once, quite well. What a funny gaspy way he had of speaking through the telephone; but then he really was a medieval relic and it was quite natural that he should be unable to get over his surprise that a human voice should issue from the thing.

Betty, meanwhile, was gently leading Pamela on to speak of her aunt. She felt that the girl wanted to get something off her chest and had no one else to confide in. Pamela's forlorn situation appealed to Betty's sense of responsibility as a married woman; she had definitely taken the girl under her wing and would look after her thoroughly.

"We were sorry we didn't see more of you at Bala," she told Pamela. "But Basil's an awfully late getter-up, and so we missed you that last morning and we had to go on that day because we'd promised to have tea with some people a long way off."

"I was awfully sorry too," said Pamela, and paused. "We set out early on purpose," she confessed suddenly. "Aunt Myra didn't want me to see you again, I'm sure. She didn't say anything, but she was very determined about that picnic and starting early. I'm rather glad to be able to talk about this, because it's been worrying me a good deal and there's no one else I can tell." There was more than her usual hesitation between one word and the next, but she obviously wanted to confide in someone. "You see, Aunt Myra was awfully good to me and gave up all her time to me when she wasn't at Oxford and was always planning for my future, but she was a bit— difficult. She didn't like it at all when I told her that Mr. Mort had been to see me. In fact, she said I wasn't to see him again; we had rather a row over it."

They heard Sally's approach and Betty wondered if this would put a stopper on Pamela's flow of confidence, but Pamela quickly noticed the look of anxiety, and as Sally entered she said, quite boldly: "I was telling your sister how Aunt Myra didn't like Mr. Mort coming to see me. In fact she went so far as to say she didn't think he was a good influence. I wanted to ask you about him. I mean, there *are* such things as dons who always try to hold hands when you coach with them; I've never met them, but I've heard of them. He didn't strike me as that sort at all. But Aunt Myra was a bit old-fashioned and she might take fright at the slightest rumour of that sort, and she never believed I could look after myself at all."

"I'm perfectly certain that the Morter's frightfully respectable," Sally assured her. "All that I ever heard about him is that he's a complete hermit and is absolutely wrapped up in the middle-ages and the strip system and that sort of thing, and walks about without ever seeing anyone who passes."

"I felt sure he was all right," Pamela replied. "And I think my first idea was right—that it was because he knew my father that Aunt Myra didn't want me to see him. He knew my mother too, he told me, and so he must have known Aunt Myra as well, years ago, and if he's been here for ages it was rather odd that she never said anything about him to me." She switched away from the subject abruptly, as the waiter came in with coffee. "Is it all right for me to call this afternoon?" she asked Sally.

Sally gave Mr. Mort's message. "I'll drive you there in the Riley and leave you and come back to tea with Betty," she suggested. "I really haven't seen much of my family since they arrived."

They sat round the fire for some time and talked in a desultory way of Bala, where Betty had first met Pamela, and of Cambridge and Pamela's work and ambitions, which she took very seriously. Sally announced that she would go and start the Riley and drive it out of the garage and round the town, to make sure she was used to it before she picked up Pamela. Betty was quite surprised at such evidence of tact.

As soon as Sally had gone Pamela began: "It's rather a relief to talk about these things to you, because I've been over and over them in my head till I thought I was probably losing all sense of proportion and getting an obsession. I hope you don't mind."

"I don't mind in the least," Betty assured her; "and if you don't ever want to talk about it again, you can forget you ever told me, and I'll forget it too. But it *does* help to clear things up if you can say them out loud to someone else."

"It's awfully decent of you to be so understanding. You see, I know Aunt Myra didn't like my father. He ran away and left my mother before I was born. Aunt Myra would never talk about him. I'm sure my mother must have had letters and photographs, but Aunt Myra destroyed them, I think, and always said there was nothing. I hate mysteries, and I don't believe my father was such an out and out rotter. I can't believe it; after all, he *was* my father, and I'm sure I should feel something bad inside me if he had been really bad. Besides, the worst things aren't so bad if you know them."

"You've never met any of your father's relatives, I suppose?"

"Not a one. It's almost as if he never existed; there seems to be no trace of him left. It's a disagreeable feeling, you know; as if you were cut off from your roots. Of course Aunt Myra must have been awfully fond of my mother, who was her younger sister, and awfully cut up when she died."

"The very nicest people can't help being terribly jealous sometimes," Betty suggested. "If your mother married someone whom her elder sister thought wasn't good enough for her, your aunt might not be able to help feeling jealous of him, and when your mother died, that would make it worse."

"Yes; I see all that. But it doesn't account for everything. Aunt Myra always seemed to want to keep me away from Oxford. It had been arranged long ago that I should go up to Cambridge and I was keen about it, so there wasn't any reason why I shouldn't come here. But when I told her that Mr. Mort had been to see me she was so furious that I couldn't help thinking that was the reason why she didn't want me ever to come here—so that I couldn't meet him. I've noticed for a long time her way of keeping people off when she didn't want me to know them—as she did with you—and at first I thought that was a kind of jealousy, but then I began to see that there was a system about it. They were always Oxford people, or people who had some connection with Oxford."

"She probably felt awfully responsible for you; even more than if she had really been your mother; and parents, you know, often think they're doing good work by trying to censor their children's friendships. It's a complete mistake," Betty declared, "but they're always doing it."

"Yes, I know," Pamela agreed. "But that doesn't account for it entirely. No; I'm sure Aunt Myra wanted to cut me off entirely from my father, and Mr. Mort is a sort of link with him, and that's the reason why she tried to keep me from ever meeting him. Well, I suppose he'll tell me about my father now—we didn't have much time when I saw him before—but I feel rather awful about it. I had hoped that somehow I could persuade Aunt Myra that it was much better for me to know whatever there was to know, and although I expected there would have to be another awful row between us, I thought that afterwards things would be easier. And now—" Pamela's lower lip trembled a little.

Betty squeezed her hand. "I'm awfully sorry, Pamela. It must be wretched. Do you really think you'd better go and see Mr. Mort to-day? Wouldn't you rather wait a bit?"

"No, really; I'd rather see him at once."

Sally, steering the Riley very decorously through Oxford, was recovering from several shocks. Somehow Burse, disguised as Aunt Myra and the tragically drowned only relative of this girl of her own age, became less of a fiend and more of a human being. And after all, Sally thought to herself, Burse was the only family she had, so I ought to help her to make the best of Burse. But how did the Morter come into it. Could he possibly know some disreputable secret about Burse's past? One wouldn't expect Burse to have disreputable secrets and one couldn't imagine the Morter having any connection at all with anyone's disreputable secrets. Or—could you? Perhaps a gay young rip might, if he repented of his youthful wildness, become just such a dried-up misanthropic scholar! But then why should the Morter be so anxious to see Pamela? Surely he couldn't be longing to betray Burse's dark past to her orphan niece? Especially if it were his own dark past as well? The whole thing was fantastic.

The whole academic world seemed to be changing its nature, putting on wigs and false eyebrows and taking part in a melodrama.

The light at Carfax changed colour and Sally carefully took a wide corner to avoid the nursemaids with prams who always consider the roadway at this point a suitable gossip stand, and drew up neatly at the door of the Mitre. She leapt out of the car and into the hotel so quickly that she did not notice Detective-Inspector Braydon strolling along the pavement. When she came out again about five minutes later, with Pamela following, he was again loitering past and paused to look very attentively at Pamela. Her appearance seemed to impress him.

A pale gleam of winter sunshine shone kindly on the weathered surfaces of the fawn-coloured stone of the college walls.

"Oxford really is lovely!" said Pamela.

Could the girl really be so impressionable, thought Sally, that Burse was right in keeping her away in case she should want to desert Cambridge? After all, if someone in possession of her senses decided deliberately that she wanted to go to the other place, where she couldn't even get a degree, surely the picturesque appearance of a few old buildings wouldn't make her change her mind. Though there was something about the place——

They halted at the main gate of Sim's.

"We can go in this way, by the Morter's garden gate," Sally explained. She guided Pamela round the quad and left her at the gate in the wall, with a cheery "Good-bye, and good luck!" for she had a vague feeling that there might be something rather unpleasant in front of Pamela, as if she were about to plunge into the mysterious depths of the university underworld.

CHAPTER XV

UNCONSIDERED TRIFLES

SALLY returned down St. Giles because it was easier to approach the Mitre from that side, bitterly regretting the speed limit as she hummed along. St. Giles is about four times the width of an ordinary street and a line of lamp-posts and islands divide the two tracks. Sally, well in the middle of the road, close to this frontier, noticed an elegant but rather dejected figure step nonchalantly from an island, cross her path and then hover uncertainly in the middle of the track. Surely it was Daphne. Sally knew that Basil was proud of his brakes and she gave a good display of their efficiency, nearly caused heart failure in the owner of a Morris Minor which was close on her tail and, when it perforce swerved round her on the wrong side, laughed heartlessly at the startled pedestrian's wild backward leap from approaching death.

Daphne stood gasping with alarm and indignation by Sally's left front wheel and remarked dispassionately: "Damn silly trick!" Then she looked at the driver. "Sally! Gosh! Whoever let you out alone in that?"

"You're not to be trusted in a road," said Sally severely. "What are you doing here?"

Owing to the width of St. Giles the traffic was able to swerve round them without much inconvenience whilst they discussed the situation.

"I saw you and just stopped to pick you up," Sally explained.

"I jolly nearly needed picking up," Daphne retorted.

"Anyway, wouldn't you like a drive in Basil's car?" Sally kindly offered.

"I'm not sure that I would, and anyway, I'm not feeling at my best. I've had a row with Owen. Have you read his new poem? It's called *Dust*, and is published by Blackwell at half a crown, and you ought to buy it because in ten years' time it may be worth ten guineas. Now, I've got that off my chest. I did promise him I'd tell people to buy it—and really it's worth it," she added generously.

"I'll tell Basil about it," said Sally. "But what's the matter with you? If reading Owen's new poem makes you feel like dirt and go mooning about in the middle of the traffic as if you were sick of life, that's not a very good advertisement."

"I wasn't mooning. It was yesterday that I read Owen's poem. It's this foul detective work that has upset everything. I asked Owen to find out something about Draga and Coniston and the penknife, and he's simply furious. I see now that it was rather a dirty trick."

"You can't have done it properly. You'd better get in and come for a drive and then we can both go back to the Mitre for tea. In fact, I think I'd better go there first because I said I'd go back at once. I've been taking Burse's niece, Pamela, to see the Morter, and Betty might wonder what had happened."

"She might, and with good reason. But why on earth to see the Morter?"

"Get in and I'll tell you." Sally held open the door and Daphne settled herself into the low seat.

"Don't go too fast, because this hat easily comes unstuck," she advised.

They were held up by the traffic lights before they could enter the Corn, and Sally was suddenly aware of a tall figure bending over the back of the car and opening a door.

"May I get in, Miss Watson? I want a word with you and I am being followed, so this is providential!"

"Oh!" gasped Sally. "I had quite a shock; I thought you were the police!"

"Well, so he is!" Daphne reminded her.

Sally exploded in giggles.

"Green light! Get on!" said Daphne.

They proceeded along the Corn.

"What do you mean about being followed?" Sally asked over her shoulder. "Is someone trying to murder *you*?"

That, of course, would be in accordance with the best thrillers, but she had never expected that the Cherwell mystery would come up to scratch to that extent.

"The hounds of the press," said Braydon gravely. "They are on my track. They seem to think that I go about dropping clues as if I were a paper chase and that by following me they'll pick some up. I was just wondering what was the best means of seeing you. If the press could report that I visited blank college and spent an hour interviewing Miss X, it would make a splendid headline, especially if Miss X were young and charming."

"I don't particularly want to be a headline," said Sally. "And Betty would hate it. But won't it make a better one if they can say 'Detective steps into fast car and is rushed by lovely young lady to'—well, anywhere—Broughton Poggs, perhaps."

"Of course it might. We must hope for the best. But are you really bound for that enchantingly named place?"

"As a matter of fact we're going to the Mitre at the moment. You might come along with us. My sister's there, but she knows all about it. Blast these lights! I suppose I can't go past them on the strength of having Scotland Yard in the car?"

Betty was not unduly surprised to see Sally return with Daphne, but when a tall dark man followed them into the room she thought that surely this must be the mysterious Mr. Mort. Why on earth—? And where was Pamela?

"This is Detective-Inspector Braydon," said Sally. "My sister, Mrs. Pongleton." She wondered whether it would be bad form to mention that Betty had helped to solve the famous Pongleton case; Betty didn't like her to talk about it; better not.

"I wanted to ask your sister one or two questions," Braydon explained, "so I cadged a lift when I saw her passing, and she brought me here."

"I'll leave you in peace," said Betty quickly. "Really—there's something I want to do——"

"It's not in the least necessary; in fact, I think that perhaps you can help," said Braydon. "First of all"—he turned to Sally— "can you tell me when, if at all, any of you told Mr. Coniston that you had found that knife, or gave him some hint that you had found it?"

Daphne turned pink. "It's my fault entirely. I asked some-one else, a friend of mine, if he could find out whether that *was* Matthew Coniston's knife, and though he didn't much like the idea, he dropped a hint to Matthew, or rather, he laid a sort of trap. He was awfully fed up about it afterwards."

"When was this hint or trap dropped or laid?" asked Braydon.

"On Saturday evening, I think. I say, I do hope this isn't serious, because it would be simply ghastly if somehow I had made—er, this friend of mine get Matthew into a mess."

"I hope, too, it isn't serious," Braydon assured her. "Can you tell me what sort of a hint your friend dropped? I'm sorry if it's painful, but criminal investigation is apt to be painful and generally unpleasant."

Daphne writhed. "As for that, I'm out of it from now on," she assured him. "I don't know exactly what was said, but I think Matthew gathered that I was in it and that I knew a knife had been found, but probably he thought the police had done the finding."

"I see; thank you. Now I hope you can put it out of your minds. At least you can rest assured that if some of you had not picked up the knife, the police would have found it, with its fingerprints intact." He knew that if Coniston's story was accurate, the knife would probably have been recovered by the owner—or perhaps would never have been left behind— but there was no need for the girls to know that.

"And remember that it won't do Mr. Coniston any good to let any gossip about that knife get about, especially as it is possible that it need never be mentioned in the case again. There is not even any proof that the knife belonged to Mr. Coniston."

Daphne heaved a sigh of relief. Sally felt some disappointment. She liked things to be tidily cleared up, and this knife affair was apparently to remain wrapped in mystery, unless Daphne had extracted more information from Owen.

"We haven't yet found out anything about the Ferry House inscription," Sally announced; "but Gwyneth was bristling with mystery this morning; I think she has some clue, and we may be able to let you know this evening. I've not had much time to cope with it. I've been occupied with Miss Denning's niece."

"Ah! The slender fair girl whom you carried off in your car after lunch?" Braydon suggested.

"So you saw us then?" Sally asked in surprise that she herself had failed to notice. "You *are* a snooper!"

"Sally!" exclaimed Betty, horrified. She had been sitting quietly in the background and they had forgotten her.

"I didn't mean to be rude," Sally explained apologetically. "But Inspector Braydon seems to dog my footsteps."

"Isn't that in accordance with popular ideas of a sleuth?" inquired Braydon. "Don't worry! I'm not offended, Mrs. Pongleton. In fact, I think I'm rather pleased to find that I escaped Miss Watson's observant eye."

"Of course that *was* Pamela Exe who got into the car with me," Sally informed him.

"Yes; I should have known her anywhere," said Braydon, almost to himself.

"So you'd seen her before?" asked Sally. Observing a denial in his expression she set her brains to work and produced an explanation. "Of course, you've been going through Miss Denning's papers with a fine comb and you saw her photograph!"

That point being satisfactorily settled, Sally dismissed it.

"Pamela has gone to see Mr. Mort." Betty explained.

There was a moment when Braydon's surprise advertised itself in his face; instantly he controlled his expression, but Betty, who had naturally been looking at him, noticed that he was taken aback by this news. Sally and Daphne, occupied with some murmured question and answer about Daphne's lunch, noticed nothing.

"Of course," Braydon remarked, "he's a friend of the family, I believe, and would know she was coming to stay with you here."

"He hardly had time to know," said Betty; "but Pamela was anxious to see him, so my sister rang him up and arranged it. Pamela is staying with us here for a day or two, if you should want to see her; but she finds it rather difficult to talk about the affair—naturally—and I'm quite sure she hasn't the ghost of a notion as to any motive or reason behind the murder of Miss Denning."

"You've talked to her about it?" Braydon inquired.

"Not much about that, but about herself and her parents a bit," Betty told him. "She seemed to want to talk to someone about things that were worrying her."

Braydon nodded and turned to Sally. "There's one other thing I wanted to ask you two; not very important, but it may help to explain a slight detail. Do you remember what state of mind Miss Czernak seemed to be in when Inspector Wythe questioned her on Friday night? You know her well and can judge best whether she seemed very upset or alarmed at being sent for."

Sally and Daphne considered. "She seemed particularly calm; not even very surprised that she had been sent for," Sally informed him. "Oh, dear! I keep forgetting that you're the police! I don't mean that she expected to be sent for, but Draga's like that sometimes. She'll take the most astounding things absolutely calmly and then she'll go off the deep end suddenly over nothing at all. She never told us what she said to Inspector Wythe; she rushed back to her room again, I think, after the interview; but it's quite likely that she started calm and boiled over in the middle of the interview and then she may have said *anything*."

"She's definitely unreliable," Daphne agreed.

"I had that impression," Braydon agreed solemnly. "Now I don't think I need trouble you any further, Miss Watson and Miss Loveridge. I believe I interrupted a drive?"

"There was one thing I *did* want to ask," said Sally; "though I don't suppose you'll tell me. What time was Miss Denning drowned?"

"It's not so much won't as can't," Braydon confessed. "If we know, you'll hear it at the inquest to-morrow."

"It was after three, wasn't it?" Daphne inquired. "I've heard about that man Bayes seeing her go downstream under the Parks bridge after three."

"Oh!" Sally exclaimed.

"There's no secret about Bayes's story," Braydon informed them.

"But do you believe it?" Daphne urged. "The man sounds very woolly! Why, first of all he thought it was a man coming down in the canoe!"

"He did, did he?" Braydon commented. "First I've heard of that."

"You see, he *is* woolly," Daphne insisted. "I shouldn't think you could count on him at all."

"Perhaps not," said Braydon sadly. "Really, I hate to keep you from your drive, and don't you think, Miss Watson, that some of the City of Oxford police may still be attending to traffic problems and may be interested in the car which you left outside the door?"

"Heavens!" exclaimed Sally, and dashed out of the room, followed by Daphne more sedately.

Braydon smiled at Betty.

"I hope my sister hasn't been a nuisance," said Betty. "I was awfully relieved when she told us that she had seen you on Saturday night and told you everything."

"I don't think they've done any harm," Braydon reassured her. "What I was more afraid of was that they might light upon something with implications that would really give them a nasty shock. One hopes, for their sakes, that no one they know is seriously involved, but one can never tell where clues, or what seem to be clues, may lead."

"I know," Betty agreed with emphasis. "I hope they'll keep out of it. I think they're only going for a drive now, because Sally wants to play with my husband's car."

"It's a satisfactory toy," Braydon agreed. "Mrs. Pongleton, I don't want to seem horribly inquisitive, though that's what I often have to be. But, you've talked to Miss Exe; I don't want to bother the girl more than need be. I don't know if there's any connection between the alleged desire of Miss Denning to keep her away from Oxford and what has happened to Miss Denning. All things are possible. Did Miss Exe say anything to explain that policy of Miss Denning's, which everyone seems to have heard of?"

"She did talk about it," Betty agreed. "It seems to have worried her a good deal. I think there's no doubt that Pamela's aunt had a definite intention of that kind. Pamela now thinks that Miss Denning's idea was to keep her from meeting this Mr. Mort, who went to see Pamela at Cambridge last term."

"For any definite purpose, do you know?"

"I think he was in Cambridge on some business and took the opportunity to look her up, because he had known her father. If he was interested in her for that reason, and Miss Denning really kept Pamela away from him deliberately, that would be a good opportunity of seeing her, of course."

"And Miss Exe was anxious to see him again?"

"Yes; she liked him, and seemed to feel she could rely upon him in some way, and yet, I thought, she was a little scared about seeing him. But perhaps that's because she seemed to have an idea that he could tell her more about her father; she wanted to know and yet was afraid of what she might hear. Miss Denning always seems to have made a mystery about Pamela's father, but I think that may have been only because she thought Pamela's mother was too good for him. Miss Denning has told Pamela vaguely that her father deserted her mother before Pamela was born. That's all Pamela knows, and naturally she is reluctant to believe that her own father was a thoroughly bad lot, and wants to hear something in extenuation, but is afraid it may not turn out like that."

"Poor girl!" Braydon commented.

"Yes; I'm awfully sorry for her. But it doesn't seem to have much connection—or has it? Of course—" Betty hesitated. "There's one thing that occurred to me; I wouldn't say it to anyone else, but perhaps it may explain a certain amount. Perhaps Pamela's father never married her mother. Pamela described Miss Denning's ideas as rather old-fashioned, and Miss Denning might think it better not to tell her niece.

But actually I don't believe Pamela would mind knowing that nearly as much as not knowing anything. It doesn't explain why Miss Denning should be so anxious to keep her away from Mr. Mort. Even if he knew, surely he wouldn't tell the girl? It would be rather caddish."

"Under certain circumstances he might feel he had a right to tell her," said Braydon, half to himself. "It's a queer story. Thank you very much for telling me. I don't know whether it explains anything, except Miss Exe's visit to Mr. Mort just now."

"Yes, it does explain that quite naturally, doesn't it?"

"Quite. Miss Exe seemed more concerned to clear up the problem of her parentage than about the mystery of her aunt's death?" Braydon asked.

"I think she discussed that a bit with my husband in the car this morning," Betty told him. "Naturally she finds it difficult to talk about that. After all, although she found her aunt rather difficult sometimes—well, people do find their parents difficult, don't they? And yet they are fond of them; and Miss Denning was almost like Pamela's mother."

"Yes; I'm sorry for the girl. I'm glad you're looking after her, Mrs. Pongleton. Thank you for the help you've given. I must be off."

Betty sat alone by the fire, thinking everything over. What she thought of was not so much what had been said but the way in which Braydon had received the various items of news. He had been definitely startled when he heard that Pamela had gone to see Mr. Mort, and he hadn't really been satisfied with her explanation of why Pamela had gone. He had particularly noticed Daphne's remark about Bayes's story of someone coming down in a canoe. But then Betty didn't know what Bayes's story was. Betty began to feel worried about Pamela, though she could not give any definite shape to her fears. It was just a vague feeling that the girl was in some danger. Who was this man, Mort? A don and perfectly respectable, Sally said. Someone you could trust, Pamela had implied. But girls were often mistaken; they could be perfect fools about men, Betty thought wisely.

At this point Sally returned.

"I took Daphne up to Cumnor," she announced. "The Riley really is a dream! I've taken her back to college now, and I've garaged the Riley, and what about tea?"

Betty rang the bell. "What about this man Bayes's story?" she asked. "Daphne mentioned it, and I'd like to know what it is."

"Funny; everyone calls him 'this man Bayes.' Daphne's told me; she had it from Owen. He asked her to lunch to tell her that, so he can't have been so awfully fed up with her, but they seem to have had a row afterwards, and Daphne is so upset that she hardly knows what she ate, and that's most unusual."

CHAPTER XVI

GWYNETH CALLS ON
AUNT SOPHIA

GWYNETH picked from amongst a multi-coloured debris on her bed a small contraption of bright blue cloth and poised it at a remarkable angle on her golden curls, so that it became a hat; not a prosaic covering for the head or shade for the eyes, of course, but something which would have been instantly recognized in Bond Street as a hat. She considered her image in the dim mirror let into the narrow door of the wardrobe.

"Definitely stir-making, but perhaps too much for Aunt Sophia," she told the image, which shook its head mournfully.

She tried another headpiece, which looked as if its creator, in despair of making it fit, had gathered up the slack at the top into casual folds and transfixed them anyhow with a quill just to keep them from flopping over the wearer's ears. Gwyneth adjusted it with great care.

"Too, too new! I don't suppose Aunt Sophia goes out into the world much, poor old dear. She might think it happened accidentally."

Gwyneth removed it tenderly. "Something definitely demure is indicated. M-m-m." She surveyed the collection and at last selected something which so far conformed to the old-fashioned idea of hat as to have a distinguishable crown and brim. She was concentrating on the correct angle at which this must be set when someone knocked at her door.

"Come in! That you, Mary? Am I appallingly late? Will I do?"

"For Aunt Sophia? I think she regards all modern clothes in the same light as Baroque architecture—unfortunate, but one must just accept it."

"O-o-oh! In that case—" Gwyneth reached for the bright blue device which she had first rejected. "It makes *me* feel good, so if it's not going to upset anyone—" She flicked off the little grey felt and turned to the mirror.

When Gwyneth faced Mary Wentworth again the latter, who was a clever girl, but not in that direction, wondered that the effect of so many minutes of careful adjustment should be as if someone had flung the thing carelessly at Gwyneth's head and it had stuck there.

"Well?" inquired Gwyneth.

"If *you* think it's all right, then it'll do. There's no absolute rightness about hats," said Mary.

"Oh, but there is!" declared Gwyneth.

"Come *on*," urged Mary. "It's nearly four."

Gwyneth snatched up bag and gloves and they started, crossing the river by the Parks footbridge and therefore just missing Daphne, who was deposited by Sally at the Mesopotamia bridge at about the same time.

Gwyneth had particularly noted Nina's remark on Saturday about Mary Wentworth's North Oxford aunt who knew quite a lot about old Lond. Mary, Gwyneth knew, was the niece of old Mrs. Daker, who was even more famous in Oxford than her deceased husband, that Professor of Metaphysical Philosophy who, it was alleged, had always bought his trousers in the Caledonian Market. Gwyneth had cunningly disinterred from some memory of a country house party a moony young man called Tim Daker, who had surely told her to call on his aunt in North Oxford, and Mary had consented to identify Tim as a cousin and agreed to take Gwyneth with her to call on Aunt Sophia that afternoon, Sunday being earmarked in Oxford for these social activities. Gwyneth was vague about exactly when and where she had met Tim Daker; it was a sheer fluke that she remembered his surname. As for the alleged request that she should call on his aunt, "It's the sort of addled thing he would say," Gwyneth told herself.

Mary was a plain, red-haired, self-satisfied second-year student. Any criticism of her was always modified by the chorus of "but she's an absolutely dead-certain first." She wore shapeless woolly jumpers and shaggy tweed skirts, and it was easy to imagine her blossoming later into one of the more notable Oxford oddities.

Mrs. Daker lived in one of those remarkable houses by which Oxford in the latter part of the nineteenth century signified its appreciation of Mr. Ruskin and the Gothic tradition. Its tall yellow brick front was diversified on the ground floor by a bay and a porch, both of which broke out surprisingly into pseudoecclesiastical stone arches, in which sash windows and fanlight were uncomfortably fitted.

The door was opened by an ancient family retainer, whom Mary greeted as "Lizzie." Lizzie surveyed Gwyneth with disfavour and seemed at first disinclined to let her in. Mary charged ahead, however, and Gwyneth followed. Lizzie caught her by the sleeve.

"There's a glass in the hall, miss, if you'd like to put your hat straight!"

Instinctively Gwyneth turned to the glass and was reassured to see, by the lurid glimmer which came through the blue and yellow fanlight, that no unkind breeze had disturbed the absolutely correct angle. She caught a malicious grin on Lizzie's ancient countenance as she followed Mary into the drawing-room.

Aunt Sophia sat erect behind a table which held an immense number of tea-cups and a shining display of silver.

"This is Gwyneth Pane, from Persephone," Mary explained. "She met Tim at—where was it, Gwyneth?"

"He particularly asked me to call and see you when I came up," Gwyneth hastily declared.

"Remarkable effort of memory on Tim's part!" said the old lady dryly. She had an extraordinarily weather-beaten face, with a long nose and whiskered chin, and the architecture of her massive grey hair was as typically nineteenth century as that of her house.

"What did you think of Tim?" Mrs. Daker continued briskly.

Gwyneth was seldom at a loss for an answer to any question that was not an inquiry for knowledge of an academic kind, but now she fumbled wildly in the dim corners of her memory for something definite about Tim. Was he the one whose pillow they had peppered? Or was he the one who had got under the sofa with her when they played Sardines?

"I liked him," she gasped feebly. "He's very nice!"

"Yes, he was nice when he came up to Oxford, and still nice when he went down. Can't take in anything, not even vice! He'll go on being nice to the end of his days. Do you like China or Indian?"

"Do I—Oh, er—China, please."

Undergraduates arrived, paying duty calls, probably because their fathers had coached with old Daker, and they created a fortunate diversion. Each of them stumbled through his answers to Mrs. Daker's fusillade of abrupt questions and found relief in handing round cups of tea and cakes. Presently Mrs. Daker again noticed Gwyneth, who was now happily telling one of the young men of the wizard time she had spent at Frinton last summer.

"What are your interests—girl—I forget your name?"

"Pane," said Gwyneth meekly. "I'm reading English."

"For lack of any definite taste for other branches of knowledge, I suppose? And that's your interest?"

"Well, of course, it's difficult to know before you come up what you *are* interested in. School work's so different. But I'm keen on tennis, and I like the river, though I haven't had a summer term yet. And—" the river reminded Gwyneth of her object in coming to see Mrs. Daker—"I'm awfully interested in old houses; I don't know much about them, but there are so many here. It makes you wonder what it was like to live here in the middle ages, you know."

"I do; a good deal," Mrs. Daker agreed unexpectedly. "Draughty and awkward and dirty. Any amount of aesthetic satisfaction and nowhere to wash! But better study old houses because you're interested, than English Lang. and Lit. because you don't know what else to read. Want any books?"

"I suppose you haven't got a book that describes Ferry House?" asked Gwyneth eagerly. "Passing by it every day we naturally get interested in it, and it looks rather—er— fascinating."

"But Ezekiel doesn't, eh? *I* know. I could show you something. Perhaps I will." She turned from Gwyneth to ask an unfortunate young man what he thought he had got out of five terms at Oxford.

The undergraduates melted away as soon as they felt they had paid for their tea by a decent period of endurance. Mary Wentworth then had to answer many inquiries from Mrs. Daker on current family affairs. At last the family had been examined and laid aside, and Mrs. Daker turned to Gwyneth again.

"What about Ferry House? Noticed the chimneys?"

Chimneys! thought Gwyneth wildly. What would one notice about chimneys, except that they smoked.

Mary came to her rescue with the comment, in a superior voice, that they were a particularly fine group, which puzzled Gwyneth, who had never thought of chimneys at all since she had ceased to believe in Santa Claus.

"I suppose you remember the island before Persephone College was built?" Mary asked, because she knew that Aunt Sophia liked to talk of this event.

"I do. And I remember how they wouldn't take my father's good advice about an architect. Adam Lond caused the sensation of his time in Oxford when he sold the island. A ladies' college—only *ladies* could receive education in those days—on Lond's land! The Londs, who would as soon shoot a woman as let her set foot on their property!"

"Shoot her! Gosh! Was that true?" Gwyneth asked.

"As true as any popular saying. The Londs had no use for women. It must have stuck in their gizzards to find that their precious family couldn't get on without 'em and that they had to admit at least one wife in each generation."

"Why did they sell it?"

"Adam was short of cash. Ezekiel's brother was a young rip; never having seen a woman except his mother, he didn't know how to deal with them when he met them; he piled up debts—and then came this offer to buy the land. Temptation of the devil, Ezekiel called it, but Adam decided to let the women have the island, doubtless hoping they'd drown themselves as I understand one of them has just done."

"Yes, our bursar," said Mary. "But it's supposed that somebody drowned her."

"Causing a nasty lot of gossip, I'll be bound. Ezekiel will be pleased. Does he live there still?"

"No, but he hangs about there sometimes," Gwyneth told her. "Please tell us more about him and his house."

"He flew into a fine rage with his father over the sale. When they began to build on the island, he went over there one night and tore down part of the wall and threw the bricks into the river—like the devil in church-building legends. But the Londs are full of talk and fine gestures; not one of them ever did anything effective. They think they must live up to the old rhyme and that's the bee in their bonnets."

"What is the rhyme?" Gwyneth asked, with a gasp of excitement. "Mr. Lond met me on the footpath a few days ago and shouted out something at me that sounded like a rhyme, but I didn't catch it all."

"It's carved on the chimneypiece—a fine piece of Elizabethan work, the carving, I've heard. I was never allowed to see it, of course, being of the hated sex and not caring to marry Ezekiel!"

"Carved on the chimneypiece!" Gwyneth gasped. "In the big room at the back?"

"Have you been in?" inquired the old lady sharply.

"Oh, no; but we—someone—did look through the window and thought they saw something. But what is the rhyme?"

"My uncle, Professor Wentworth—name wouldn't mean anything to you, of course, but if you read history you might know that he's still thought something of—he, being a bachelor, was let in; in fact, was on quite good terms with Adam Lond. He memorized the rhyme and entered it in his commonplace book. Adam noticed him looking hard at it; then the fat was in the fire. Adam, poor fool, thought some curse would come on the family if the rhyme became common property; he couldn't see that his idiotic family were bringing their own curse on themselves."

"But what is it?" Gwyneth implored, unable to contain her curiosity.

"Don't be impatient! Sense of values is what all you girls lack! The point of this story is not the jingle of words, but the store that the old Londs set on them. Consider your own hat!" Mrs. Daker suddenly advised Gwyneth. "You think a North Oxford frump doesn't know anything about modern hats, but I know that if that were put in a museum it wouldn't give anyone a hundred years hence the ghost of a notion of what you look like, unless it were set at the right angle on a millinery model with the proper *coiffure*. Isn't that so?"

"You've absolutely got it taped!" Gwyneth declared, thinking that this was one in the eye for Mary.

"And have you got it taped about this rhyme?"

Gwyneth was slightly dazed.

"The important thing," Mary explained, "is how it came to be carved on the mantelpiece in Ferry House and how it influenced the lives of the Lond family and how great-uncle Gilbert came to write it down."

"Just so. Ferry House is Elizabethan, and a fine example of its type. It ought to be properly preserved, but I'll guarantee Ezekiel is letting it fall into ruins; shiftless lad he always was. The Elizabethan Lond who built it had the rhyme carved there, worked into an intricate leaf pattern. It doesn't stand out plainly; I really don't see how you could recognize it from looking through a window." She regarded Gwyneth suspiciously. "If Ezekiel had the wit to realize that only a connoisseur of carving would ever notice it, he could let hordes of trippers through his house, and get a good revenue from them, and never lose a wink of sleep over the secrecy of his family motto!"

"Did your uncle keep the copy that he wrote out?" Gwyneth asked anxiously.

"My Uncle Gilbert had no intention of mutilating his commonplace book, however much Adam might rage, but he had old-fashioned ideas of honour, and respected Adam's superstition, so he never published the rhyme and only showed it to a few members of his own family and friends. He hadn't the modern idea of making money out of private information, no matter how you may have gained it."

Gwyneth was wriggling with impatience but terrified of diverting the old lady once more to Elizabethan days or modern fashions. "Does it give a clue to any secret?" she asked.

"Stuff and nonsense! A mere boasting jingle! I've got it here." She half-rose. "Hm! I don't know——"

"We'd love to see it," Gwyneth ventured.

"Of course you would! Because it's private!" She bent towards Gwyneth fiercely. "How do I know you're not Lady Pauline Pry of the *Sunday Gossip*? I might see the Londs' rhyme in print next week."

"You'd know quite well if you could see me trying to write an essay!" Gwyneth maintained. "I never write a word more than is necessary."

"Good—if you're sure you know what is necessary! Well, I'm not such a fool as to ask for promises, but I rely on you both not to make any improper use of this!"

Mrs. Daker went to one of the tall bookcases which flanked the fireplace and took out a small fat volume bound in vellum. She returned to her chair and browsed over the pages, covered with tiny sharp writing, faded brown. "Here it is!" She handed the open book to her niece, and Gwyneth seated herself on the sofa beside Mary and bent over the book with her. They read:

"Inscription carved on a chimneypiece in Ferry House, Oxford, and believed by Adam Lond, the owner, to have some magic significance. I have given him my word that this shall not be published. 1867.

> "*I Lond hold this Ilond*
> *As Deare to me as Lyf*
> *No Woman heere may Woo man*
> *Save shee be wedded Wyf,*
> *Shee who this rede gainsayth*
> *Atones onlie in Dethe.*

"The family tradition is that Giles Lond, who built Ferry House in the days of Queen Elizabeth, carved this himself. I opine that the popular saying 'The Londs who would as soon shoot a woman as let her set foot on their land,' comes from a misreading of this inscription. The intended meaning was probably that a woman who trespassed on the island would not be forgiven in her lifetime. But owing to the sinister significance popularly attributed to the inscription, the Londs have an aversion to its becoming common knowledge. The puns are typical of the era."

Gwyneth skipped hastily through Professor Wentworth's wordy comments and read the rhyme again and again, hoping her memory would prove as good as his. When Mary had finished reading, she took the book from her and pored over it.

"It's queer writing, but very neat," she said, hoping to gain time.

"It doesn't say that no woman may set foot on the island, but only that she may not 'woo man' there," Mary pointed out.

"The Londs probably considered that the mere approach of any woman to their vicinity constituted wooing!" Mrs. Daker suggested.

"And, of course, an Elizabethan would say anything for the sake of a pun," Mary commented.

"Originality in orthography was also admired," Mrs. Daker added. "Giles Lond did pretty well in that respect. Here! Let me have it!"

Gwyneth parted reluctantly with the book.

"Thank you so much for letting us see it. It really is thrilling—to know the whole story of it," Gwyneth finished hastily. She was repeating the words to herself feverishly, praying that she and Mary might be able to take their leave at once, before the necessity of making further conversation should drive the verse from her mind. Fortunately Aunt Sophia was quite willing to let them go.

"Come again! I'd like to see your next hat!" she told Gwyneth graciously as the two said good-bye. As soon as Gwyneth got back to Persephone College she rushed to her room, snatched up a note-book which, according to its label, dealt with Beowulf, and wrote down the Lond family motto. Then she hurried off to find Sally.

CHAPTER XVII

PAMELA AT THE BACK END

SALLY'S feeling about dons was that although they might sometimes be pitied they should never be admitted to friendship or treated as equals. It was not altogether their fault, poor things, but if they cultivated their intellects so assiduously it was only to be expected that "the humanities"—to borrow an academic term—would suffer. So Sally would have been quite shocked to observe how Pamela, installed in Mr. Mort's bookwalled room, was pouring out tea for him and treating him as a human being. She had quite forgotten that he was a don.

Even Pamela, who was not a conceited girl, could not help noticing that he was pleased to see her. He questioned her now in an eager way about Cambridge, her work and friends and future plans. Yet sometimes she thought he wasn't really listening to her answers, he gazed at her in such a dreamy way, as if he were seeing something else. And she wasn't sure if she really caught a queer, twisted look on his face now and then, or whether it was only the effect of the yellow light of a sensational sunset, mixed with leaping glares from the fire.

"You know," she said, "I've been worrying a lot about the way Aunt Myra would try to manage my life for me, and specially about the way in which she tried to keep me from having anything to do with Oxford. She was awfully angry when I told her you had called last term. Somehow I felt that was a kind of crisis and that things might be explained. But they weren't. I feel that only you can explain now, and I want you to."

Denis Mort rested his chin in his hand and turned his head away from Pamela, staring into the fire for some moments, frowning. Then he turned rather wearily towards her and relaxed into his high-backed chair, so that his face was shadowed by it.

"The fact that your aunt never did explain makes it difficult for me now. You see, don't you? You know that there was an old quarrel between us; that we felt differently, thought differently. She had only bitter memories of your father, and because of—of my friendship with him she did not wish you to meet me. It is an old, unhappy story, Pamela. Can it do any good to speak of it?"

Pamela was strangely moved by those words which came slowly and brokenly from the man whose face she could no longer see. But she could not leave it at that.

"I hate mysteries!" she declared vehemently. "Surely I have a right to know about my father, and perhaps you are the only person who can tell me."

"I'm not sure, Pamela. I thought I had a right to see you, because I felt a great interest—no, I may as well be honest—a great affection, for your mother's daughter. But perhaps I was wrong; I seem to have made new difficulties for you."

"Oh, no!" Pamela assured him. "The difficulty had been there for a long time; your visit focused it, as it were. I didn't mind the row itself so much; we were bound to have one some day. But I really was most awfully glad that you came to see me. I have been counting on seeing you again and getting you to tell me about my father. You seem to be my only link with him. And it wasn't only because of that that I was glad you came. You were—well, understanding."

Denis Mort got up from his chair and crossed the room with long strides to the farthest wall of bookcases; he turned and strode back till he stood almost over Pamela.

"Perhaps you had better know, Pamela. Probably it will not matter so dreadfully to you. Your father and mother were not married. But he intended to marry her; you must give him credit for that."

Pamela looked up at him calmly. "I had guessed that. I wasn't sure, but it seemed to fit in with the facts as far as I knew them. I don't mind dreadfully; if I do mind at all it's only very little; what I mind about terribly is whether he really loved her."

"That's the one thing you can be perfectly sure of in this world."

"Then it wasn't true—I never really believed it could be true—that he left my mother before I was born, because he didn't care? That seemed to be why Aunt Myra hated him so."

"He did care, Pamela. You're quite right. That mattered, and still matters, more than anything else. Your father was weak; I think that was his greatest sin. He was very young and circumstances were too difficult for him. He and your mother were both under age; your Aunt Myra and your father's mother were both against the marriage. They thought it imprudent. Your father was still at college; he had little money but great expectations from an uncle who might be expected to disapprove strongly of such an early marriage. But your aunt felt even more strongly against the marriage; she seemed to wish to prevent it at all costs."

"She was jealous, you mean?"

He was startled by her insight into the past. "Yes; I suppose she was. Jealousy may catch the best of us, you know. They were orphans and Myra had been like a mother to Pamela—your mother—and this was the first time that Pamela had seriously gone against her sister's wishes and—worse still—had cared for anyone more than Myra, and had been ready to give up everything, even Myra, for someone else's sake."

"But I don't understand, about why he left her."

"It was a strange thing, Pamela. There were those two sisters; Pamela was about your age, nineteen; Myra was about twenty-five; both strong-willed, with their wills set so stubbornly in opposition, yet compromising on a plan of action. Pamela did not want to harm her lover; she had great faith in his career and was afraid he might wreck it for her sake. She loved him too much, if you can understand that, Pamela; perhaps, as her daughter, you can. So she tried to take Fate into her own hands. She did not tell him that she was expecting a child, and she agreed to Myra's plan to go away to a remote village in Devonshire, where the child should be born and no one should know. Goodness knows what Myra intended to do after that!"

"So my father never knew about me—that I existed?"

"Yes; wait. Your mother wrote to him, telling him that she would not interrupt his work, but would see him again when he had finished at Oxford. She gave him no address and found an opportunity to get letters posted in a town some way off. Pamela, you must always remember that if your father was weak your mother had courage of the rarest kind, the courage that can refuse help and face loneliness and be content to be quiet."

"Content to be quiet," Pamela repeated. "You speak of my mother as if you were very fond of her."

"Yes." He dropped the word slowly into a deep silence. "And then you were born and she died. Myra wrote to your father the most terrible letter that a man could receive. Yet I don't think it mattered to him, after what had happened. Then the war broke out. Your father enlisted at once; like many other weak men in difficulties, he thought that the war solved them. Really, it only postponed the necessity for solution. He—was—glad to die."

"It's terrible that they couldn't be happy together any longer, my father and my mother. Tell me about my mother."

"You are very like her, and yet she seemed younger than you; less sophisticated; perhaps it is just the difference between two generations."

Pamela realized that he was so lost in his memory of that other Pamela that he intended no criticism of her. Yet somehow she minded a good deal what he thought of her.

"I'm not really sophisticated—not in the hard, worldly way. But other people all seem so much more grown-up than I; I have to try to be grown-up, too."

"Yes; I suppose youth generally strikes an attitude and plays a role. Just now it is the attitude of worldliness, and perhaps that makes life easier."

"But I want to know more about my mother," Pamela persisted. "Not just what she looked like, but what she was like herself. She wasn't like Aunt Myra, was she?"

"They were both very resolute and both courageous. They were not much alike in other ways. Pamela had a heavenly sense of humour and a restless, active mind. She was adventurous, intellectually as well as in other ways. I never knew an honester person. 'We must live truthfully,' she used to say; and she was never afraid to know the truth. You are like her; I think you have an instinct for the truth, as she had. My dear child, even now it is difficult to talk about her; perhaps more so because I have not talked of her for so long. She was young and sweet and—lovable."

The room was almost dark except for the moving, uncertain light from the fire. Pamela felt that she herself had gone astray in the time before she was born. The middle-aged scholarly man who was again striding about his dark library with jerky spasms of energy, yet always softly, speaking in jerky difficult sentences, had dragged her back with him across twenty years. Pamela sat with her eyes half-closed, almost believing that if she looked up she would see her mother, who was so real and living in that room.

Suddenly Denis Mort stopped his striding and sank into the high-backed chair.

"I'm frightfully grateful to you for telling me about her," said Pamela timidly, afraid that he would not hear her voice across the desert of years that separated them. But as she spoke the past slipped back to its distant place.

"I had always tried to imagine them, putting together what I had heard, but they were only people I had made up. Now

I know them. You have given me a father and a mother; I don't suppose you can realize what that means to me, but it's a lot."

He only said: "We ought to have some light," and switched on a reading-lamp, tipping its shade so that the radiance flowed out away from him and towards Pamela.

"I have some photographs of her, some of which you may not have seen," he continued, and went to his desk to find them.

• • • • •

Meanwhile, at the Mitre, Sally and Betty had finished tea and thoroughly discussed plans for the Easter vac. before Basil returned.

"Oh, Basil, lamb!" Sally greeted him. "Your car came in very useful, and I was most frightfully careful with it. There was a slight schemozzle in the Giler, but nothing was touched. Now I must get myself back to college somehow, because Gwyneth is sure to be there by now, and I'm dying to know what she was up to this afternoon."

"Which is a hint, I suppose," said Basil resignedly. "All right. Come along before I settle down."

"I'll come, too," Betty announced. "I'd like to see Oxford by night."

"There's nothing to equal Piccadilly Circus," Basil assured her; "but come if you really want to. We'll see what Sally has done to my car."

They deposited Sally at the front door of Persephone College, swept round the drive and returned over Mesopotamia bridge.

"Don't you think we might go and fetch Pamela?" Betty suggested. "I'm really quite worried about her; I don't know why, but we've had a curious afternoon."

"You haven't let my sylph run into danger?" asked Basil in concern. "I thought she'd gone to call on a highly respectable old don who coaches Sally?"

"Yes. But I'm sure that detective didn't like the idea of her being there. I could see it in his face. I can't think why, unless he thinks Mr. Mort will worry Pamela by talking about her aunt. But *he* wouldn't be likely to think of that. No, I can't see any reason for worry, but I thought Pamela herself seemed almost frightened to go, though she suggested it."

"You're all worked up by this pack of girls and their beastly detective work," Basil assured her. "But Pamela must be about ready to come home. Where does the man live?"

Betty explained as much as she had gathered, and Basil thought he understood, but it was not surprising that he turned along Norham Road instead of Norham Gardens, and thus approached Mr. Mort's house by its private drive, little used except by tradesmen's cars, instead of through the college quad. They left the car at the gate and entered the garden, but in the darkness took the path to the back door. This led them past the library, where the curtains had not been drawn, so that they saw Pamela sitting in a pool of lamplight, talking earnestly to a man who sat in the shadow.

"There she is!" cried Basil cheerfully, making a loud scrunch with his heel on the gravel as he halted.

The man heard, for he started up and came towards the window, crossing the path of light as he did so. Betty, anxious to see him, peered in and she noticed a strange look on his face; was it alarm, horror or merely surprise? In a moment he was in front of the lamp, opening the window, and had become merely a featureless silhouette.

"We've called for Pamela," Basil explained. "Sorry we lost our way and went blundering round your garden. We'll come round to the door."

Mr. Mort murmured something and shut the window.

CHAPTER XVIII

SCOTLAND YARD GOES UP
THE RIVER

It was Monday morning and Braydon sat in consultation with the superintendent. Braydon was considering a sheet of paper covered with neat notes.

"Extraordinary amount of coming and going on Friday afternoon along that route from the Parks, over the foot-bridge, to Ferry House and Persephone College," Braydon remarked.

"Rather odd how none of these people met each other, isn't it, sir?" Wythe inquired.

"Take a look at the time-table," said Braydon, flicking the paper towards him.

Miss Denning leaves Perse. Coll.	
boathouse	1.45
passes under Parks bridge	a bit before 2
ditto, return journey	?2.47
arrives Perse. Coll. boathouse	4.16
Bayes on Parks bridge	a bit before 2
ditto, return journey	?2.47
Lidgett in fields by river	2.15–3.5, roughly
meets Bayes in field	?2.40
Draga Czernak crosses Ferry House	
footpath	about 2.15
Parks bridge	" 2.20
reaches Sim's	" 2.30
leaves Sim's	" 3.30

Parks bridge again	about 3.40
Ferry House footpath	” 3.45
Mort leaves Sim's	2.45
Parks bridge	2.55
Ferry House footpath	3
ditto, return journey	4.5
Parks bridge	4.10
Sim's	4.20
Lond arrives at Ferry House (possibly) via Ferry Road and the lane	3.30

Wythe studied this for some moments.

"Seems to me, sir, that Mr. Mort should have overtaken Lidgett in the fields between the Parks bridge and the lane, but he declared in his statement that he saw no one besides Bayes in those fields," Wythe commented.

"It's still possible that Bayes was right in his first idea that he crossed the bridge the second time just after three and that Lidgett came rather more slowly along the bank on Friday than he did with you yesterday. Then Mort might have got across the bridge before Bayes arrived there and would have been well ahead of Lidgett."

"Yes, sir." Wythe studied the schedule. "It seems impossible that anyone could have moved through those fields more slowly than we did yesterday."

Braydon laughed. "Anyhow, it's certain that unless the canoe really passed under the bridge *after* three, Lidgett couldn't have run after the canoe and murdered Miss Denning in those fields, because Mort would have seen him. Even an unobservant man could hardly miss a murder right in his path."

"That's true," Wythe agreed disconsolately.

"There's another thing about that schedule," Braydon continued. "Miss Czernak's times, as they stand, don't help us at all. It's rather odd how they avoid overlapping with all the others. But they have only been guessed at by Coniston and may be all out. I'm going to see her and try to check her schedule. Now, here's a pretty thing!" He handed Wythe a page from Gwyneth's Beowulf note-book, on which she had inscribed a fairly accurate copy of Giles Lond's rhyme.

Wythe studied it earnestly. "It doesn't seem to mean much, except that someone, apparently Lond, can't spell and that a woman is dead. Did he write it?"

"One of his ancestors carved it on the mantelpiece, in the days when nobody cared whether they could spell or not, and Ezekiel Lond chipped it off on Saturday night. The Londs have always had a superstition about this rhyme and thought it would bring them bad luck if it became generally known. He knows that we were suspicious about him and has wit enough to guess that we would search his house. I think he got into a panic about it, perhaps thinking it would draw still stronger suspicion upon him, and so he removed it."

"At the same time, if he *had* brought death upon some woman, as the rhyme says, he might think it was a kind of evidence against him and want to remove it for that reason; at least, so it seems to me, sir," Wythe suggested.

"It's possible," Braydon agreed. "The thing can be explained either way. It's not evidence, but I'm quite glad to know what he was doing when those girls looked through the window. What is far more to the point, I believe, is this." Braydon took up Miss Denning's bank pass-book, which Wythe had obtained for him on the previous day from a bank manager reluctantly stirred from Sunday sloth. He took from between the pages a long slip of paper covered with figures and dates. "I've had the manager on the telephone this morning, but he knows nothing about these payments except that they have continued at irregular intervals for years. It's not his business, of course, to be inquisitive, but he thinks Miss Denning remarked on some occasion that the money was paid to her for her niece. Miss Denning obviously paid all the girl's expenses—school fees, college fees, doctor's and dentist's bills and so forth—from her own private account and gave the girl a small monthly allowance as well. There's no trace of trust money or anything of that kind, so far as I can see, but I'm going to make another inquiry on that point."

"You mean, sir," Wythe asked, "that Miss Denning received money from someone in cash and used it for her niece's education and keep?"

"That's the idea," Braydon confirmed. "What she received in cash has been more than enough, for some years past, to cover her outlay on behalf of her niece—so far as I have been able to isolate that expenditure from the rest. But she was a careful woman, I should judge. She made small investments from time to time and some of these probably represent the balance of what she received in these cash payments. There's nothing in her pass-book to show that they were earmarked for a particular purpose, but I shouldn't be surprised to find some private record—though I haven't lighted upon it among her papers yet—keeping a tally of what she received for her niece, what she paid out and what she invested."

"Then she doesn't seem to have made much personal profit out of the affair—whatever it was?" asked Wythe. "That's queer, isn't it?"

"I'm not sure that it is, from what I hear of Miss Denning," said Braydon meditatively. "The accumulation of money for someone she was very fond of might have been as powerful a motive with her as private gain would be to someone else. Also there's another point, which I'll come to in a moment. But just now the point is that for many years these sums, generally not very large—fifty pounds seems the maximum— have been paid by Miss Denning into her account, *in notes.* We know what that looks like."

Whatever it looked like did not seem pleasing to Inspector Wythe, who indeed had received all this information with an expression of doubt. "Of course, sir," he suggested, "the bursar of a college handles large sums of money. Undergrads have all sorts of funny little ways; some of 'em might pay their fees in cash. Without suggesting any hanky-panky—which we might look for in a case of suicide, but which doesn't seem to come into this—isn't it possible that she found it convenient to pay money into the college account by cheque and——"

"Wythe! You're an incurable romantic!" Braydon interrupted. "You're longing for a solution in which a crazed old man, a deserted Elizabethan house and a rhymed curse carved therein, shall all figure. You reject anything so sordid as blackmail, without really bringing your mind to bear on it. *Think*, man! The bursar might find it convenient to take cash which was paid to the college and use it for her personal expenses, replacing it by her own cheque; but you can't pretend that there would be any point in paying that cash into her own account, unless she were embezzling it. There's no indication of that. We must trace where that money came from."

"Yes, sir," Wythe agreed meekly. "Somehow blackmail—well, it's difficult to fit in with my ideas of these university dons."

"I know," said Braydon. "We're all apt to get fixed ideas about people; classify them and label them and say 'this lot are liable to go in for such and such crimes'; 'this lot don't.' But we've got to remember all the time to allow for the exceptions."

"You've got some idea, I take it, as to where that money did come from?" Wythe inquired more amenably, soothed by the Scotland Yard man's generalizations.

"Yes, I have. To begin with, I suspect that it came to her in larger amounts; she may have kept some for her own use and paid only the balance into her bank account. Or she may have paid it all into her bank in instalments. I think she avoided paying in large bundles of notes, with the idea that that would be too noticeable. So what you may find is withdrawals of larger sums in notes, at longer intervals. If you can find the account of Mr. Denis Mort of St. Simeon's College, I think you will trace that money."

Wythe gazed aghast at Braydon. "Mort!" he muttered.

"I'm afraid I haven't been quite fair," Braydon confessed. "But until last night the pieces of the puzzle didn't fit together to make up the picture. I still thought there might be some quite different solution, and I was trying to test the other possibilities. What first directed my ideas towards him was his apparent reluctance to answer any of my questions directly, the first time I saw him."

"Did you have any suspicion before you went?"

"Not really," said Braydon. "As I told you at the time, it seemed, from what the girls said, that he had been near the river at what might have been an important time, and there was a possibility that he could tell us something useful. I *did* give some thought to a chance remark of Miss Watson's, that he turned up for the coaching in very shabby old trousers and shoes, his gardening kit which he'd forgotten to change, he told her. But she said, when I asked her, that she didn't notice that they were particularly muddy, except for the shoes. *They* could have picked up mud anywhere—but of course there was the mark on Lond's bank to consider."

Wythe frowned over this. "I don't quite follow it yet," he admitted. "But just how did he answer your questions, sir?"

"Of course one had to consider the character of the man; an accurate scholar is often vague on practical everyday matters. But it struck me that he very carefully avoided saying exactly what he did on Friday afternoon. He answered with generalizations, as if he didn't want to say what actually happened but didn't find it easy to lie. I asked, 'Did you take the footpath?' and he replied, 'One naturally takes that path.' That sort of thing. It seemed to be rather more than mere donnish vagueness. The only thing he was quite certain about was the Ferry House boathouse is hidden from view in every direction. It's significant, you see, that a man who isn't normally very observant should have noticed that so particularly."

"Yes, I see. But what I don't see yet, sir, is the connection between this man Mort and Miss Denning," said Wythe, frowning.

"I've picked up scraps of evidence here and there and I feel pretty sure that Mort is the illegitimate father of Miss Denning's niece."

"So that was the pull she had for her blackmail!" Wythe exclaimed. "But I shouldn't have thought that a man like that would have jibbed at providing for his daughter."

"That's the other point I mentioned just now," Braydon remarked. "I think that the sense of power over this man, heightened by the atmosphere of intrigue, which the situation gave Miss Denning, was probably as important to her as the actual getting of money. Doubtless she *could* have received the money in some more businesslike and regular way, but I think she didn't want to. Mort isn't a business man, and if Miss Denning didn't choose to help him he probably saw no way of financing the girl secretly, until she was of age."

"You mean to say, sir, that she actually chose to go up the river by canoe, to see him and collect the money from time to time—for I take it that was what she did go for?" Wythe exclaimed, incredulously again.

"I'm sorry," Braydon apologized again. "It *is* rather a queer story, but I believe that's the fact, and I think she probably enjoyed it. Mind you, the evidence is by no means complete, and if we give the alarm too soon, Mort may remember to destroy something which perhaps it is still possible to find. Keep this very quiet. I'm going to test the time on the river and make a few inquiries and see what I can pick up. I'll leave you to think out just how it happened, and to go through Miss Denning's room and see if you can find anything that looks like a record of that money. It's not in her bureau, but it may be concealed in some place where you wouldn't expect to find it. Will you have Miss Denning's canoe taken back to the college boathouse and put in the water there. I shall probably be ready to embark in an hour, or less. Oh, you needn't be anxious! I have some skill with the paddles."

Braydon went first to the Mitre and sent a message to Mrs. Pongleton. In a few minutes Betty appeared in the lounge.

"Good morning, Inspector," were her words. But her voice and look said, "What on earth do you want? Is there any trouble that concerns Pamela?"

"Mrs. Pongleton, I want to ask Miss Exe a few questions about Miss Denning's financial affairs," Braydon explained. "I don't think they will be very difficult; she will either know the answers or she won't. You can be present if you think that will reassure her, and then you can see that I don't try any third degree!"

"Yes, I think Pamela might find it less alarming if I were there," Betty agreed, reassured by his friendly smile. "She and I are just finishing breakfast. If you will go up to our sitting-room, where you came yesterday, I will bring her along."

Betty, with Pamela, followed close on Braydon's heels. Pamela gave him a long, searching look from her blue eyes when Betty introduced him.

"I'm sorry to interrupt your breakfast," he apologized, "but one small point in connection with Miss Denning's financial affairs has cropped up, which you may be able to settle for us."

"I-I knew practically nothing about Aunt Myra's m-money matters," said Pamela. "She p-paid my college fees and everything and gave me an allowance."

"Do you happen to know whether your aunt held any money in trust for you? Or was there any other trustee, perhaps, of money that may have been left for you by your parents?"

"T-that's rather difficult," Pamela confessed. "B-but I'm sure no one else held money in trust for me. I d-don't think there was exactly a t-trust at all, but I know that my father left some money for me; Aunt Myra once told me that."

"He left it to your aunt, perhaps; and it was at her discretion to use it as she thought best, for your education and so forth?" Braydon suggested.

"Y-yes." Pamela obviously felt that there was something here which demanded explanation, but she made no comment.

Braydon caught Betty's puzzled look. She, also, was struck by the thought that this was an unexpected arrangement, considering the antagonism which had apparently existed between Pamela's father and her aunt.

"I'm sure Aunt Myra had charge of the money," Pamela continued, after a pause. "You see, I think she had an idea that I sh-shouldn't bother about money until I was of age, and so she d-didn't tell me details, though I d-did ask because I thought it was better that I should know how I stood. Aunt Myra would only say that there was plenty. Sh-she was awfully generous to me. I sometimes wondered if she wouldn't tell me because there was really very little and she was making it up from her own." Pamela paused again, and then added:

"I'm sorry. I haven't explained at all well, but really it was so vague!"

"Thank you very much. I think that *does* explain it. Now I'll leave you to your coffee and marmalade. I hate to be interrupted myself until I've finished my sixth cup. Good-bye!"

Betty followed Braydon downstairs and when he parted from her in the lounge he held her hand a moment after taking his leave.

"Look after that child!" he added hurriedly. "I'm very much afraid that the solution of this business may give her an even worse time than she has had already. In fact, if you could get her away from Oxford immediately after the inquest, it might be as well. Keep her with you somewhere for a day or two, but let me know where you are."

With that he was gone.

He walked rapidly along the High, turned up Cat's and strode on to Persephone College. Here he asked for Miss Cordell and was presently shown into the principal's study.

He noticed her strained look as she turned from her bureau to face him. In truth she was suffering not only from worry over the mysterious death of Miss Denning and the ensuing publicity, which alone was enough to make her nights miserably wakeful. Worse still was the sense that she had lost a friend on whose personality she had become dependent.

"Good morning, Miss Cordell. I want to ask if I may have a few words with Miss Czernak. No—" Braydon continued hastily as he saw her expression of anxiety—"nothing wrong, but she may be able to tell me something that may help to fix a time."

"Unfortunately," said Miss Cordell, "the Slav race has an ill-developed sense of time; I have noticed it when travelling in eastern Europe and I see it again in Draga Czernak."

"But still, I may be able to get something useful," said Braydon cheerfully.

"Of course, of course," Miss Cordell replied abstractedly. "I will send for her at once. But, of course, she may have gone to a lecture." After ringing the bell she looked uncertainly at Braydon, wondering if it would be improper to ask for information. He saved her the effort of deciding.

"I'm afraid I cannot tell you much, Miss Cordell. I believe that I may be on the point of solving the problem, but nothing is yet certain. After I have seen Miss Czernak I propose to go up the river in Miss Denning's canoe, which has been brought back here for that purpose. I want to make some tests of time and distance."

Miss Cordell nodded. A maid answered the bell and received instructions to find Miss Czernak.

"I shall welcome an end to this dreadful uncertainty," the principal said, "and yet I almost fear what the solution may be."

Braydon was taken aback. "There is nothing further you can tell us, Miss Cordell? Nothing that would help us?"

"Oh, no, no! I have not the faintest idea what can have happened. I only mean that, try as one can to imagine that the death of my colleague was the result of an accident, one is forced to the conclusion that there is something—something sinister and terrible to be discovered, something that may be even worse than uncertainty."

"I am afraid the explanation of an occurrence of this kind is bound to be terrible," Braydon agreed gravely, feeling profoundly sorry for Miss Cordell.

There was a knock at the door and Draga appeared.

"Inspector Braydon wants to speak to you, Draga. Probably you would like to go to the small common-room?" Miss Cordell suggested to Braydon. "Draga, will you show Inspector Braydon the way?"

He took his leave of Miss Cordell and followed Draga, noting her composed appearance and remembering Sally's warning that this might suddenly break into storm.

"I suppose that you have come to ask me to tell you the whole truth, as Mr. Coniston has told me I am to do," Draga remarked when she was seated opposite to him.

"We do prefer the truth," Braydon agreed amiably. "It gives us less trouble. I came to ask you if you can remember at what time you returned to college on Friday afternoon, after visiting Mr. Coniston at Sim's."

"The time!" exclaimed Draga in annoyance. "In England you do everything by the clock! To me that is finally tiresome."

"It *is* rather a bore," Braydon agreed. "But if you could think of something that would make it certain, it might help us a great deal. What time do you have tea in college?"

"At a quarter to four the bell rings," Draga said.

"Well, do you remember whether you heard the bell ring after you came in on Friday? Did you go to tea?"

"Yes, I went to tea. I acquire the habit," Draga admitted with some pride. "Now, I will think. Ah! They were already eating tea when I arrived."

"So it was certainly after a quarter to four. Now can you remember how much later it was. Did you hear a clock strike four by any chance? You can hear Sim's chimes from here, can't you?"

"I know!" said Draga suddenly, after a period of meditation. "I came home because it was the time for tea! When I was talking to Mr. Coniston I looked at my little clock and saw that it was a quarter to four. I did not come away at that moment; we talked for a little more; but I came soon after."

"Then it would be five minutes past four, or even later, when you got here? Did you walk across Ferry House garden?"

"Yes; the lane is so long. But I still do not know the time when I arrived here!"

"Do you walk fast?" Braydon asked.

Draga looked vague. "How can I tell?"

"You don't know how long you take to walk from Sim's?"

Draga shook her head hopelessly. "I try to tell you the truth," she declared, "but that I do not know."

"Well, never mind; perhaps you know this. Did you meet anyone on the bridge, or in the lane after the bridge, or on the footpath or between that and your front door?"

"No, no. I know that, because it was—not dark, but so dim. I was rather frightened of the footpath, because Gwyneth had told me of that terrible old man. I am sure there was no one there."

"Now you could help me a great deal if you would walk up to Sim's this morning and then walk back, just as you did on Friday, and look at your little clock before you start and when you get here and see how long it takes. And I hope you're not worrying any more about your curse, because really I feel sure it had nothing to do with Miss Denning's death and I don't think anyone need know of it."

"Thank you," said Draga gravely. "I will do as you say, and will you come again so that I can tell you?"

"Yes, I'll come again," Braydon promised as he took his leave.

Braydon next proceeded to the boathouse and found Miss Denning's canoe, the *Faralone*, with its two paddles, waiting for him there in the charge of a constable.

"Will you go up to Norham Road and wait around there for me, near the entrance to the Back End—you know the house? I think you had better bring a car," Braydon directed the man.

Braydon got into the canoe, noted the time by his watch, and paddled vigorously upstream. He skirted the west side of the island, passed the fork of the New Lode where the spiky-headed willows overhung the water, continued along the Parks bank and soon sighted the footbridge. As he passed under this he noted the time again. Only ten minutes from the start. He was probably going a little too fast, and certainly his muscular right arm was aching.

He slowed down slightly and in rather less than a quarter of an hour from the bridge he passed the backwater up which lay Sim's college boathouse. Braydon carried on, paddling steadily, past Sim's gardens which border the Cherwell behind tall iron railings, until he came to another backwater on the same side. It was narrow, with reedy shores, but there was a fairly clear passage wide enough for a punt. He swept the canoe round to the left and began to paddle gently through the stagnant, muddy water, looking ahead with a slight frown to where the backwater apparently ended in a hedge. As he came nearer he saw that the channel curved sharply to the left, and when he rounded the corner the channel was clearer.

He stopped paddling and looked at his watch. It was eighteen minutes since he passed under the bridge and twenty-eight minutes since he started. He plunged the paddle straight down into the water. It struck mud when the blade was little more than fully immersed, and when he drew it up the lower edge was clogged with thick, blackish lumps.

Braydon surveyed the scene. Directly ahead of him was a substantial boathouse with a sloping landing-stage in front of it, which blocked the end of the backwater. The right bank of the channel had been straightened, cleared of reeds and shored up with stakes. A thick hedge on the bank obscured any view in that direction. The left bank was even more carefully edged with boarding, and beyond it stretched the garden of the Back End. It was a garden thick with shrubs and trees, and roses trained on posts, but above this growth Braydon could see the irregular slopes of the roof and one tall chimney of the house. He stepped out on to the bank, and when the canoe, freed from his weight, rose in the water its gunwale was level with the ground.

Tying the canoe to a post, he surveyed the bank carefully and then strolled up to the landing-stage and paced across its lower edge, measuring the width of the backwater. About six feet, he reckoned. At the side of the boathouse he found a door, fastened with a padlock which opened easily to one of his skeleton keys.

Inside it was dark and he drew out a torch and flashed it around. A punt, bottom upwards, filled most of the space.

There were cushions, poles, paddles; all the paraphernalia one would expect. He looked for a rug, but found none.

Some garments hung on a peg on the wall. Braydon took them down and examined them. An old tweed sports coat, out at elbows; a pair of grey flannel trousers, faded and stained and rather muddy at the hems. He looked at them closely and scratched at the mud with his finger-nail. It was quite dry and was of brownish colour. He hung up the trousers on their peg and continued to peer around the boathouse, sweeping the space systematically with the ray of his torch. In a corner he found a pair of thick shoes, scratched and dirty, and evidently long unpolished. There was a good deal of mud on them, but again it was dry and brownish. He carried the shoes out to the side of the backwater, where the *Faralone* was moored and, kneeling down, he examined the boarding which shored up the bank. There were clots of dry mud there too, but that was blackish, like the stuff that had clogged the blade of his paddle when he had thrust it into the river bed, only paler because it was dry.

Braydon carried the shoes back to the boathouse and set them down where he had found them. They, and the coat and trousers were just the things a man might keep for messing about with his punt, or in the garden. Apart from the coat, they were just the things that Sally had described as worn by Mr. Mort at the coaching on Friday afternoon.

There was a cupboard on the opposite side of the boat-house and, opening this, Braydon found the big punt cushions, doubled up. He hauled at their unwieldy bulk and they sprawled out on to the floor. There was something left behind, which seemed to have been stuffed in untidily beneath them. Braydon pulled out another pair of grey flannel trousers, which he spread on the punt and examined carefully by the light of the torch. From the upper part, which was unsoiled, one would judge that they were fairly new and had been well pressed, but from some inches above the knees, downwards, they were smeared with mud of a blackish colour, or grey where it was partly dried. Much of it was still soft and the trousers were damp. He investigated them inch by inch and presently he found what he half expected, a long, fair hair.

Braydon returned to the cupboard and his ray of light disclosed a pair of shoes. These were clotted, not only outside but inside, with wet, black mud, and the leather was dulled and discoloured and damp with water. Yet apart from the havoc wrought by mud and water, they seemed to have been a better pair of shoes than the first pair he had come across.

He rolled up the trousers carefully and pondered for a minute. Then he lifted the edge of the punt and pushed shoes and trousers beneath it. He replaced the punt cushions and left the boathouse, shutting the door but not snapping the padlock. After another look at the *Faralone* where it lay moored in the backwater, and a glance round the deserted garden, Braydon followed the path up to the house and found the front door. A brisk, middle-aged woman answered his ring.

"Mr. Mort is out," she told him. "Lectures and so forth. He'll be home to lunch. Will you leave a message?"

Braydon looked at her closely. "Do you happen to know if Mr. Mort has lost a rug? Rather an old rug, with a sort of plaid pattern in various shades of brown?" he asked.

The woman frowned. "There was an old brown rug that Mr. Mort sometimes uses in the punt, but he hasn't been out on the river lately, not this term, I should think. I haven't heard that it was lost. Are you from the police, sir?"

"Yes. Detective-Inspector Braydon. You don't know if the rug is in the house?"

"Mr. Mort generally kept it in the boathouse, so's it would be handy when wanted. Has he reported it lost?" She was evidently puzzled. "If you was to show it to me—" she began, slowly. "But I don't know; rugs are much alike."

"I haven't got it with me now. Never mind. Please tell Mr. Mort when he comes in that Inspector Braydon called, and that I came by the river."

The path from the front door to the gate into Norham Road led near the boathouse, and Braydon secured the shoes and trousers and strolled out into the road. There was the police car, with a constable at the wheel. Braydon deposited his bundle carefully on the floor and got in.

"Straight back to the station," he directed.

CHAPTER XIX

A MAN GETS FREE

THE hall of Persephone College, although not forty years old, achieves by means of good proportions, panelled walls, plain, round-arched windows and general simplicity, a certain Augustan dignity. Here, on Monday afternoon, the University coroner conducted the inquest on Myra Denning.

Miss Cordell found some relief in the fact that, since the university retains the right to conduct its own inquests, this function was a very academic affair, and the police court element, represented by Superintendent Wythe and Detective-Inspector Braydon, was distinctly subdued. The jury, composed of fellows and tutors of the college, the dead woman's colleagues, under the foremanship of Miss Cordell herself, was sombrely formal in caps and flowing gowns.

The members of the Lode League sat in a row, in their abbreviated undergraduate gowns and medieval, square black caps. Nina was struck by the fact that although Miss Cordell, as foreman of a jury, ought really to be more official than usual, nevertheless, if you considered her face and movements rather than her academic dress, she appeared in the guise of a human being who could claim sympathy, instead of playing a role which gave one the right to do one's best to baffle and mislead her.

"Poor old Cordial!" Nina murmured to Sally. "I really am sorry for her; this has knocked all the stuffing out of her. I believe she must have been *fond* of Burse!"

"I'm sure she relied on her a lot," Sally replied. "And I suppose they are all human, after all."

Even the deep distress which Miss Cordell felt did not free her from a rather fussy anxiety as to how her students would conduct themselves on this semi-public occasion. It was some relief to her that a university inquest was dignified and ballasted by a long train of precedent; there were rules of procedure to guide herself and her colleagues. But undergraduates were capable of going to ridiculous extremes either to uphold a tradition or to smash it; you never could tell how it would affect them, but in either case their behaviour was liable to be exaggerated. She had long ago decided that they were more highly developed in the brain than in the heart and had little hope that grief would exercise any repressive influence.

Sally and Nina and Daphne could be relied upon, she thought; she hoped that Gwyneth would not get excited and squeak in that ridiculous manner of hers. But Draga, whose presence the coroner had insisted upon, was as dangerous as a lighted squib. She was sitting placidly enough beside Nina, but the presence, on her other side, of a dark, ugly man in an undergraduate gown was disturbing. Fortunately a table prevented Miss Cordell from seeing that Matthew Coniston was holding Draga's hand.

By one o'clock, an hour before the inquest was due to open, Braydon's case had still been incomplete in minor details and this gave him an excuse for deciding to let these academic people carry on according to plan and conduct their inquest as a rather unimportant formality, from the police point of view. At the back of Braydon's mind, too, there was a sense of relief that he was able to spare them from having to give a verdict of murder against one of their own colleagues.

The inquest opened with evidence of identification given by Pamela in a low voice. Draga was then called and asked to tell how she had seen Miss Denning go down to the boathouse to start on her last journey. Miss Cordell held her breath and gripped the table.

"From where I sat in the library," said Draga distinctly, "I observed Miss Denning go across the lawn towards the boathouse with her two paddles, as I have seen her go before. It would appear to be, in England, an ordinary procedure."

The coroner, who had been given a lurid account of Draga's idiosyncrasies, asked no questions. Miss Cordell audibly let out her breath and Miss Steevens, looking anxiously at her principal, observed that she was unwontedly red in the face. The evidence proceeded dully. By means of simple questions the fact that he saw a woman paddling up the river and, later, down again, was extracted from Bayes without any confusing details. The members of the Lode League described with fitting gravity the finding of the body; the superintendent told of his arrival on the scene. Medical evidence was then given.

"Would you give it as your opinion," the coroner asked, "that the evidence precludes the possibility of death having been accidental?"

"As to that," Dr. Odell replied, "the death itself might have been caused accidentally. There is nothing to show whether Miss Denning received a deliberate blow, which rendered her unconscious, and was then pushed, or fell, into the water, or whether she fell, by pure accident, into the water and in doing so hit her head. The subsequent removal of the body from the water and packing of it into the canoe indicates, obviously, the presence of some other person. That is all I can say."

"Thank you," said the coroner, and Dr. Odell stepped down.

"In this grievous and, unfortunately, mysterious affair," the coroner summed up, "all that we here can decide is the cause of death. We must hope that the police will earnestly pursue their investigations into matters which are now beyond our scope and will lay clear what is now dark. Ladies of the jury, on the medical evidence you should decide that the cause of death was drowning, you may add, if you so decide, that the deceased had first been rendered unconscious by a blow on the head. You must also decide, if you can, whether the blow and the drowning were accidental or were caused by some person or persons unknown. If you are unable to come to any conclusion upon this question, you must return an open verdict."

The jury retired to consider their verdict because Miss Cordell felt that it would be undignified for them to remain in their places and whisper together.

Their discussion was short.

"We can't really decide anything," declared Jean Steevens, the vice-principal, "unless we agree, as the coroner suggested, that Miss Denning must have been drowned whilst unconscious from a blow on the head. That seems reasonable, since we know she was a strong swimmer and unlikely to drown if in full possession of her faculties."

They agreed to this, Miss Cordell silently deploring Miss Steevens's breezy manner.

"As to the rest," Miss Steevens continued, "there was obviously someone present who did all he could to conceal what had happened and where it had happened, but I feel that we ought to consider the possibility that the actual happening was accidental. That means an open verdict."

"But," put in another don, Miss Purden, "surely no man would have done all that unless he was guilty. Ought it not to be a verdict of murder against a person unknown?"

"I can't see that we've got real *evidence* for that," replied Miss Steevens impatiently. "We must work on the facts we've heard."

They agreed upon this and returned a verdict accordingly.

The coroner paid the usual tribute to the subject of the inquest.

"You have lost a valued and respected colleague and will wish me to express our profound sympathy with the relatives of the deceased. Miss Denning's long record of devoted work on behalf of her college is well known, and not only the university, but the city also, owes her a debt for her energetic action towards the preservation of some of the green and pleasant land around us from the defacement of ill-considered building."

Sally, listening to the stilted, conventional phrases, thought: "Poor Pamela! It doesn't do her much good. She'd probably much rather have her aunt alive and building skyscrapers all over the city of Oxford!" Looking round for the object of her sympathy, Sally noticed that Pamela, Betty and Basil had quietly slipped away.

The assembly dispersed, with a general feeling that the inquest had been rather disappointing. No sensation and nothing decided. Jean Steevens and other members of the senior common-room of Persephone College were inclined to be breezily fatalistic about Miss Denning's death. Very unfortunate and all that, but we must just make the best of it. They could not feel any real regret for the loss of Miss Denning, much as they deplored the manner of it and paid tribute to her competence. The bursar's hard efficiency in her own affairs and indifference to those of other people, and the curious satisfaction she seemed to find in her solitary and sometimes peculiar occupations, had not attracted friendship. Only Miss Cordell had penetrated to something softer and more tolerant in her colleague. Perhaps it was because the principal, with her uncertain grasp of business matters and affairs of organization, had provided the bursar with an opportunity for domination which she had enough discretion to exercise tactfully.

Miss Cordell was sensitive of the unsympathetic attitude of the rest of her staff; she longed to talk things over with someone who could understand her distress of mind and the difficulty of presenting a placidly dignified face to the world. That Scotland Yard man, she felt, really seemed more understanding than anyone else; it did not occur to her that his genius for giving people this impression was the secret of professional success. There he was, talking to Draga again, and he seemed to have a wonderful influence on that girl.

"Were you able to carry out that little test for me?" Braydon was asking Draga.

"That is so," Draga replied, very pleased with herself. She handed him a scrap of paper. "I wrote down the times, that I might not forget. Twenty minutes I walked from Sim's to our college."

"And you started some minutes after a quarter to four? May I see your watch?" He compared it with his own and found it, to his surprise, correct.

"It is a good watch, and I take great trouble that it shows me the right time," Draga told him, "because it is so important here that one should be always punctual."

"That's good. Did you time yourself from Sim's gateway?"

"Yes, from outside the gate."

"So you would have arrived at Persephone College at about ten minutes past four on Friday?" Braydon asked.

Draga thought a moment. "I think so. Not sooner."

"And you are sure you met no one?"

"In the Parks I am not sure, but from that tall bridge to our door, no one."

"Do you know Mr. Mort, who coaches Miss Watson?"

Draga considered. "Ah, yes! The gentle one, from Sim's."

"Gentle!" Braydon commented doubtfully. "You really know him?"

"I know what he looks like," Draga maintained. "He has light hair and a look as if he were worried."

"You didn't meet him on your walk on Friday? Not even in the Parks?"

"Oh, no; I would remember that, because I know him," Draga declared.

"Thank you very much," said Braydon. "That is what I wanted to know."

He returned with Wythe to the superintendent's room at the police station.

"That girl's story is one more point in the evidence against Mort," said Braydon, after telling Wythe what Draga had said. "Miss Watson confirms the fact that he left the college a minute or two after four, but he wasn't seen anywhere on the way to Sim's between ten to four and ten past."

"He could get over that by saying that he followed the lane all round Ferry House, instead of crossing the stile," Wythe pointed out. "And I think you said, sir, that he didn't state definitely to you that he *did* cross the stile?"

"He did say that he had never been round by the lane," Braydon recalled. "But we've really got remarkably little evidence, and yet the case is as clear as daylight."

"That housekeeper must know something," Wythe mused. "But I suppose she's not saying anything. When you arrest a real low-down criminal there are plenty with a grudge against him who'll fall over each other in their anxiety to tell you something, but with a man like this it's different."

Braydon nodded thoughtfully. "I don't mind confessing that I hate to lay hands on him."

"I quite understand, sir. We're used to running in an undergrad now and again for a minor offence, but with one of these dons it's different. However, it's got to be done." He half-rose, with an inquiring look towards Braydon.

"A few minutes makes no difference," said Braydon. "I'm anxious to hear the doctor's report on that hair from the trousers."

"My men have got that house, the Back End, guarded as if it was the Crown jewels," Wythe declared with some pride. "So it's all right as far as that goes."

"Whilst we're waiting I want to have a look at that account book of Miss Denning's which you've discovered for me and at Mort's pass-book," Braydon said.

Wythe took from a drawer two pass-books and a cheap, red-covered note-book and handed them to Braydon, who turned over the pages, comparing one book with another.

"I've checked Mort's withdrawals of sums in notes, generally a hundred pounds at a time, with Miss Denning's payments of cash into her account over the last two years," said Wythe, "and they seem to tally." He handed over a page of neat figures.

"And Miss Denning, in this private account book of hers, seems to have recorded—without giving away any names—all those sums received and every penny she spent on her niece, and all the balance which she invested from time to time. What a meticulous woman! Undoubtedly honest in her own way. I wonder if she ever showed Mort this note-book or whether she preferred to leave him in uncertainty as to whether all his money was really being used for his daughter's benefit?"

"If you've a minute or two to spare, sir, there's one or two things I don't quite understand yet," said Wythe diffidently. "That man Coniston——?"

"His story is quite true," said Braydon. "It struck me first of all that anyone who had to invent a story would normally invent something more easily credible. On the other hand, I realized that Coniston is clever; clever enough to invent a story so fantastic that you feel almost sure no one *would* invent it and hope to be believed. It did pass through my mind at one time that Mort knew or suspected that Coniston was involved and might be trying to shield a member of his own college."

"You say you got a line on Mort when you saw him on Sunday morning. That was after Bayes's evidence, which all pointed downstream, as it were," Wythe suggested.

"All the time I was looking for a clue above the bridge which would fit in with the time the watch stopped, which suggested that the drowning happened about half an hour's paddle upstream. Bayes mentioned a rug and thought there was something under it. He was inclined to withdraw that when we questioned him, you remember, but my impression was that he did notice a rug covering something, and if Miss Denning was drowned above the bridge, the something could only be her body, and the murderer in her hat and coat was presumably paddling the canoe."

"And yet you suggested yourself, sir," cried Wythe in reproach, "that it was only the spare paddle under that rug!"

"Yes, I know. It *might* have been only the spare paddle. I wanted to test every possibility. There was still old Lond to be accounted for, and Lidgett. But when I came to work out the times they fitted extraordinarily well, taking the earlier time, as given by Lidgett, for Bayes's second crossing of the bridge. And then I happened to hear that Bayes, when he told his story to his friends, said that when first he saw the canoe coming down the river he thought there was a *man* paddling it."

"He never said that to us!" Wythe declared. "Well, we've got a funny lot of witnesses! There's Bayes, who isn't sure of anything; he did all right at the inquest, but what'll he be like when he has to face cross-examination? As for that Yugo-Slav young lady—!" he paused, then continued: "But there's another thing I don't quite get at, sir; that is, why Mort parked the canoe under Ferry House garden, as I suppose he did, and then ran the risk of returning to it."

"He was evidently pressed for time and the quickest thing was to moor it. If he were more than a few minutes late for a coaching that would certainly be noticed and remembered; he couldn't risk that. The canoe was safe there, too; no one goes down the New Lode, and Mort probably didn't even know that Lond sometimes hangs about Ferry House. He had satisfied himself that Lond's boathouse was completely hidden from chance observation. Then I think his idea may have been, when he went back to the canoe and pushed it off, that it would drift much farther, below the island, perhaps go over the weir, and he thought that would completely confuse the trail."

"Yes, I see. Very neat. But if Mort planned this beforehand, he ran it pretty fine—the whole time schedule, I mean."

"I'm pretty sure he didn't plan it ahead. In fact, I'm not sure yet that he's guilty of murder. I'm trying to see some point that may be evidence of that, one way or the other. Of course, concealing what happened and all that, gives ground enough for an arrest."

"The evidence of those books," Wythe remarked, indicating the two pass-books and the red note-book, "gives motive enough for murder, to my way of thinking."

"It may show that he had reason to dislike and fear her," said Braydon slowly. "I shouldn't expect him to be the kind of man to knock a woman over the head, but it's conceivable that if he merely threatened, or perhaps pushed her, she may have fallen backwards into that narrow channel and struck her head on one of those stakes on the opposite side." He paused. "I don't know. It may be a weakness, but I like to know what I really believe a man to be guilty of before I arrest him."

Dr. Odell entered with his report. "Those hairs on the trousers," he announced, "—there's more than one—are as certainly the twin brothers of the hairs on Miss Denning's head as you can ever tell. Of course, no one can *prove* their identity, one way or the other," he added helpfully.

"So now for the Back End," Wythe suggested.

The little house, with sunshine printing the blurred arabesque of bare branches on its plastered walls, looked very peaceful in its bushy garden.

"Mr. Mort's resting," the brisk housekeeper told them. "He hasn't been at all himself these last few days. I gave him your message, sir." She looked at Braydon. "But you never said anything about when you'd come back. As for that rug, Inspector, Mr. Mort hasn't made any complaint himself about it being stolen, I'm sure, and it's not a very big matter if it was."

"This is very important," Braydon informed her. "More important than any stolen rug. I'm afraid we must insist on seeing Mr. Mort. Will you tell him, please."

"He gave orders that he wasn't to be disturbed," said the woman doubtfully. "Couldn't you come back later? I think he's gone off into a nice nap and there's no doubt but that he needs it."

"He hasn't been sleeping well lately, I expect?" Braydon suggested.

"Since you say it, and he may have mentioned it to you, sir, I don't believe he slept a wink last night. Walking up and down he was, all the night long. So you see, sir, I don't like to disturb him now."

"And he's none too easy a man when orders are disobeyed, I believe?" Braydon continued.

"It's not my place to discuss my employers," the woman replied stiffly.

"Quite right," Braydon agreed. "Now will you go and tell Mr. Mort that I want to see him. I'm afraid we must insist. The matter is important and urgent."

"Well, if you say so," she agreed doubtfully and left them in the hall.

In a few minutes she returned, looking scared.

"I can't wake him! He's taken some sleeping medicine, I think. These things do send you into an unnatural sleep, I've heard." She was obviously trying to allay her own fears. "I don't quite know—" she added doubtfully.

"I think we had better see him," said Braydon gravely. "It may be wise to send for a doctor, but I have some knowledge in these matters."

The woman's hostility towards them had vanished and she seemed glad of their presence. She led the way into the library where Braydon had first seen Denis Mort. He lay there now, in a low wicker chair, with one arm bent upwards and the hand beneath the cushion on which his head rested. The sprawled legs, the body turned to one side, were the attitude of a man in a deep sleep. Braydon made a quick examination and turned to Wythe.

"Will you call Dr. Odell? He has got free." The last words were spoken quietly and the housekeeper, standing near the door, did not hear them, but she caught the mention of a doctor. She clutched her hands together tightly.

"Oh, sir, is it—is it——?"

"Yes," said Braydon. "There is nothing that a doctor can do now. We must take charge, you understand."

The woman gave a sort of gulp and blundered out of the room. Wythe followed her, to find the telephone. Braydon prowled round the room and found on the desk an envelope addressed to himself, which he put in his pocket. The photograph which he had studied so attentively on his first visit was missing.

CHAPTER XX

DENIS MORT GIVES A VERDICT

THE letter opened without preamble.

"I write to you as a man rather than as a detective, because I feel that some explanation is advisable, and I trust your judgment as much as I appreciate your tact. The chloral hydrate was obtained some years ago in a perfectly regular way, for my mother in her last illness. I have kept it because I have thought more than once of taking this, the weak man's way out of an unbearable situation. My own weakness has brought misery to myself and worse than misery to others, from first to last.

"What distresses me most of all now is that this sordid blackmailing story may be made public. I see no way to avoid it. Blackmailing is what it will be called, but it differs from the usual case of blackmail in that I was willing enough to give the money for my daughter's education and support, and I am satisfied that it has been used, or set aside, for that purpose. I want to be fair.

"I did not premeditate murder, although murderous thoughts, never translated into a plan of action, have been often enough in my mind. I have tried to force myself into action; not murder, but disclosure of all the story to my daughter, known as Pamela Exe, who was, I thought, old enough now to be trusted with the knowledge. I planned to end Miss Denning's power over me by wiping out all secrets and to find some way of putting the money in trust for Pamela. But my own weakness and procrastination defeated me again and the power of action only came to me when action was useless.

"I had asked Miss Denning not to come on that particular Friday afternoon because my time would be limited by that extra coaching. When she came I wanted to have time to tell her all this. That, I felt, would be only fair. Nevertheless she came, as I half expected she would, and I was in the garden in case she should come. I was in an evil fury that she should come when I had no time to explain what I intended and that she thus forced me to prolong the situation which I was determined to end. I rushed out at her as she stood at the edge of the backwater. She had seldom seen me in that state of anger and, as I afterwards realized, I had a pruning knife in my hand. She may have feared the violence that was far from my mind. She was certainly startled and stepped back into the water and fell. She lay right across the backwater, with her head just under the water on the far side, but at first, with the splashing and the churning of the mud, I did not realize that her head was under water. I waited for her to begin to struggle out; I felt a kind of mean triumph and then anxiety as to how I could get her into the house and give her the opportunity of obtaining dry clothing without making her visit public.

"Suddenly I realized that she was not moving; I don't know what happened but I suppose that she struck her head on one of the stakes that shore up the bank. I actually stepped into the water and then hesitated. Apparently my housekeeper had heard nothing. There was no sign from the house. I turned away and strode about the garden, raging in impotent fury. She has killed herself, I told myself, or if she has not killed herself yet, she is doing so. She has hounded me, taunted me, kept me away from my daughter, shown me no mercy.

Why should I go to her help when even the law does not require me to do so?

"I was unjust, of course; it is I who have spoilt my own life. I had power over it, had I been strong enough to use it.

"An evil curiosity drew me to the backwater again. There she lay quietly under the water. I was afraid, and I walked in and dragged her out. She was dead. The best plan seemed to be to put her into her canoe, and I had some idea of pushing it out into the river. Her coat lay in the canoe and I removed this and recovered her hat which was floating on the water.

"Then I remembered that I was to coach Miss Watson at three and, thinking things out, I made the plan of taking the body down in the canoe. I gather that you have found my rug, which I took from my boathouse to cover the body and which I afterwards flung into the bushes in Ferry House garden. You have also found the wet and muddy trousers and shoes, which I discarded in exchange for the old ones I usually keep in the boathouse for gardening. Miss Watson may remember those. I worked out further details of the plan as I paddled down.

"When I left Persephone College at four I returned to Ferry House garden, where I had moored the canoe near the derelict boathouse. My idea was to upset the canoe, so that the body would be found in the river and a verdict of accidental death returned at the inquest. In that way, I thought, there was no danger that either I or anyone else would be suspected. I pulled the canoe a little way up above the fork of the New Lode to a bank beneath which, I thought, the water was deep enough for the body to be swept out into the stream, but I was unable to carry out even this plan to its conclusion. I slipped on the bank and the canoe floated away beyond my reach, without upsetting. I could do nothing more but fling the paddles after it.

"No one is in my confidence. My housekeeper, Mrs. Bingham, knows nothing.

"What is the use of facing a trial and giving, not only my own private affairs, the muddy sediment of my life, but many things also which others should be allowed to keep secret, to the public to gape at and conjecture upon? Technically I am not guilty of murder, yet how can I stand up to fight that charge when my conscience gives the verdict: *Morally guilty?*

"Do you consider that such self-recrimination as this is extravagant, if what I have written is true? Although you are well acquainted with crime, you may not realize the effect upon the mind of a man who has a particular abhorrence of crimes of violence, of the conviction that he is morally guilty of one. Myra Denning's relationship to my daughter, Pamela, intensifies the horror of this idea, round which my mind has revolved during three frightful days and nights. I have faced Pamela once since Friday afternoon, but I cannot face her again.

"In the top right-hand drawer of my desk are some letters and photographs for Pamela. I cannot write to her. I had planned a conversation with her in which she would learn the whole truth and would be as honest and generous as her mother always was. When the opportunity for that conversation came, it had become impossible to tell her the truth.

Yet perhaps she knows. I can only pray that she may show that same high courage which her mother had, and that she may make her own life so fine an achievement that in the general scheme of things it may be counted as atonement for her father's failure."

THE END